Monuments in Darkness

Also by Nicholas Kaufmann

Novels
Hunt at World's End
Chasing the Dragon
Dying Is My Business
Die and Stay Dead
In the Shadow of the Axe
100 Fathoms Below (with Steven L. Kent)
The Hungry Earth
The Stone Serpent
The Mind Worms

Collections
Walk in Shadows
Still Life: Nine Stories

Monuments in Darkness

Nicholas Kaufmann

Hippocampus Press

New York

Published by Hippocampus Press
P.O. Box 641, New York, NY 10156.
www.hippocampuspress.com

Cover art and design © 2025 by Daniel V. Sauer, dansauerdesign.com.
Hippocampus Press logo designed by Anastasia Damianakos.

First Edition
1 3 5 7 9 8 6 4 2

ISBN 978-1-61498-471-9 (paperback)
ISBN 978-1-61498-472-6 (ebook)

Contents

The Fire and the Stag

I have always believed in God, even from a young age. Maybe not the commonly imagined old man with a long white beard sitting among the clouds, not Yahweh or Christ or Buddha, but I've always sensed there was *something*—some infinite mystery—at the heart of the cosmos. Is it benevolent? Is it kind? Does it love us, watch over us, protect us?

I don't think so.

There's nothing kind about nature; and what is nature but an extension of the infinite mystery, the embodiment of its will? If nature were kind, every animal would be a vegetarian. Instead, they hunt each other, kill each other for food. It is perhaps the greatest irony of this world that its inhabitants must kill in order to live. This is the cruel game nature devised for us. This is our pitiless God's design.

When I was eight years old I survived a wildfire. My parents were wealthy and provided everything for me and my older sister April, including a lavish house in the wooded hills of Southern California. All week we'd been able to smell smoke, but the wildfire was far away and wasn't supposed to spread in our direction. A sudden shift in the wind changed that. I don't remember much of what happened, and what I do remember I don't like to think of often—running from my bedroom in the middle of the night through heat and smoke, eyes stinging, lungs hacking, praying Mom and Dad would find me. Somehow, in the midst of it all, my sister did. April was only ten years old, but she was smart and didn't panic. She grabbed me by the hand, and then we were outside, running away from the house down the long, twisting driveway. We stopped at the bottom and turned to look back. I had expected Mom and Dad to be right behind us, but I didn't see them anywhere.

I kept my grip on April's hand, paralyzed by fear as we watched the ravenous, towering flames engulf the forest, our house, everything. It lit the night with an otherworldly orange glow. Neither of us had ever seen anything like that fire—its enormity, its insatiable hunger.

Nor had we ever seen anything like what came charging out of the burning woods toward us. It was a huge stag, its body shrouded in flames, the branches of its immense antlers blazing orange and trailing thick black smoke. It looked like something from another world, a creature made of fire. I squeezed April's hand tighter, a scream locked in my throat. The burning stag ran past us, blind and bellowing, so close I could feel its heat against me, its pungent smoke in my nose. The stag collapsed a few yards away from us, and my scream finally released itself. I clutched my sister, unable to take my eyes off the burning beast. It was on its side, but its legs were still moving, as though it were still trying to run. It lifted its head on its thickly muscled neck, a branching crown of fire raging above its skull, and then it fell back. There was no running from the fire anymore. The stag had become the fire, and the fire had become the stag. There was no escape, except death.

I had learned about wildfires in school—all California children did—and I knew most of them weren't started by people. They were natural occurrences, part of a cycle intended to remove the old, dead trees and make room for new ones, to clear the ground so sunlight could reach the soil and help new plants grow. It was all part of nature's plan.

That was what terrified me. That was why I couldn't stop screaming.

Because in that moment, even before I learned our parents were dead and our lives would change forever, I understood that within the unknowable mind that turned the gears of creation, the gears of the cosmos itself, there was no mercy. No pity. No humanity. Only fear, and suffering, and death.

I understood, at only eight years old, why we are born into this world screaming.

April was forty-four when she disappeared.

Although our adult lives had taken us on different paths, neither of us had married. We'd both thrown ourselves into our careers at the expense of our social lives—professor of anthropology at UC Davis for her, and sporadic psych ward inpatient diagnosed with major depression for me. Over the years we continued to lean on each other, to rely on each other as much as we had as children after our parents died. That never changed, not even when I moved across the country to New York City, where I could get the best treatment, paid for by the inheritance Mom and Dad left me in the form of a trust fund managed by April. She was never stingy with the purse strings and always made sure I could see the best doctors, be admitted to the best hospitals when things got bad, and still have enough money on hand to cover my living expenses.

My depression was a dark, smothering curtain that constantly hung over me, waiting to drop. The last time it did was the worst it had been in a long time. It forced me back into the hospital, and April dropped everything to fly out and see me. She slept in my Lower East Side apartment and visited me in the psych ward every day for the two weeks I was there, sitting across from me in the visitors room and making exactly the kind of small talk I needed at the time, making me feel normal instead of broken. It was only afterward that I discovered exactly how much she'd sacrificed to be there. She'd been up for a promotion to the head of the UC Davis Anthropology Department, but by staying in New York for so long she'd missed several important interviews. In the end, she didn't get the promotion—I assume it went to somebody who didn't have a broken, needy headcase for a brother—but she never blamed me, not once.

"It's what big sisters do," she said.

A few months later April walked into the Appomattox-Buckingham State Forest in Virginia and never came out. She'd flown there on a university-funded expedition to find evidence of a lost indigenous nation— one so old its name wasn't even known anymore, and so reclusive it appeared only in the oral legends of the Rappahannock, who called them "the Strange People Who Came Out of the Forest." She was determined to find out what had happened to them and if they'd left any signs of their civilization behind. Through her research she deduced that the ancient woods where this lost nation dwelled would have been roughly in the same location as the state forest.

She checked in with me constantly while she was in Virginia, from the moment her flight landed until she vanished two days later. I grew concerned when she stopped answering my calls and texts. It wasn't like her to drop out of touch. Once I learned her colleagues at UC Davis hadn't heard from her either, my next call was to the Virginia police. They spent the better part of a week searching the forest but didn't find her, nor any remains that might have been her. They didn't even find her campsite. Desperate, I begged them to keep looking, not to give up. They explained that the forest covered nearly twenty thousand acres and they'd searched it as thoroughly they could. I hung up on them.

The idea of April all alone in the middle of twenty thousand acres of merciless nature, lost or injured, was more than I could bear. She'd been there for me, selflessly, during my darkest time, and I intended to be there for her in hers. Despite my intense dislike of air travel, I booked a flight, packed a bag, and left the safety of New York City, where nature is wisely kept to a minimum. I flew into Richmond, then took a long bus ride to Chestnut Grove, where I'd reserved a motel room close enough to the state forest that I could get there easily first thing in the morning.

On the bus I looked again at my last text exchange with April. I'd asked, *So did you find your missing tribe yet?* Normally she would have responded right away that tribe wasn't the proper term—I knew this, although I loved to tease her—but instead there had been no answer at all. Then, hours later, in the middle of the night while I slept, a text from April had come through. It was only one word. My name.

Kenny

I was Kenneth to the rest of the world—my doctors, my landlord, the distant relatives who used to call to check up on me but had stopped a long time ago—but April still called me by my childhood nickname. To her I would always be Kenny, the little boy whose hand she held while our house burned down with our parents inside. April was the only one who was allowed to call me that.

Two hours later, another text came while I still slept. It was the same.

Kenny

Two hours between texts. What had occurred during that time? I couldn't say. Another hour passed in the night before a third and final text arrived, her last message before she vanished.

They're still here.

* * *

It took every ounce of courage for me to enter that sprawling Virginia forest. I stood at the edge of it, the morning sun throwing my shadow into the mouth of one of the forest's major trails. My backpack was filled with trail mix, nutrition bars, bottles of water, a flashlight, and an external battery in case I needed to recharge my smartphone. Before me, the oaks, hickories, and pines towered like giants. Their leaves rustled in the wind, their branches swayed like grasping arms. I hadn't set foot in a forest since the wildfire. Hell, I'd even carefully avoided Central Park back in New York, and yet here I was, about to enter the woods for the first time in decades. I took a deep breath and forced myself forward.

The state forest was dotted with approved campsites and crisscrossed with hiking trails, but I knew April wouldn't have used any of them. If there were evidence of a lost indigenous nation to find, the only place it could still exist was off the beaten path, in the parts of the forest where no one went. That was where she would have gone, so that was where I had to go.

A posted sign warned visitors to stay on the trails for their own safety. Like a foolish child in a fairy tale, I ignored it and stepped off the path. I couldn't let myself think too much about what I was doing or I would surely turn back. Any excuse not to step willingly into nature's violent clutches. But there was no one left to find my sister now that the police had failed, only me, so I pushed down my fear and walked into the trees.

I activated the GPS on my phone, knowing how easy it would be to get lost in these woods. On the screen I was a tiny dot, vulnerable and exposed in the middle of a huge, unnerving expanse of green. Low branches scratched at my arms as I walked deeper into the forest. Undergrowth tried to tangle itself around my feet. It was a warm day, but the sweat that slicked my palms and beaded on my brow had nothing to do with the weather. Every snap of a twig or rustle of leaves, every movement in the corner of my eye, made me jump. I thought of the wildfire again, and the burning stag. Around me insects fought to the death under the carpet of leaves and birds snatched small rodents off the forest floor, as if to remind me I was at nature's mercy—and it had none.

Was that what had happened to April? Had she been caught up in nature's cruel game, killed by some wild animal, her remains devoured until there was nothing left for the police to find? I couldn't stand the thought. Not April. But who would have protected her from such a fate? Not God, surely. Not the pitiless, sadistic mind that spun the gears of creation. The answer was no one. There was no one to protect her.

Or me.

I grew tired quickly. I was forty-two with a lifelong aversion to exercise, and hiking through the woods didn't come naturally to me. The lumpy, uneven forest floor, where layers of dead leaves covered treacherous holes and tree roots, was nothing like the flat concrete sidewalks of New York City. I tripped a few times and went down cursing. I cut my hands and bruised my knees, but I always got back on my feet and pushed forward. Time seemed to stretch and warp in the forest. Sometimes I would check my phone to discover only a few minutes had passed since the last time I looked; other times, hours passed without my realizing it. I stopped to eat and drink some water, and looked at the GPS again. The flat expanse of green filled the whole screen like an infinite wilderness. What the hell was I doing out here? What if I'd made a terrible mistake? What if April wasn't even in the forest anymore?

As the sun inched toward the western horizon and the air grew colder, I thought about turning back. My plan had been to search the forest until dusk, return to the motel, and start again in the morning. But turning back felt like giving up on April, and I couldn't do that. She had never given up on me. I pushed myself to keep walking, telling myself just a little farther, just a few more minutes. I tripped over a tree root and fell forward, crashing through a web of thin branches. I landed on my hands and knees. My sleeve was torn, and my arm bled where the branches had scratched it. I got back on my feet, cursing and wondering if I should turn around after all before this place killed me, but then I saw I was in a clearing.

At the center of the clearing was a small lake, its waters still and glassy. The rest of the clearing was full of grass, tall weeds, and wildflowers. Off to one side was a tent tilted at a precarious angle, as if the wind had knocked it over. It was dirty and covered with fallen leaves. It looked as if it had been there for weeks.

I didn't know if it was April's tent. After all, the Virginia police had told me they couldn't find her campsite. I approached it cautiously. There was no sound from within, no movement. The flap at the front of the tent was open, and inside I saw an unrolled sleeping bag, a pillow, two empty water bottles lying on their sides, and a backpack I instantly recognized as April's. It was the same purple one she'd had since grad school, with the same corny "Anthropologists do it in the field" patch on its outer pocket. For the first time since she disappeared, I had hope that I might find my sister after all.

I looked out over the clearing, cupped my hands around my mouth, and shouted, "April!" Was she still nearby? I shouted again, "April!"

The only answer was the wind through the trees, a sound so lonely it made me shiver.

I took out my phone to call the police, but the GPS had drained the battery. I plugged it into my external battery and fumed while it charged. I had found April's campsite on my first day of looking. Why hadn't the police? Had the lazy bastards bothered to look at all? As soon as my phone came back to life, I made the call. The reception was muddy and kept cutting out on me, but I managed to ask for Sergeant Donahue, the man in charge of the search for my sister. When he came on the line, it took a great deal of willpower not to yell at him. Instead, I remained calm and simply told him I was in the forest and had found April's campsite.

I expected him to sound guilty, like a child caught in a lie, but instead he sounded surprised. "Where? Can you give me the coordinates?"

I launched the GPS app again and gave him my coordinates. The reception cut out a few times, and I had to repeat the numbers more than once before he finally had them.

"Are you sure these are right?" he asked.

I checked the GPS again. "Yes, I'm sure. Are you sending someone?"

The line went dead for a moment. Then Sergeant Donahue's voice came back in brief blasts of sound. "Can't be . . . puts you . . . middle of the north parking lot."

"What?" I looked around me. "I am most definitely not in a parking lot. Sergeant, can you hear me? Sergeant Donahue?"

But the line was dead, and this time the sergeant's voice didn't return. I tried to call again but couldn't connect. I decided to let the phone charge, and if the sergeant didn't send anyone I would try again later.

I brushed the leaves off the tent, set it upright again, and crawled inside. How much time had passed since April had been here? I touched the pillow at the head of the sleeping bag and found it moldy and damp. Rain, I figured. That wasn't a good sign. April was too fastidious to have left the tent flap open to the elements and risk ruining her belongings.

Unless she'd left in a hurry. But to where?

I removed my backpack and dropped it next to hers on the tent floor. Mine was just as old, just as scuffed and dirtied, and together the two bags looked like weary old siblings leaning against each other in quiet contemplation. I'd felt a constant, simmering despair ever since April disappeared, but now it boiled over into panic. I sat on her sleeping bag, and for a long moment all I could do was breathe. Where was she? Where was my sister?

I rummaged through her backpack, but there wasn't much inside. She'd eaten all her food, and there were no water bottles left. Her phone was gone. Had she taken it with her and run out of battery? I wished I knew. I dug deeper into the backpack, pushing aside a layer of empty nutrition bar wrappers, and found a hardback notebook at the bottom. I snatched it up and flipped madly through the pages. April's familiar handwriting comforted me—the swoop of her Cs, the way she crossed her Ts with an upward-tilting slant, the rushed dot over her lower-case i that always slashed forward to look like an accent mark—and I managed to get my panic under control again.

I skimmed through the notebook, hoping to find some clue as to what had happened, and discovered it wasn't April's field notes, as I'd first assumed. It was her diary. I felt a brief sting of shame to be looking through her private writings, but I knew it was my best chance to find answers.

She wrote quite a lot about someone named Josh Glover, and at first, given the frequency with which she mentioned him, I thought he was her boyfriend. Upon closer reading, however, I learned he was a translator she'd hired to assist with her research. Apparently one of the last remaining members of the Rappahannock nation had written down his ancestors' oral legends shortly before he died, including the story about the Strange People Who Came Out of the Forest. Unfortunately, he'd written it in one of the Algonquian languages, which April couldn't read.

Josh was very patient with me all afternoon. Most of my questions probably sounded ridiculous to him. If I'm being honest with myself, I desperately wanted to impress him. I want him to think I'm smart and accomplished and amazing and [illegible word heavily crossed out]. Ugh, this is so ridiculous! I should just bite the bullet and ask him out, right? We get along so well, we make each other laugh, and he's so goddamn hot. He's not wearing a wedding ring and so far he hasn't mentioned a girlfriend, but on the other hand he's also at least ten years younger than me. I know I don't look forty-four, but the gap between our life experiences is so painfully obvious sometimes. At one point, when we were both growing frustrated with the translation, I mentioned that I needed a drink so badly I didn't care if I had to down a bottle of vanilla extract like Uncle Ned on Family Ties, *only he had no idea what the hell I was talking about. I don't think I've ever felt like such an ancient hag as I did in that moment.*

Note to self: Edit all this out when I turn my research into a bestselling nonfiction book. Maybe in the movie version Josh and I will have a steamy romance.

Kenny called. He's in his dark days again and wants me to come visit. Sometimes I really wish he'd get his shit together. I can't drop everything and go out there every time he hits a snag. Especially not now, when I'm so close to finishing the translation. I can't let myself get distracted. If I'm successful, if I find proof that this lost nation existed, this is what I'll be known for. This is what I'll be remembered for long after I'm gone. Kenny can wait.

I stopped reading, taken aback. It didn't sound like the April I knew. There was a bitterness to it that I'd never seen in her before. She'd always been there for me, always been my rock, but . . . was this what she secretly thought of me? That I was a nuisance?

Maybe she was right. Maybe I'd leaned on her too much over the years. I'd already cost her a promotion; who knew what else she'd had to give up because of me? Who knew what else I'd ruined for her?

She would have been better off pulling mom and dad out of that burning house, not me.

*　　*　　*

The translation work has been slow and frustrating. The problem is that there are numerous Algonquian dialects but no standard writing system that's used for all of them. Worse, over the centuries each dialect developed different writing systems from a range of influences, including other languages, so one might have certain words or concepts that another doesn't. But we're making headway, and so far two things stick out.

The first is what Josh said about the name "the Strange People Who Came Out of the Forest." Apparently this particular usage of the word strange doesn't mean the same as it does in English, like odd or weird. It's more akin to the word other. I asked if that meant the same as foreign, if perhaps they'd migrated from somewhere else, but he said no, there would be a different word for that. He couldn't explain it further.

The second thing that stuck out was where it's written that the Strange People Who Came Out of the Forest "mirrored" the Rappahannock. I assumed it meant they took on some of the Rappahannock's customs and laws. After all, the Strange People were described as naked when they came out of the forest, so perhaps they adopted the Rappahannock custom of wearing tanned hides as clothing. But Josh isn't so sure. He's starting to doubt whether mirrored is the right word.

I stopped reading when it got too dark out to continue. I'd lost track of time and the sun had set. I thought about heading back to the motel, but trying to find my way out of twenty thousand acres of forest at night with only my phone's GPS to guide me sounded terrifying.

Since April's tent was already set up and her sleeping bag was already unrolled, I decided to stay where I was. I ate dinner by the light of my flashlight, then tried to make more calls, first to Sergeant Donahue, then to the Anthropology Department at UC Davis to see if they'd heard from April. Neither call connected. Whatever meager signal I'd hooked into before was gone.

I took the small pill bottle out of my backpack and shook out a capsule into my palm. My new prescription anti-depressant worked better than the last one; so far, it had kept that dark, smothering curtain from falling again. But I hated the drowsiness and fuzzy-headedness that came with it, which was why I only took it at night, before bed. I swallowed the pill, then kicked off my shoes and slipped fully clothed into April's sleeping bag. The damp mustiness of the pillow bothered me, but the pill's side effects kicked in quickly and I was asleep before I had a chance to read any more of her diary.

I awoke in the middle of the night with the uneasy feeling that I was being watched. Someone was in the tent with me; I heard them breathing. I opened my eyes and saw a shadow crouched beside the sleeping bag, peering down at me. I stifled a scream, worried that if I made a noise it would attack. I snatched up the flashlight and switched it on, pointing the beam into the intruder's face. It was April. Her eyes stared wildly down at me.

"Jesus!" I cried, startled. I sat up quickly. "April, are you all right?"

She was naked, her hair hanging in long, tangled strands over her thin chest. I turned away quickly. It's one thing to see your sister naked when you're children innocently bathing together, but it's quite another when you're adults. It upsets the order of things. It means something is very wrong.

"What happened to you?" I asked.

She darted out of the tent like a frightened animal, slipping through the flap I'd forgotten to zip closed. I sprang to my feet and ran after her. She couldn't have had more than a five-second head start, but there was no sign of her in the moonlight. I pointed the flashlight in every direction, but all I saw were trees and weeds and the lake at the center of the clearing.

"April!" I shouted.

A flickering orange light moved between the trees on the outskirts of the clearing. It reminded me of fire, and I froze in place. But it was nothing like the wildfire; it was smaller, more controlled. A torch, maybe? But why would April have a torch? What happened to her flashlight?

"April!" I called again.

I hurried toward the edge of the clearing, but I wasn't used to going barefoot, especially in nature. Every rock, twig, and stiff, unyielding weed cut into the tender soles of my feet. The orange light flickered and moved deeper into the darkness, away from me. I paused at the edge of the trees, unable to take another step. But it wasn't the pain that kept me from going any farther, it was fear. Stumbling through the woods during the day had been frightening enough, but at night it would be madness. And yet, April needed me. It didn't matter what she secretly thought of me. She'd saved my life the night of the wildfire, and a hundred more times in ways that I'm sure felt small to her but were so big to me. I owed her. So, against all common sense, I threw myself into the dark woods to follow her.

The light continued to move through the forest and I ran after it, weaving around trees and underbrush, the beam from my flashlight bobbing unsteadily in front of me. Sharp rocks and sticks stabbed my feet. I shouted April's name, but to no avail. Finally I had to stop to catch my breath.

The flickering orange light returned, moving closer. I saw it through the trees, saw what it was. My breath caught in my throat.

Enormous antlers blazing with fire.

It was impossible. I closed my eyes tight, certain I was seeing things, maybe even dreaming, and when I opened them the fiery antlers were gone. I ran forward, pushing my way through a cluster of saplings. On the other side, the stag's hoofprints burned in small fires upon the ground. I followed them, desperate to understand how this could be happening. The burning hoofprints circled through the trees and returned to the clearing, where they approached the lake. They ended at the water's edge.

I knelt down on the bank and shone my flashlight across the lake. The water looked as black as oil, and yet it wasn't completely opaque. Something moved under the surface—a shape I couldn't make out. Without thinking, I dipped my fingers into the water. Something brushed against them, smooth and slimy like the skin of an eel, but also freezing cold, bitingly cold. My fingers went instantly numb, and when I pulled my hand back and turned the beam of my flashlight on it, my fingers looked red and frostbitten. I flexed them a few times until the feeling came back, then shone my light into the water again. All was still. Whatever had moved beneath the surface was gone.

The flaming hoofprints were gone too, as if they'd never been there.

After Mom and Dad died, April and I went to live with our grandparents. Their house was small for the four of us, but it was a warm, comfortable home and they made sure we never wanted for anything. I was fascinated by the antique lionskin rug that lay on the floor of their living room. It was a real one, with the head still attached, the lion's face frozen in an angry snarl, its lips pulled back to bare enormous teeth. As fascinated as I was, I was also repulsed by the violence it implied. Someone had hunted this majestic creature through the grasslands of Africa, tracked it, and killed it, but for what? So it could become a rug in someone's house? I knew nature was cruel and thrived on death, I'd known it ever since the wildfire, but we humans were supposed to be better than that, weren't we?

One day I lay down on the floor beside the lionskin rug as one might beside a beloved pet. I stroked the mane that ran from its forehead down to the middle of its hide. The hairs were stiff and bristly, and though I knew the lion was real, the hairs felt wrong, fake, as though they'd been replaced with something synthetic.

"Poor lion," I murmured sadly. "Look what they did to you."

April, then twelve years old and sporting a mouthful of metal braces, lay down across from me on the other side of the rug. "It's dead. It doesn't care."

"You don't know that," I said. "Wouldn't you care if you were dead?"

"Probably not. I didn't care before I was alive, so why would I care afterward?"

"It's different," I said. I stroked the lion's mane again as I struggled to explain what I meant. "You have friends now, and things you like to do. All that would be gone."

"But either I'd be in heaven, which would be better than everything else, or there's nothing after you die, in which case I won't be around to care."

"Which do you think it is?" I asked. On some level I understood we were talking about Mom and Dad, even if neither of us wanted to admit it. "Heaven or nothingness?"

She shrugged. "Ask the lion."

I looked into its glassy, unseeing eyes, but they held no answers. Its eyes were replacements too, I realized, like the hairs of its mane. This wasn't the same lion that had died on the grasslands. It had become something else, something that only looked like it.

After chasing phantoms through the woods, sleep was out of the question. How much of what I'd experienced was real? I was still getting used to the side effects of my new pills. The burning stag had to be a hallucination, but what about April? I'd seen her in the tent with me, but more than that I'd heard her breathing even before I opened my eyes. Did that mean she was real? If so, why had she run away? And where the hell were her clothes?

I sat on the sleeping bag inside the tent, remembering to zip the flap closed this time. My bare feet were bruised and bleeding from the forest floor, but my fingers hurt even worse. I thought of the fish I'd touched in the water, or whatever it was, and how unbelievably cold it had been, like touching dry ice. That had definitely not been a hallucination. I flexed my fingers again to ease the pain and then picked up April's diary. By the light of the flashlight I resumed reading.

Josh finished translating the story of the Strange People Who Came Out of the Forest, and it doesn't end happily. Although, perhaps fittingly, it does end strangely. Details are scarce thanks to the story being passed down orally for generations, but apparently before the Strange People returned to the forest they killed several members of the Rappahannock. "Poisoned them so that they wasted away to dust," according to Josh's translation.

The Strange People had described to them where they lived in the forest, including the lake that was the center of their territory, but when the vengeful Rappahannock pursued them into the woods they couldn't find the lake. Or as Josh translated it, "There was no lake," which sounds a lot more conclusive.

What had kept the Rappahannock from finding the Strange People Who Came Out of the Woods?

What had kept the Virginia police from finding April's campsite?

As I continued with the diary, it became unexpectedly poignant to read about April's growing infatuation with Josh, a sentiment she never shared with him but instead kept safely locked away in the pages of her diary, not unlike her unspoken frustration with me. At one point she even entertained the idea of asking him to come with her to Virginia, secretly hoping that the shared experience and close quarters might lead to romance, although in the privacy of her diary she used a far more vulgar term than that. Something about these passages brought me to tears. They made her seem so alive, so full of hope and longing, that her absence hollowed me out all over again. I cried until I didn't have anything left.

"Come back, April," I whispered. "I need you."

I flipped through the diary's remaining pages, but what I found there was much darker in tone than what had come before, an increasing obsession with finding evidence of the lost nation. By the time April left for Virginia, she wasn't even picking up when Josh called. She refused to let anything distract her, even her own feelings.

The final page of her diary startled me. She'd written many things that were crossed out—not just struck through like errors, but scratched out so violently it was as if she had wanted to remove them from existence altogether. I couldn't read any of it, save for three snippets. The first was toward the top of the page:

so weak, can't keep anything down

And further down:

has to be the same lake

And lastly:

mirrored

My fingers ached. I put down the diary and flexed them again. The frostbite was gone, but I was surprised at how shriveled and pruned my hand looked. I balled it into a fist. My joints felt stiff, and several of my knuckles cracked in unison.

A sudden sharp pain tore through me and I doubled over, dropping the flashlight. Its beam winked out when it hit the tent floor, leaving me in darkness. The pain was like nothing I'd experienced before, as though my whole body were being crushed, and I had the strange thought that it was spreading from my hand. Out of nowhere I heaved and regurgitated everything in my stomach. The floor of the tent ran with watery vomit. I curled up on the sleeping bag amid the awful stench, not knowing what was happening to me. In my weakened, delirious state I cried and begged April to come back and help me.

Footsteps approached the tent. I wept with pain as my body cramped and seized, and I wept again when I saw, silhouetted by moonlight against the tent walls, the shapes of men. I heard the zipper of the

tent flap start to pull. Weak and disoriented, all I could do was curl into
a ball and remember the last text April ever sent me.

They're still here.

Dark shapes pressed into the tent and dragged me out. I screamed
and thrashed, but I didn't dare look at their faces. I didn't want to see.
Their hands were cold and wet. I didn't want to think about what that
meant, but on some level I already knew. I'd known from the moment
I followed those burning hoofprints to the edge of the lake.

They didn't carry me far before they dropped me on the grass. I
curled into a ball for self-protection, waiting for their blows to rain
down, waiting for them to kill me. I hadn't counted their number, but I
figured there were at least half a dozen of them—more than I would
have been able to fight off even if I weren't sick and in pain. But they
didn't attack. When I finally dared to look up, they were gone and I was
alone on the bank of the lake.

I tried to stand, but I was too weak. My clothes hung loosely off my
frame as I continued to wither away, the strange illness draining my
strength like a leech draining blood. I forced myself to my knees and
saw I wasn't alone anymore. In the middle of the lake, standing impossibly upon the water's surface, was the burning stag.

Its bright orange flames reflected across the dark water. It turned its
fiery head toward me, its enormous, branching antlers raging like
torches. But instead of fear, all I felt was anger.

"Where is she?" I demanded. "Where is my sister?"

The burning stag stared at me, and then it was gone. Standing in its
place in the middle of the lake, as naked and motionless as a statue, was
April.

Only it wasn't my sister. I knew that without a doubt. This was
someone else, the creature that had been in my tent. Watching me while
I slept. Studying me.

I understood then the error Josh Glover had made in his translation.
The Strange People Who Came Out of the Forest hadn't *mirrored* the
Rappahannock. They *mimicked* them. Such an easy mistake to make, and
yet such a fatal one.

"You're not her," I told the creature that looked like April, although

I needn't have spoken aloud. That it had taken the shape of the burning stag told me it was already inside my head. I gave a weak laugh and added spitefully, "You're not even half the person she was."

With a pang of guilt I realized I'd spoken of my sister in the past tense for the first time. I supposed I had always known she was really, truly gone, but that was when I finally accepted it.

I wished I'd never entered the forest. I wished I'd never found this place, but then, I hadn't stumbled upon it by luck. I understood that now, too. This was a secret place, a hidden place, but like April I'd been *allowed* to find it. The only thing I didn't know was why.

I should never have put my fingers in the water, should never have let the creature touch me. That was my mistake, and probably April's, too. Somehow that was what made us both sick, poisoned like the Rappahannock.

A large bubble formed on the surface of the lake next to the creature that looked like April. Another one of them was rising up, a dark and formless mass that slowly solidified into the shape of a man.

The pain gripped me again, and I doubled over with a cry. My hands became bony and gnarled, my limbs as thin as sticks, my cheeks hollow and sharp. I was wasting away to nothing, and at the same time, in the gray light of the approaching dawn, the naked, featureless male figure began to develop a face. My face.

The horrible truth dawned on me. It wasn't just mimicking me; it was *feeding* off me. It was nature's cruel game, the law of the wild. Everything had to kill in order to survive, even them. That was why they'd let me find them, and April before me. They were hungry.

Poisoned them so that they wasted away to dust . . . Was that what had happened to April? Was she nothing but dust now, blown by unforgiving winds through twenty thousand acres of forest, invisible and forgotten? Was that what would happen to me?

Or was it possible, just this once, that there could be some mercy in nature's horror? When the process was complete would I join them, the devourer and the devoured becoming one, like the fire and the stag? Would I be reborn in a new and better body, one that had no chemical imbalance in its brain, one that never suffered from the dark curtain's smothering weight? Could that be April standing upon the water after all, inviting me to join her in a place that was better than everything else?

I could feel the creature rooting around in my head, icy fingers picking through my mind. I didn't resist. I welcomed it, opened myself to it. I felt my body shrivel, felt myself leaving it, but to go where? Was this transference or death? Heaven or nothingness? I prayed: *Just this once, just this once . . .*

But the curtain was still there—the heavy, dark, smothering curtain that was always with me. The icy fingers touched it and recoiled in disgust. The creature withdrew from my mind. The male form stopped reshaping itself and melted like candlewax back into the water.

"Wait," I rasped, my voice thin and feeble.

And then April followed, sinking slowly and silently into the lake. Her expression remained blank. Utterly indifferent.

"Wait!" I shouted with the little strength I had left.

She sank straight down, the glassy surface of the lake barely rippling as it came to her waist, her chest, her neck, her eyes. Then she was gone.

I collapsed to the ground, weak and empty, though I could feel my strength start to return. They'd rejected me. I was too damaged for them, too broken. There was no point in continuing the process.

"Come back, April," I whispered. "Take me with you."

But the surface of the lake remained still. I lay there beside the water as the sun lit the empty clearing. The wind blew lonely through the tree branches, and birds swooped down from the air to catch their prey, and armored insects fought like gladiators in the dirt, and the cruel, pitiless, infinite mystery at the heart of the cosmos looked down upon me and, seeing nothing of interest, looked away.

The Rest Is Noise

When Andrew opened his eyes, he was surprised to find himself lying on the worn Oriental rug in the living room of his cramped Manhattan apartment. He tried to pick himself up off the floor, but his arms and legs barely contained the strength to move. Inside his ears, something wet and sticky sloshed. The faint smell of copper came to him.

On the rug beside his hand, his smartphone was still on, still talking to him. The outgoing message of the number he'd called—had he dialed a number?—was malfunctioning, stuck in a warped, maddening loop.

"I can't answer your call right now. Please leave a message . . . I can't answer your call right now. Please leave a message . . . This is Justin Valentine . . . I can't . . . leave . . ."

Finally the call disconnected and the phone's display screen went dark.

He didn't remember what had happened. How had he wound up on the floor with his phone dialed? The delirium he felt was a familiar sensation, like coming out of a high, but he hadn't done drugs in twenty years, not since he was an undergrad at NYU. He looked at the phone again, inches from his hand. Why had he called Justin Valentine? They hadn't spoken in years outside of the occasional rushed greeting at industry events, Justin being a label exec and Andrew a journalist for *Bebop*, one of the few remaining jazz magazines in the nation. Their estrangement pained him at times, but it was the way of the world. It didn't matter how close you were once; college friends grew apart over the years—a slow, tectonic drift that seemed to start the moment you threw your caps in the air.

The stark white cord of Andrew's headset had been ripped from the jack in the top of his smartphone. Red droplets dotted the earbuds. Blood, he realized. The wetness in his ears, the coppery smell—it was blood.

What was happening to him?

It came back to him then: the mysterious email from Justin Valentine, blank but for a single attachment: an MP3 file. An advance review copy of an album, Andrew had guessed, but then he'd seen the name of the artist. This was what he'd been listening to, had been listening to for days now, unable to stop, each note so perfectly honed it sliced through him and plucked his soul like a harp.

He had to hear it again. It was like an itch, a compulsion. Each moment without it felt squandered.

He reached for his smartphone, surprised to find he had the strength to move after all, but the overwhelming need to hear that amazing music again gave life to his limbs. He plugged in the headset cord and slipped the earbuds into his blood-slick ears. His fingers slid across the touch screen desperately until he found the MP3 file again.

Through the Gates of Hamelin by Indigo Mantooth.

Christ, he could hardly believe it. He hadn't heard that name in so long. It had been a decade since the last Indigo Mantooth album—a decade since anyone had seen him alive, including Andrew.

A memory came to him then, Indigo smiling the grin that always put Andrew at ease, no matter what mischief they were about to get into, and saying, *"If this shit doesn't make you see the face of God, you're doing it wrong."* In one hand he held a record, *Duke Ellington at Newport,* and in the other a plastic baggie filled with hashish. Even now, some twenty years later, Andrew still couldn't be entirely sure which one Indigo was referring to.

His finger paused above the glowing Play icon. This feeling was familiar too. It was the moment before you lit the pipe, or licked the tab, or snorted the line; it was the delicious anticipation before the high. This music was unlike anything he'd heard before. It was a drug, more powerful than any he'd ever tried.

He tapped the Play icon and closed his eyes.

As Indigo's trumpet began to blare in his ear and he drifted away, some renegade part of him wondered how many times he'd listened to the album now. He'd lost count.

He wondered what day of the week it was. He'd lost track.

But most of all, he wondered what those *things* were that had begun growing out of his back.

Andrew's memories of college consisted of a four-year haze of drugs and music. Hash, angel dust, ecstasy, magic mushrooms, acid—whatever he, Justin, and Indigo could get their hands on cheaply. It was the late 1980s, and their classmates were tossing back Buds at parties and playing the latest from R.E.M. or U2 on their CD players, but not them. Instead, the three of them would sit in Indigo's dorm room on West 10th Street, so high their heads felt like balloons no longer attached to their bodies, and as they tripped they spun vinyl on Indigo's authentic 1972 Bang & Olufsen Beogram 4000 turntable. What came roaring out of his top of the line Bose speakers was Mingus's *The Black Saint and the Sinner Lady,* Coltrane's *A Love Supreme,* Davis's *Kind of Blue,* Monk's *Misterioso.* The music took them to places far, far away.

They were inseparable throughout their time at NYU. Some professors called them the Three Musketeers, others the Three Stooges, but always it was the three of them. Yet as the years rolled on, Andrew would sometimes walk in to find Justin and Indigo already high, a record already spinning on the stereo, having started without him. He would find them talking in conspiratorial tones, and they would stop when he came in and refuse to tell him what they'd been discussing. In those moments, Andrew's world constricted on itself. The Three Musketeers reduced itself to the Two Musketeers and Andrew, the outsider.

During winter break of his junior year, he flew to Louisiana to visit Indigo at home, a desperate and poorly masked effort to strengthen their friendship so he'd never be left out again. Indigo lived in an old, ramshackle house in a humid backwoods bayou, its wooden walls rotting from the wet and leaning at odd angles, as if the house were in a constant state of collapse. Andrew wondered how someone who lived in such a setting could afford a first-rate stereo system like Indigo's, but he didn't pry. He did, however, voice his concerns about the house falling on their heads while they slept.

"Didn't you hear? This house is magic," Indigo teased him. "These old walls ain't never gonna come down."

He was only half joking. Indigo often claimed his parents were mediums who communed with the spirits, though the only evidence Andrew saw of anything unusual was the five-pointed stained-glass star that hung in the front window. That, and the rats.

At night the rats came from all over the bayou and congregated like parishioners on the front porch of the house. Andrew saw them the first night he was there, hundreds of little hairy bodies so tightly packed together that they seemed to undulate like water, their long, wormy pink tails thrashing.

He sank lower in the window, keeping his eye on the rats. "What are they doing?"

Indigo shrugged nonchalantly. He was clearly used to them. "God only knows. My folks say they're drawn here because this house is on the border."

Andrew scowled at him. "What border? You're miles from Texas."

Indigo grinned and wiggled his eyebrows. "The border between our world and the spirit world." He laughed and pulled out a joint. "Now smoke up, and maybe we'll see some more weird shit."

Indigo didn't talk to the spirits as his parents did. But as they sat on the couch that night, stoned and watching the smoke curl along the ceiling, he told Andrew that he thought growing up in this house had given him a spiritual appreciation of music that few others shared, one more in tune with what he called the cosmic jam. He didn't just want to study music, he said as he stubbed out the joint, he wanted to create it.

When winter break was over, Indigo returned to school with an old, battered trumpet he bought at a garage sale. It was the same horn he would play throughout his career.

It was, in fact, a trumpet that had ignited Andrew's fascination with the intangible power of music.

He'd been ten years old when his parents dragged him to Italy for a family vacation. There, in the Medici Chapels in Florence, he'd stood beneath Panizetti's massive painting *L'Ascensione di Gabriel* and marveled. One look at the archangel Gabriel's titanic form, his head amid the clouds, his wings all but blotting out a sky that roiled red with wrath and awe as he blew his trumpet to call mankind to worship, and Andrew had been overcome with the idea that music was, at its heart, an unknowable mystery.

What reason was there that a seemingly random assortment of sounds should make the listener feel something? The honking of a car horn didn't stir your soul, and yet the exact same note blasted from Indigo's trumpet at just the right moment could make your spirit soar. That was music's power. It was what drew Andrew to its study. It was why he and Justin had tried to start a band with Indigo after he brought the trumpet to school, though they quickly gave up after discovering they didn't have an eighth of Indigo's talent.

Yet the question continued to itch at him throughout his adult life: How could simple sounds touch you so deeply? The first humans who'd picked up a rock or stick or hollow bone and tapped out a beat had to have been moved by something. What had made them do it?

All Andrew knew for sure about music was that it was unknowable.

What he suspected was that it came from God.

The growths on his back had started as six small, red, perfectly circular bumps. He noticed them in the mirror the morning after his first hearing of *Through the Gates of Hamelin*. They'd grown bigger since, forming stiff protuberances like small cones of flesh with tiny puckered blowholes at their ends. He had no idea what they were or where they'd come from, only that he refused to take a moment away from listening to the album to see a doctor about them.

He hadn't shaved in days. The unrecognizable, hairy-jawed thing that stared back at him from the mirror had hollow eyes and a crust of dried blood in its ears. His clothes were filthy. When was the last time he'd changed them? When was the last time he'd eaten anything? Had he checked in with his editor at *Bebop*? Called Mary from the coffee shop for a second date? He couldn't remember. All he wanted to do was listen to the music, over and over again.

And oh, what beautiful music it was! The ten-year wait since Indigo's last release had been worth it, he thought. More than worth it. *Through the Gates of Hamelin* was divided into two twenty-minute-long tracks, and he could imagine how it would have played as a traditional vinyl record, a single track on either side like Mingus's *Town Hall Concert* or Albert Ayler's *At Slug's Saloon*. The first track, "Rider on the Tides," was a blast of freeform improvisational jazz, a cacophony of sound as jarring as it was smooth, as much sandpaper as velvet. The second track, titled "Answer the Call," was a soundscape so riveting he couldn't tell if there were other trumpets involved or if Indigo had somehow managed to clone himself into four, five, six separate trumpeters, each one weaving notes around the other to form an aural web, its final sustained note like a knife tearing through the membrane-thin barrier between the Earth and the heavens. In a word, the album was sublime.

The music took him to places far, far away. Often he fell asleep listening to it and dreamt he was in a desert, surrounded by the ruins of an enormous marble building. Half-broken columns protruded from the sand at odd angles like grasping finger bones. What remained of the building's domed roof lay half buried in a nearby dune. Above, the sky was as red as a rose petal, with no sun or stars, though somehow he could see. There weren't even any clouds, just an unbroken plane of crimson from horizon to horizon. In the dream, something shifted underfoot. A bulge appeared under the sand and started toward him, six long, spiky protuberances breaking through the sand like sharks' fins.

He would wake then, always at that same moment, with something unseen racing toward him beneath the sand.

The three of them took different paths after college, though each was still guided by his love of music. Justin went the corporate route, earning an MBA and venturing into music distribution and promotion. Andrew attended Columbia to study journalism and landed magazine gigs that eventually led him to *Bebop* magazine.

Indigo went on to play the meanest horn this side of the guy who blew down the walls of Jericho.

Album after album topped the jazz charts and won Grammy nods. For a decade Indigo Mantooth was the face of American jazz. Then, in 2001, he had his first flop, an album titled *The Call*. Considered a failure by fans and critics alike, it lasted a week on the charts, then plummeted, dragging Indigo down with it.

Shortly after, he disappeared. Rumors of his death spread quickly through the smoky jazz clubs of Manhattan, though Andrew stubbornly refused to believe it, despite the fact that by then he and Indigo had lost touch. But there was no obituary, no public death certificate or record of burial. Still, Indigo never resurfaced to put the rumors to rest, never returned Andrew's phone calls or responded to his emails and letters. It was as if in failure Indigo Mantooth had been erased from the world.

Andrew woke from a dream of the strange desert to find himself standing in a dark, empty hallway. The smell of dust and stale air stung his nose.

Startled, he nearly fell over, and grabbed the wall for support. It took a moment for him to get his bearings, and for his jackhammering heart to calm. The wall was dusty under his palm, its plaster crumbling from neglect. Cobwebs hung in the corners and a row of empty light sockets lined the ceiling. Spray-painted graffiti marred the walls and ceiling. The window at the end of the hallway was boarded up, the only light source the sunlight that squeezed through between the planks of wood.

How long had he been here? How had he *gotten* here?

As his mind cleared, the hallway became eerily familiar. He'd been here before, he realized suddenly, been here many times, in fact. He looked at the door directly in front of him and knew, even before he saw the faded ghost of the room number in its chipped paint, that it was Indigo's dorm room.

He'd heard that the old NYU dormitory on West 10th Street had been closed and scheduled for demolition in favor a new facility, but the recession had put the plan on hiatus, the job only half done.

Why had he come back here?

More to the point, *how* had he come here? The last thing he remembered was falling asleep at home listening to *Through the Gates of Hamelin*. Was he sleepwalking now, on top of everything else?

The floor was carpeted with a thick layer of dust that showed two pairs of footprints. One was fresh, his own, ending where he stood before the door. The other was older, the prints salted with a light coating of new dust. They were flat, treadless, like the soles of dress shoes, and they continued into the room. Someone else had been here.

Terrified, he turned and ran, fleeing down two flights of stairs to where he remembered the exit was. He burst through the plywood-boarded door, the padlock jangling uselessly on its broken chain, and out onto West 10th Street. The pedestrians walking by didn't give him a second look. Greenwich Village was already filled with men in filthy clothes and scraggly beards; what was one more?

It was only then that he realized Indigo's trumpet was still blaring in his ear. He was still wearing the earbuds. He'd grown so used to them he didn't feel them anymore. But how could that be? It had been early morning when he'd tapped the Play icon for the umpteenth time and let the music carry him away, but judging from the position of the sun in the sky and the fact that the sidewalks were crowded with people heading home from work, it was now late afternoon. Christ, how many times had he tapped Play in his sleep?

He looked back at the old dorm, its shuttered windows like dead eyes. He hadn't been back since graduation. Why now? West 10th Street was more than twenty city blocks from his apartment. Something had drawn him there, compelled him to walk a full mile on foot in his sleep.

He took the subway home. There, he took the earbuds out of his ears for the first time in . . . he couldn't remember how long. Since he'd charged the phone last night? No, he'd continued listening even then, with the phone connected to the outlet. The earbuds were so coated with blood they looked as if they'd been painted red. It was jolting to see, but even more jolting was being cut off from the music so suddenly. Over the past days—weeks?—every note had become such a part of him that its absence felt like a yawning pit.

The dorm. Why had he gone back to the dorm?

He was losing it. That was the only answer. Something inside him was broken, and all that was left were disjointed fragments spinning off in every direction.

He dropped onto the couch, and the outgrowths on his back ached when they hit the upholstery. They'd grown bigger, stretching his dirty, sweat-soaked shirt away from his back. If they kept growing like this, one day soon he wouldn't be able to fit a shirt over them. Then what? How big would they get?

What were they?

What was happening to him?

One day at NYU, their music history professor asked the class, "Who is the greatest musician of all time?"

The students responded with a variety of names—Beethoven, Thelonius Monk, Jimmy Page, Rush (that one earned a titter from the class)—but the professor only shook his head dismissively.

"Wrong," he proclaimed. "The greatest musician of all time is the Pied Piper."

The class erupted with noise, some laughing to pretend they were in on the joke, others harrumphing indignantly like grand dames who'd found a spot on the silver. Andrew was one of the laughers, and he turned to Indigo beside him, expecting to see him laughing too, but Indigo sat listening intently. From Indigo's other side, Justin glanced over at Andrew, ran a finger around his ear, and whispered cuckoo noises.

"The thing about the Pied Piper," the professor said, "the thing most people don't know, is that the earliest versions of the folktale tell of a mysterious piper who shows up in a village one day and, without reason or explanation, leads all the children away with a song, never to return. Imagine that. Hearing his music was all it took for every child in the village to fall under his spell and leave their homes forever. Mozart, Beethoven, Bach, even Thelonius Monk at the height of his game couldn't do that."

The room fell silent. Indigo picked up his pen and started writing feverishly in his notebook.

"It was only centuries later that the story was changed," the professor continued. "The piper became a rat catcher hired by a village to lure plague-carrying rats away with his magic pipe. This is the story you all know, this bastardized version where the villagers refused to pay him afterward and he retaliated by turning his magic pipe on their children to lead them away just as he had the rats. But it's bullshit." Another titter ran through the class, a nervous one this time. "The new version was an attempt to fix a tidy and understandable moral on the original, far darker tale. The Pied Piper was never a rat catcher. He didn't catch rats to save villages from the plague. He *was* the plague. He was catastrophe, tragedy. He was death, and his motives were unknowable. But this much I do know; this much I can tell you with certainty, and if you take nothing else away from this class or your time at this university, *this* is what you should remember."

Indigo looked expectantly at the professor, as if the man possessed secret knowledge.

"It wasn't the pipe that was magic," the professor said. "It was the music that came out of it."

After graduation, while Andrew was studying journalism at Columbia and Indigo was playing the jazz clubs and getting noticed, Justin Valentine was rising quickly through the corporate ranks. Eventually he worked his way up to CEO of the Verve Music Group, ushering in the label's most profitable years ever, until it all came crashing down.

Unlike Andrew, Justin had never stopped doing drugs. The tabloids printed pictures of him raging half-dressed through the streets of Southampton, or at a Grammys after-party with traces of white powder ringing his nostrils. A video surfaced of him smoking crack with one of the label's artists, and that was the end of his career at Verve. Since then, there had been five arrests for drug possession, various hospitalizations, multiple stays in rehab, and rumors about him starting his own label.

Andrew had lost track of him somewhere in the cycle of abuse and detox, until Justin's email came out of the blue with the new album from Indigo Mantooth attached. It opened an old wound. Indigo had never responded to Andrew's attempts at contacting him, not even to let him know he was still alive. Yet he had clearly been in contact with Justin, possibly even working with him on the new album, and neither of them had thought to let Andrew know until now.

It was like opening that dorm room door and finding Justin and Indigo doing their thing without him all over again. The Two Musketeers and the outsider.

"This is Justin Valentine. I can't answer your call right now. Please leave a message."

"Goddamn it, pick up!" Andrew shouted, gripping his phone with shaking fingers. The lumps on his back burned as they rubbed against the fabric of his shirt. They were still growing, stretching his skin like taffy. "Please, Justin, I've got to talk to you."

". . . can't answer your call right now. Please leave a message."

Justin's voicemail was still malfunctioning, caught in an endless loop. Andrew winced, squeezing his eyelids tight. The pain was excruciating. His whole back felt as if it was going to split open.

"What did you do to me, you son of a bitch?" he yelled into the phone, though he knew it would do no good.

The outgoing message only warped and stuttered in reply. *"This is Justin Valentine . . . please . . . I can't leave . . ."*

Andrew's body began to spasm. He dropped the phone and fell onto the floor.

The voice on the phone said, *"Please . . . help me . . . where am I? Why can't I leave?"* And then the line went dead.

Andrew spat great sobs of laughter into the rug. He was going crazy, that was all. Loony tunes. The men in white coats were coming to take him away, ha-ha.

The room spun and grew dark. His eyelids fluttered, his eyes rolled back in his head, and then he was in the desert again. It was just as he remembered, hot sand and red sky, but this time the domed building stood tall and proud, whole and untouched by the ravages of time, not yet reduced to the ruins he'd seen before. It was a temple, he realized, a shrine devoted to something unknowable that dwelt within it.

Music, the most beautiful he'd ever heard, floated out from the darkness at the heart of the temple, winding its way between the mighty columns and filling the desert with its sound. He recognized it immediately. He'd heard it enough times to know innately which note followed which. It was Indigo's *Through the Gates of Hamelin* coming from inside the temple, but instead of confusing him, it put him at ease. He didn't belong anywhere else but here.

He saw then that he wasn't alone. Shapes surrounded the temple, walking on two legs like men, but they were taller, bonier, and their joints bent at wrong angles. Their hides were a matted, mangy gray. The eyes in their terrible, rodentlike faces were rolled back, just like his, blank and empty in religious ecstasy. They swayed and writhed to the music, and their pointed ears bled. Six long, fleshy extrusions sprouted on each creature's back, identical to the ones on Andrew's.

From behind him, a voice spoke suddenly, making him jump. "He remakes us in His own image so that we may better serve Him."

Andrew knew that voice, and hearing it here in the desert, in his dream, filled him with horror. He turned around slowly and woke up on the floor of his apartment. His heart still pounding, he pushed himself up into a sitting position. The lights were out, though he didn't remember turning them off. Had he been sleepwalking again?

The tumorous swellings on his back ached. They twitched with each breath he took, as though their roots had dug so deep inside him they'd latched onto his lungs. He could feel the small holes at their ends puckering with each exhalation.

A murky shadow moved among the other shadows in the corner of the room. Andrew gasped and scrambled backward along the floor until his back hit the couch, sending a sharp pain through the growths there. The figure stayed in the shadows, resolving into the silhouette of a man in a long coat, but his identity remained as hidden as his face.

"Hello, Andrew," the figure said.

Andrew started at the unexpectedly familiar voice. The same voice he'd known so well in his youth. The same voice from his dream.

"Justin?" Andrew reached for the lamp on the table beside the couch.

"No, leave it off," Justin said. "The light hurts. I'm not used to it anymore."

Andrew let his arm drop, leaving the room in darkness. "How did you get in here?" He looked down the short hallway that led to the front door, but the corridor only ended in darkness.

"I've missed you, Andrew. We both have," Justin said.

Andrew got to his feet. "What's happening to me?"

"You are being lifted. He is lifting you. I was like you, confused and frightened when He first came to me. But oh, the things He showed me, Andrew. The ecstasy of it all. I understand His need now. His role for you and me."

"Damn it, Justin, just tell me what's happening to me! What are these *things* on my back?"

"The price of admission."

A sharp pain shot through Andrew, and he doubled over, gripping his stomach. "It's the music, isn't it? It's changing me. Putting these things on my back. Making me sleepwalk. Giving me those insane dreams."

"Not dreams," Justin said. "Glimpses into another world. He can show you more, Andrew. He can take you there."

Andrew sat down on the couch, still hugging himself. "You're out of your mind. You've done so many drugs you've lost touch with reality."

"I regret nothing. The drugs opened my mind, expanded my consciousness enough to receive Him when He came to me. He played His music for me, His incredible music, and at last I understood."

"Bullshit. Why would Indigo reach out to you and not me? I was his friend too."

"So little has changed. Are you really the same insecure college kid who thought his friends were going to leave him behind?"

"It looks like you did. How long were you working together? Why didn't either of you tell me he was recording a new album?"

"He created that album just for you, Andrew. There was no recording session, He *willed* it into being, out of thin air. That's how powerful He is."

Andrew shook his head. "You're fucking high."

"He had to make sure you'd hear. This was the best way. *Through the Gates of Hamelin*. I thought you would appreciate the reference."

"This is crazy. This is just some drug-fueled psychotic break. What did you do, slip me something?"

Justin laughed. "What He offers goes beyond drugs, Andrew. Way beyond them." He stepped forward, into a slash of light from a streetlamp outside the window. Andrew had seen plenty of junkies in his time; it came with the territory when you wrote about musicians, and Justin certainly looked as if he was still using. His face was pale, his cheeks scruffy, unshaven, and sunken beneath sharp cheekbones. Dark circles shadowed his eyes. A white cord drooped from his ears into his coat pocket. He was bleeding around the earbuds, dark, dried blood painting the sides of his face.

It was like looking in a mirror. If Justin was still using, then so was Andrew, only their drug of choice had changed.

"His music is a higher art form. Transcendent. Transformative," Justin said. "It's a beacon, a summoning, and the call has already been answered. He chose me, Andrew. And now He's chosen you too. It'll be just like old times. The three of us, remember? We're getting the band back together."

Justin was wearing dress shoes, Andrew saw. Flat-soled. He wondered if he inspected them closely if he would find dust on their soles. He closed his eyes, wishing that would make everything go away. The growths on his back twitched.

"There are so few of us, Andrew, the ones who truly understand what music is. Where it comes from. Why it moves the soul the way it does. He knows."

Andrew opened his eyes. "You said Indigo came to you, but where had he been? He was gone for ten years."

Justin grinned. It made his gaunt, pale face look like a skull. "Find out for yourself. He wants to see you."

Andrew leapt off the couch. "Indigo is in New York? Where?"

"You know where." With that, Justin turned and walked to the door. From beneath the back of his coat, six large, tubular shapes bulged against the fabric.

The last time Andrew had seen Indigo was during an interview for *Bebop* magazine. As they'd sat across from each other at a table in the lobby of the Waldorf Astoria, the miniature voice recorder blinking silently between them, Andrew almost hadn't recognized his old friend. Indigo looked gaunt, as if he hadn't eaten for weeks. His eyes had sunk deep in his head, and his skin, once the color of smooth mahogany, now looked ashen and pale. Andrew asked if he was all right, and Indigo just nodded and said, "Let's do this." So they did.

"In several of your interviews, you've called music 'the celestial language,'" Andrew said.

"That's what I believe, yeah. If music can bridge the gap between human beings, black, white, yellow, and brown, and bring them together with a kind of universal language, why can't it bring *all* life together everywhere?" Indigo seemed to come alive as he spoke, the color returning to his face. "The universe is a big place, man. You really think we're the only ones making music? Earth's kind of a primitive planet. What about the more advanced civilizations out there?"

A half-smile grew on Andrew's face. "Are you talking about aliens?"

"Aliens, spirits, angels, gods, whatever you want to call them. Radio and TV waves are floating out there from our little blue ball, so why not music? Music lifts the soul. It joins everything together. I know they're out there, listening. Riding the tides of the universe and just grooving on the beat."

Andrew chuckled. Now *this* was the Indigo he'd known in college. He decided to play along. "Have you ever heard any of *their* music? Are they communicating with you?"

Indigo laughed too. "Oh, yeah, I've heard it. We play together sometimes, me and that rider on the tides. A cosmic jam session that lasts for days at a time. Ain't like nothing you've heard before. It would blow your mind. I can't even listen to regular music after that. Compared to this, man, the rest is noise."

Still grinning, Indigo looked at him expectantly, ready to keep going. Andrew took a deep breath. He knew what he had to ask next, and he was dreading it, but his editors at *Bebop* would never forgive him if he didn't. So he steeled himself, checked his notes, and said, "Let's come back down to Earth for a moment. Your latest album, *The Call*, didn't connect with your fans the way your previous albums did. Sales numbers were pretty low. Reviews labeled it too experimental, too out there to catch on. The *New York Times* called it, and I'm quoting here, 'a cacophony of seemingly random trumpet notes that should never have been recorded, let alone packaged for sale—'"

"I know what they called it," Indigo interrupted. The grin was gone, and it was like he'd been shut down. His face grew closed, drawn, like a gate falling over his features.

Andrew felt as if he'd stabbed his old friend in the gut. Hoping he sounded more sympathetic than mercenary, he said, "That's got to sting."

Indigo glared at him for a long time. Andrew wondered if he'd insulted him, if Indigo would get up and walk out, but finally he just shrugged and said, "I don't care what they say. I didn't record *The Call* for any of them, not the fans, and definitely not the critics. It's something different, something special, you know what I mean?"

Andrew frowned. "Then who did you record it for?"

Indigo didn't answer. His expression was unreadable.

"Indigo, seriously, if not your fans or the critics, who did you think would be listening to it?"

To Andrew's surprise, a smile grew on Indigo's face. He winked.

The next day, Indigo Mantooth disappeared.

He was alive. Alive and in New York City. Andrew almost couldn't believe it. It was too good to be true.

Yet as much as he wanted to see his old friend, he was terrified. The things he'd seen (another world, Justin said; was that even possible?) and the things that were happening to him (the blackouts, the sleepwalking, the things growing out of his back—*"He remakes us in His own image"*): it all scared the hell out of him. And if Justin was right, somehow Indigo was at the center of it.

He needed something to calm him down. Out of habit, he picked up his smartphone and flipped to the MP3 of *Through the Gates of Hamelin,* but the file was gone. It had vanished from his phone as surely as if Justin had walked out of the apartment with it.

Oh, no. Shit shit shit, he needed that music. He'd dropped everything, ignored everything, his personal hygiene, his job, his *life* for that music—and now it was gone.

No, not gone, he realized, not entirely. Indigo still had it. He was the source of it.

For a while he fought his need for it with the same ferocity a junkie does when he's been away from the needle long enough to muster his strength, but the compulsion was undeniable. That music was the strongest drug he'd ever been addicted to. And if Andrew knew anything about drug addiction from his own history, it was that sometimes it's stronger than you are.

When it finally got to be too much and he gave in, he at least had enough presence of mind to grab a steak knife from the kitchen drawer and slip it into his boot before leaving the apartment.

"You know where," Justin had said.

Yes, he did. Of course he did. It was where he'd always gone to see Indigo.

Andrew returned to the old, shuttered dorm on West 10th Street, slipping inside the unlocked front door and following the two sets of footprints—his own and Justin's—up two flights to Indigo's dorm room. He stood in front of the door and reached for the doorknob. Suddenly frightened again, he pulled his hand back.

His gut told him to run, and that seemed like a pretty good idea until he heard the music playing softly from inside. It invaded him, overwhelmed his senses, and silenced his instincts. Lured by the music, he twisted the doorknob and as the door opened, he stepped through.

Beyond the door, the room was completely black. The air was hot and thick with humidity. He heard the buzz of insects and the croaking of frogs. As his eyes adjusted to the dark, lit only by sudden starlight overhead, he realized he was standing not on the wooden floor of a dorm room but on grass and mud. Before him was an old house, its slowly collapsing walls leaning at dangerous angles. A five-pointed stained-glass star hung in the front window.

Indigo's family home, the house on the border. Seeing it again now put a bolt of terror in his chest, but he couldn't turn away. Though the windows were dark, the music was coming from somewhere inside it, calling to him like a needle dangled in front of a junkie.

Andrew walked up the steps onto the porch. A furry carpet of rats squealed and ran from his boots, jumping off the sides. He turned the knob on the front door. It was unlocked and opened easily. He stepped inside.

The music stopped abruptly. Andrew's mind reeled. He thought, not for the first time, that he was going mad.

He stood in a vast desert. Above him the sky was the color of fire, of lava and blood. The ruins of a great domed building dotted the landscape, and in the middle of it all, sitting on a plain high-backed wooden chair on the sand, was Indigo Mantooth. His ears were bleeding and he clutched a battered old trumpet in his hand.

"Indigo?" Andrew said.

Indigo looked up. His fingers played with the piston valves along the spine of the trumpet, pressing and releasing them like a nervous tic. "There is a silence that hangs between the stars," he said. "A silence that yearns to be filled."

"Jesus, Indigo," Andrew said, starting toward him. "Are you all right? What happened to you?"

"The void must be filled with music." Indigo's fingers clacked along the piston valves again. "Music isn't just sound, you see, it's transformation. Evolution. It is the key, and it is the doorway."

In mid-step Andrew's knees gave out and he fell on all fours, gasping. The air was so hot and thick it felt like soup. He was choking, losing oxygen, and then the growths on his back twitched to life. They opened their little holes, filtering the air they pulled into him, and suddenly he wasn't so lightheaded anymore and could stand. It felt as natural as breathing, and it disgusted him as there was nothing natural about it.

The sand shifted under his weight, sliding away to reveal a stark white skull near his foot. It was human-sized but elongated, with obscenely large incisors at the front of its jaws. It reminded Andrew of the rodentlike creatures he'd seen in his dream, swaying and writhing around the temple, and he gasped and scrambled back from it. "What is this place?"

"Once, long ago, He was worshipped as a god here," Indigo said.

"He? Who is *he?*" Andrew demanded, still on edge, every nerve in a heightened state of alarm.

"Eventually His followers went the way of all things mortal, lost to the inevitable decay of death," Indigo continued, ignoring Andrew's question. "For millennia He sang His songs alone, unheard, driven nearly to the brink of madness with no one to worship Him. His song reached out to fill the space between the stars, a summons that none answered."

Andrew realized his mistake then. He'd assumed Justin had been talking about Indigo back at the apartment. He hadn't been. His pulse quickening, he looked around quickly, remembering what he'd seen in his dreams. There was something else here, something under the sand. He wished he could pull his feet up like a kid scared of monsters under the bed, but there was no place to put them. The sand was everywhere.

"Then, at last, He heard another lonely soul call out from far, far away, call out with music, and in that music He heard an echo of His own. He is so powerful, Andrew, so awe-inspiring that His consciousness was able to cross millions of miles of darkness just to answer that call."

"It was *your* music it heard," Andrew said breathlessly. "That's who *The Call* was for. You were communicating with it!"

"His consciousness followed the notes like a trail of breadcrumbs, and we became one. God and prophet. Musician and instrument. For years we played together here in his domain, but He needs more followers, Andrew. One could never be enough for Him."

"So you—you *told* it about us?"

"There was no need. He'd already seen inside my mind. Justin came willingly. He had nothing left to lose, and the drugs had turned his mind to putty. You have been harder to summon. But now that you're here, will you stay? Stay, Andrew, and hear His music as you've never heard it before."

Indigo smiled, but there was no mirth in it, none of the warmth Andrew remembered from their days together at NYU. His eyes were hollow and glassy, and a chill crept up Andrew's back as he realized the man in the chair wasn't Indigo Mantooth. Not anymore. He was completely under the control of the thing beneath the sand, a drone to its queen bee. There was nothing of his old friend left, only a mindless disciple speaking on behalf of his mad, lonely god.

"No," Andrew said, backing away in horror.

"Through His music He transforms us, puts us in tune with His will," Indigo said. "Through His music, we worship Him anew. And He needs worshippers, Andrew. He needs us to look after Him, to rebuild His great temple. A god without worshippers is like a tuneless song, empty and without purpose. Join us, Andrew. Worship Him."

"No," he repeated. He stumbled on the loose sand and quickly righted himself.

"His music has already transformed you, made you ready to serve Him. He has given you but a taste of the music to come. Why refuse His gift?"

Andrew spun around, ready to run out through the door he came through, but it was gone. He'd been a fool to think it would still be there. In its place was Justin.

The protrusions on Justin's back had grown, thickened, and torn through his coat to extend like tree branches. The white wires of his headset hung from his bleeding ears and the sharp, tinny sound of a trumpet seeped from the earphones. *Through the Gates of Hamelin.*

"Worship Him," Justin said. His eyes were rolled back into his head in religious ecstasy. The growths on his back moved in time with his breath. Andrew remembered the strange things he'd heard on Justin's voicemail, his confusion at being trapped somewhere, his cry for help— a side effect of the unearthly music, perhaps, or a warning from Justin somehow, one last gift from an old friend he'd thought had deserted him—and he realized there was nothing left of Justin either in this drone that stood before him. There was only one Musketeer left.

A loud, sustained trumpet note blared through the silent desert. Andrew turned and saw Indigo rise out of his chair. The growths on Indigo's back unfurled, thick as organ pipes, to extend over his shoulders and out to the sides like bony wings. Andrew put his hands over his ears to keep the music out, but it was no good. It grew louder, sneaking in around his palms, between his fingers, through his skin. Blood oozed out of his ears. He looked at Indigo and saw to his horror that he was holding the trumpet at his side. The sound wasn't coming from his horn. It wasn't coming from Indigo at all.

Andrew's gorge rose, and he understood now that it wasn't Indigo he'd been listening to on the album. It was Indigo's god, the thing under the sand, playing the same siren song that had turned Indigo and Justin into its followers. And now it wanted him.

He felt his mind slipping, felt a sudden desire to stay in this strange and lonely desert and fulfill his destiny. It took every ounce of his strength to push the thought away. He started running, but his boots couldn't get any traction in the sand and Justin grabbed him easily. Andrew pulled the steak knife out of his boot and slashed at him. One wild swing caught Justin in the face, and he turned away with a ribbon of red on his cheek. Andrew slashed again, catching the side of one of Justin's growths. It trickled blood, and Justin howled in pain and finally let go, backing away.

Andrew put his hands over his ears again and ran. He knew there was nowhere to go, no way to get back home unless the doorway opened again, but he ran anyway, his frail, weakened body clumsy on the sand. He risked a glance behind him and saw that Indigo and Justin hadn't moved. They just stood there watching as they grew smaller in the distance.

The sand shifted under his feet, and he nearly fell again. Instinctively he yanked his hands away from his ears to balance himself, and the deafening trumpet blasts drew more blood from his ears. Ahead of him, an enormous shape bulged in the sand. Six long, spiky protuberances broke through, like the conning tower of a surfacing submarine.

And then the rest of it rose up, so huge that the sand fell from its body in great pouring sheets like water from a falls. The titanic shape kept rising up and up, casting him in shadow. Massive protuberances spread winglike, all but blotting out the roiling red sky, and the trumpeting that emanated from them called them to worship. The sound swept into him like an inexorable series of waves and took root there.

Andrew dropped the knife and stared up at Him in all His revealed glory. As the ecstasy came over him and his eyes rolled up into his head, he thought of how wonderful it would be to join his friends again, the Three Musketeers reunited, and to listen to music all day every day, just as they'd always wanted to, until their time was up and the sand blanketed their bones. How foolish he'd been to fight it. Why had he ever wanted to resist something that made such beautiful music? There was nothing to fear.

Music had always taken him to places far, far away.

It was no longer an unknowable mystery, not now, and what he'd always suspected about music had at last been proven true.

It came from God.

Lucienne

During the whole of the dull, dark, and soundless time that Ray was unconscious, he dreamed he was back at Romano's with the guys. They were in their usual booth, talking shit and cooking up plans around the beer-slicked wooden table, a haze of cigarette smoke in the air. Then Ray stuttered awake, blinking his eyes against a painfully bright light. He wasn't at the bar; he was sitting in the kitchen of someone's house—a kitchen so much bigger and cleaner than the filthy, cluttered kitchenette of his studio apartment that at first he didn't know where he was. It took a moment for the events of the evening to come back to him. He was still in the house he'd broken into. The house that was supposed to be empty but clearly wasn't.

"Good. You're awake."

Ray's eyes focused on the old man who sat across from him. He was in his seventies, with shaggy mop of gray hair and a beard to match. He was fat, too, with a wide girth that filled the chair to overflowing. A birdcage hung from the ceiling behind him, and inside it a canary sat on the wooden perch and watched Ray with black, beady eyes. The clock on the kitchen wall read 11:30.

Shit, Ray thought. How long had he been unconscious? He'd left Romano's a little after 8:00 and couldn't have gotten to the house much later than 8:30 . . .

"You picked the wrong house to rob, kid," the old man said, "and definitely on the wrong night."

Ray cursed under his breath. The guys had told him no one would be home. Did they get their facts wrong or was this a setup, a way to screw the new guy by sending him to rob a house they knew wasn't empty? The house belonged to a fence named Visconti, one of the best in the business, and they'd told him there would be all sorts of loot for the taking in the vault in his basement—jewelry, electronics, antiques. Easy pickings. Those sons of bitches. He should have known it was too good to be true.

Still, the old man wasn't holding a gun on him, which Ray took as a good sign. Once he got out of here, he would give those old, washed-up Mafia assholes at Romano's a piece of his goddamned mind. He tried to get up, but his arms were bound behind the chair with thick ropes. More ropes encircled his torso in a complex web that ended with a nooselike coil around his neck. The noose wasn't tight, but its presence made him nervous. He strained against the ropes, trying to pull his arms free.

"Don't bother," the old man said. "You're not the first person I've tied up. I know how to do it right."

A knifelike pain cut through the back of Ray's head, fading to a dull throb. "The fuck happened to me?"

"A little bump on the head, that's all. I learned a long time ago it's easier to tie people up when they're unconscious. They don't struggle."

Where had this fat old bastard come from? There had been no sign of him when Ray first got to the house. It was dark and quiet, no lights on, nothing. It looked as empty as the guys told him it would be, so he jimmied open the sliding glass patio doors in back. He waited a moment for the shrill klaxon of a burglar alarm to sound, but none came. Downstairs, at the electronically locked door to the vault, he punched in the code the guys gave him, and sure enough the door opened. Inside was a treasure trove of Visconti's loot. Ray had stood stunned in the doorway like a kid given the run of a candy store before he busied himself shoving anything that looked valuable into his duffel bag. When the bag was full, he made his way back to the patio doors, but that was where his memory cut out.

The old man—who could only be Visconti himself—must have been hiding in the dark and clubbed him on the back of the head. Which meant he'd already been hiding with the lights out when Ray got there, waiting for him. The thought put a knot in his stomach. There was only one way Visconti could have known he was coming: the guys at Romano's had given him a heads-up.

Maybe it wasn't a setup. Maybe it was some kind of initiation, a trial by fire. The thought made him sit a little taller in the chair. After all, they wouldn't bother putting him through a rite of passage like this if they didn't intend to make him one of their own, would they?

That was all he'd ever wanted, to be one of them, but it was hard to join the Mafia when you weren't Italian. Being poor, Irish, and not from the neighborhood didn't help. The guys loved to rib him. They called him "leprechaun," "Mick," and "Paddy," but still, they never kicked him out of Romano's, never told him he couldn't drink with them. As the whiskey flowed, they regaled him with stories of the good old days when the Italian families ruled this part of New Jersey, and even though he knew they would never elevate someone like him to a made man, he still hoped one day they would make him an official part of their crew. When they told him about the fence's house sitting empty, just waiting for a thief like him to take advantage, he'd jumped at the chance to prove himself to them. They must have known he would. He'd made it all too easy for them to set up this little prank.

"Real funny, pops," Ray said. "But the joke's over, okay? You hit me too hard. My head hurts like hell. I should probably get it looked at."

"You think this is funny?" Visconti said. "Breaking into my house, trying to steal my shit, you think that's *funny?*"

Ray watched Visconti's face, waiting for him to crack a smile or laugh reassuringly, but his angry expression didn't change. The silence stretched out, growing heavier with each passing second as the two men stared at each other from their chairs. Ray's confidence slipped. Maybe he had this wrong. Maybe this wasn't a prank.

"Fine, you caught me, you win," Ray said, trying to sound properly contrite. "I've heard about you, Visconti. You're the best fence in the state, but you didn't get where you are without being smart. The smart thing to do now would be to turn this situation to your advantage. A man in your position could probably use someone to do his legwork. I could be that someone for you. Pay off my debt for trying to rob you. Just tell me what you want me to do."

If there was one thing Ray had always been good at, it was fast-talking. It had saved his ass more than once. He could talk his way into any establishment, any crew. Hell, he'd talked his way into Romano's, hadn't he? But Visconti was unmoved. Holding Ray's wallet in one beefy hand, the old man opened it and looked at the ID inside.

"Your name's Ray Quinn," Visconti said. "Look at that, you've still got your Boston driver's license. You're a long way from home, Irish. I'm surprised no one taught you not to bring your ID on a job. If the cops catch you, it'll take them exactly two seconds to find out who you are. It's a rookie mistake. It tells me you haven't been in the game very long."

The fat old man leaned back in his chair, shifting his considerable bulk, and stuffed the wallet into his pants pocket. Ray fumed. He wasn't stupid; of course he knew better than to bring his ID on a job. It was just that this job had come out of nowhere, an unexpected, blink-and-you'll-miss-it opportunity. There hadn't been any time to prepare.

"What are you, nineteen, twenty?" Visconti asked.

"Twenty-two."

"Of course you are." He leaned his bulk toward Ray, breathing heavily as though even the small shift in position had left him winded. "Listen up, Irish, I've been a fence since before you were born. Hell, I made my first sales when your dad was still in high school jacking off to pictures of Kathy Ireland."

"Who?"

He rolled his eyes. "Christ, don't make me hate you more than I already do. You young shits. Back in the day, we knew how to play the game, but you new guys, you never stopped being juvenile delinquents. You're all hotheads. You have no discipline, no respect for those who came before. You don't even know what's worth stealing and what's not. Case in point, I bet you don't know what this is."

He picked up a hardcover book from the floor next to his chair, a thick volume bound in leather, its pages edged in gold. Ray remembered seeing it in the vault, but it hadn't looked like anything so he'd left it behind.

"It's a book," Ray said. He would have shrugged if it weren't for the ropes. "Nobody gives a shit about books anymore."

The look Visconti gave him could have cut glass. "Don't make me hit you on the head again, Irish. This isn't just *any* book."

Ray looked at it more closely. The title was stamped into the thick, brown leather of the cover in gold letters.

Complete Stories and Poems of Edgar Allan Poe.

Visconti flipped through the pages. Ray was surprised at how gingerly his thick, sausage-like fingers treated the thin paper. "I've read this book a lot since it came into in my possession, cover to cover and back again, and you know what I discovered? Poe was obsessed with dead women. Half the shit he wrote is about women who died and men who are too hung up on them to let go. 'Morella,' 'Ligeia,' 'Berenice,' 'Annabel Lee.' He loved writing stories about dead women, but more than that he loved *naming* stories after dead women."

He stopped turning the pages and smiled. "Ah, here we go. Out of all the stories in the book, this one's my favorite. 'The Fall of the House of Usher.' It was her favorite, too."

Ray squinted at him. "Her?"

"The original owner of the book," he said. "I must have read 'Usher' a dozen times. You probably read it in school, yeah?"

Ray hadn't bothered much with schoolwork and hadn't stuck around high school past his sophomore year anyway. What was the point when there were plenty of crews in Southie hiring school-aged kids as mules and runners? It was easy work that got him respect on the street and a pocket full of cash.

"Never heard of it," he said. He twisted and wiggled his wrists behind the chair. The ropes bit into his skin, but he kept the pain from showing on his face. The best thing he could do was keep the old man talking while he worked to slip out of the ropes. "What's it about?"

Visconti grinned as if he was hoping Ray would ask. "A guy goes to visit his childhood friend, Roderick Usher, only to find he lives in a shitty old house, and worse, he's a complete nutcase. So is Roderick's sister Madeline, who dies while the guy is visiting. So they bury her, but Roderick is terrified that Madeline is going to come back from the grave to kill him. The guy tries to tell him it ain't possible, but Roderick doesn't believe him." Visconti read a passage out of the book. "'Have I not heard her footstep on the stair? Do I not distinguish that heavy and horrible beating of her heart? Madman! I tell you that she now stands without the door!'"

Visconti stared at Ray, but if he was expecting a reaction, Ray didn't give him one.

"So the doors blow open with a gust of wind, and it turns out he's right," Visconti said. He read another passage from the book. "'But then without those doors there *did* stand the lofty and enshrouded figure of the lady Madeline of Usher. With a low moaning cry, she fell heavily inward upon the person of her brother, and bore him to the floor a corpse.'"

Ray stopped twisting his wrists in the rope and shuddered. The story was pretty tame compared to those *Purge* movies he liked, but something about it got under his skin.

"That's fucked up," he said.

"It's just a story, Irish. Just harmless words. That's what we tell ourselves, isn't it? That stories can't hurt us?" Visconti slammed the book closed. "No, the fucked-up thing is that when you went through my vault looking for shit to steal, you didn't bother looking at the book. If you had, you would have seen this."

He opened the front cover to reveal white endpapers, on which someone had written in black pen:

For my darling daughter Lucienne, on the occasion of your 11th birthday. Sorry I missed your party. I'll make it up to you. Daddy promises.

All my love,

Sal Toscani

"Holy shit." Ray blanched. He'd heard the name before from the guys at Romano's during their stories about the glory days. "Sal Toscani was a legend."

"You can say that again. I worked for him back in the day. I knew him and his family well."

"No shit, really?" *Keep him talking,* Ray told himself, and went back to trying to loosen the ropes. He felt a coil slacken around one wrist. Not enough to shake off the ropes, but it was a start.

Visconti shifted his weight in the chair with considerable effort. "His daughter Lucienne—there was something wrong with that girl.

You could tell just by looking at her. As tall and skinny as a scarecrow, with straight black hair that came all the way down her back. Long, long nails painted jet black. But the creepiest thing about her was her eyes. They were as dark as midnight, and it felt like she was looking right into you, all the way to your soul. I'll be damned if I ever saw that girl blink."

Visconti looked down at the leather-bound volume in his lap. "Lucienne loved this book more than anything in the world. I think she liked the way Poe wrote about obsessive characters, because it was like a mirror for her. She was obsessive about a lot of things herself—her room had to be just so, she had to run the comb through her hair a specific number of times—but she was especially obsessed with this book. She wouldn't let anyone else touch it. She took it with her wherever she went, even as an adult. She was never without it when she was alive."

The ropes around Ray's arms loosened more. He was almost there. "So she died?"

Visconti nodded. "The night before her wedding, she was murdered by Tommy Costanzo, a young hothead who was looking to prove himself to the higher-ups in his family. He shot her dead in the hotel where she was staying. June thirteenth, 1999. I'll never forget it."

June thirteenth, Ray thought. Why did that date sound familiar?

"Tommy Costanzo tried to make it look like a robbery gone bad, took her jewelry, her money, and the big purse she always carried with her," Visconti went on. "I don't think he knew the book was in her purse when he took it; he just grabbed everything and ran. There's no way he could have known how valuable it was. If he'd bothered to check, he would have discovered the leather was genuine, and the gilding on the pages and the stamp on the cover were done in real gold. But what made it really valuable was the fact that Sal Toscani had signed it to his daughter himself. The big man's signature made it a one-of-a-kind copy. To the right person it would be worth tens of thousands of dollars."

Ray was disappointed in himself that he'd passed it over so quickly in the vault, but his disappointment died as soon as the ropes slid off his raw and bleeding wrists. Before he could move, the loosened coils triggered a response in the complex web of ropes that somehow slipped the noose tighter around his neck. Ray choked and clawed at the rope.

"Ah, ah, ah," Visconti taunted, waving a pudgy finger at him. "I told you I know how to tie a man up properly."

He tied Ray's hands behind his back again, releasing the pressure on his neck. Ray coughed and gasped until he was breathing normally once more.

Visconti sat down. "You gonna behave now? Because I need you to listen to what I'm telling you. It's important."

Ray nodded mutely. He was fucked and he knew it. At least Visconti was still talking instead of putting a bullet in Ray's head.

"After Lucienne died, Sal was out of his mind with grief. He went after Tommy Costanzo to have his revenge, as was his right, but the Costanzos moved Tommy far away to protect him. Sal couldn't reach him. It drove him crazy that he couldn't kill the man who'd murdered his daughter, but it turned out he didn't have to. A year after Lucienne's murder—one year to the day, in fact; June thirteenth, 2000, the anniversary of her death—the police found Tommy Costanzo dead in a house down the Shore. He had scratches all over him like he'd been attacked by a wild animal. They said his eyes were still open and he had a look of sheer terror on his face, like the last thing he saw put the fear of God in him.

"Sal spent every day since Lucienne's funeral going to the cemetery and sitting on the steps of the family crypt to pay his respects. On the day Tommy Costanzo was found dead, Sal went to the crypt as usual, but this time, through bars of the gate, he saw something on the floor inside. It was Lucienne's book, the one Tommy had taken."

Ray looked up at Visconti. His throat was still too raw for him to speak, but his disbelief must have registered in his eyes.

"Hand to God," Visconti insisted. "We Italians are superstitious. The Devil, the Evil Eye, all that shit. We believe a loaf of bread has to be put on the table face up or it's bad luck. We believe a bird inside the house means someone's going to die. We're crazy like that."

Ray glanced nervously to the birdcage hanging from the kitchen ceiling. The canary stared back at him with eyes as round and black as the barrel of a gun.

Visconti followed his gaze to the birdcage and chuckled. "Relax, Irish. The superstition is about a bird *loose* in the house, not in a cage.

That's why I never let her out. Ain't that right, Sofia?" He made whistling noises at the bird. It ignored him and pecked tiny pellets out of its bowl. "I named her after my mother, like any good Italian boy would. Unfortunately, she won't sing for me, won't even chirp, no matter how much I ask. Women, right? They don't give a shit what anyone else wants. That's why I live in this big house by myself. Never found a broad worth shacking up with."

Ray swallowed painfully through his bruised throat. There was no doubt in his mind now that Visconti was going to kill him. There was clearly something wrong with the old man, dementia maybe. It didn't matter. Ray had to get free of these damned ropes. He had to kill Visconti before Visconti killed him.

"Anyone else might have taken the book home with him for sentimental reasons, but not Sal," Visconti continued. "Being properly superstitious, he left it in the crypt. After all, it was Lucienne's book, not his, and in life she had loved it more than anything.

"Sal died a few years later. He was only sixty-eight. The Costanzos never got him; it was his ticker that did him in. So Gina, his widow, started visiting the family crypt every day in his place, paying her respects to her husband *and* her daughter. One day she found the crypt had been broken into. All the tombs inside had been busted open. The thief took everything he could carry—jewelry, watches, rings, even Lucienne's book.

"This was no random robbery. The name Toscani was written big as can be over the crypt's door, and believe me, back then *everyone* knew that name. Whoever broke in knew exactly who they were stealing from. Gina figured it had to be some new hothead looking to make a name for himself—not unlike you, Irish—since no one else would dare rob them so brazenly. And desecrating the dead like that? Forget about it. She called the whole family together to hunt this fucker down, but nobody knew who it was. The grave robber didn't belong to any of the other families. Nobody could find the guy. They waited for him to slip up, to start bragging to his buddies or trying to sell the loot in town, but it never happened. Eventually, other things took priority and Gina gave up the search. I'm telling you, that thief was the luckiest man on the planet."

Ray glared at Visconti. His throat burned where the rope had strangled him. His wrists stung where the ropes rubbed them bloody. All he could think about was getting free and killing this fat son of a bitch with his bare hands, just so he wouldn't have to listen to him talk anymore.

"However," Visconti continued, "a few months later, the police got called to a house across town. Inside they found a dead body, a young Spanish guy with a history of break-ins and burglaries. They said he had scratches all over him, just like Tommy Costanzo, and the same look of terror on his face. All his belongings were scattered like someone had tossed the joint, so the cops assumed it was a robbery. That same day, Gina Toscani went to the family crypt as usual. And what do you think she saw through that gate, sitting on the floor inside the crypt?"

Ray shook his head. He laughed, either out of disbelief or spite, or because he was losing his mind tied to this fucking chair. The laughter hurt his throat, and he stopped.

"Hand to God, the book was back, just like before. And the date? June thirteenth. The anniversary of Lucienne's death. Poor Gina nearly had a heart attack like her husband Sal. Unfortunately, she wasn't superstitious like him, so she took the book home with her. Not for sentimental reasons. No, she was ice cold, that woman. She took it because she knew it was valuable with Sal's inscription inside. That was a big mistake, because one year later—"

"Come on," Ray rasped. "Enough with this bullshit already."

"One year later, on June thirteenth, Gina Toscani was found dead in her house. They said she was lying on the floor of her bedroom, all scratched up, eyes wide open and terrified, just like the others. The house had been ransacked. This time the police assumed it was a hit job masquerading as a robbery, but there were two problems with that theory. First, no one would dare go after Sal Toscani's widow. Even the Costanzos wouldn't sink so low. It's just not done. Second, something *had* been taken from the house."

He tapped the book in his lap.

"This is bullshit," Ray said.

"Of course it's bullshit! It's *all* bullshit!" Visconti said. "It's just another story, right? People in our line of business love to tell stories. The dead body that disappeared. The stoolie they were sure they'd killed but who showed up in court the next day. The guy who stole his dead grandma's ring off her finger and then was mauled to death by her dozen cats. Everyone's got stories, even Poe's got his dead-woman stories. But sometimes there's truth in those stories, and sometimes, even if there isn't, a story can leave an echo in the world, some part of itself that sticks around. The murders of Tommy Costanzo, the grave robber, and Gina Toscani really happened, just the way I told you. So how can we know? How can we be sure what's real and what's not?"

He turned in his chair to look at the clock. It was ten minutes to midnight.

"The thing is, Irish, I've been a fence for a long time now. Over the years, better thieves than you have brought me all sorts of loot. Most of it I could move pretty quickly and for a good price. But imagine you're me, and after someone drops off their shit you find Lucienne's book mixed in with the rest. Imagine finding it and knowing exactly what it is, exactly who it belonged to. Knowing its story.

"I'm stuck with the damned thing. I can't sell it. It's got value, but everyone who would buy it on the black market already knows its history and won't touch it. I can't just donate it to the library or leave it at a bus stop because it's got Sal Toscani's goddamned name inside it. Believe me, people still know that name in this town, and if it's ever traced back to me, well, let's just say I would be forced to answer for some things that I'd really rather not. I can't burn it or bury it or rip it up because that won't save me, you understand? It'll only make her angrier."

"Make her angrier?" Ray scoffed. "You don't really buy into this shit, do you?"

Visconti met his eye, his gaze hard as steel. "We're all animals in the end, Irish. We like to think we're something more, but we're kidding ourselves. When an animal is faced with danger, its fight-or-flight instincts take over. It's the same with people. It's built into us. But what if you can't do either? What if it's something you can't fight and something you can't run from? What then?"

Ray was wrong. Visconti wasn't suffering from dementia. The old man was straight-up crazy. It was only a matter of time before he tried to kill Ray. He had to get free, but the ropes held him fast, and he knew if he slipped them off his wrists again the noose would tighten around his neck. There had to be another way, but he couldn't think straight. Visconti's story had him all turned around.

"Come midnight," Visconti said, "it'll be June thirteenth."

Fuck, Ray thought. That was why the date sounded familiar. It was tomorrow.

"Circumstances being what they are, I did the only thing I could," Visconti said. "I set a trap. See, my buddies at Romano's told me there was a new, young thief in town, a Mick from Boston looking for a big score to make a name for himself. So I had them tell you a story about an empty house with a vault full of loot just waiting to be plundered." The fat old man shook his head, his face reddening with anger. "Only you didn't take the fucking book! You were supposed to take it home with you, but instead you just left it in the vault like an idiot! So I was forced to improvise. The guys told me you weren't too bright. They didn't lie."

"Fuck you," Ray snarled. "And fuck all this bullshit!"

Visconti stood, groaning as he lifted his heavy bulk.

Ray shrank back in the chair. "Don't you fucking touch me!"

"It's not me you gotta worry about, Irish."

Visconti dropped the book onto Ray's lap. It felt unnaturally heavy, as if its pages were crowded with memories, with the crushing weight of obsession. The old fence took another length of rope off the kitchen counter and tied the book to Ray's lap, securing it with a tight knot under the chair seat.

"Every year, on the anniversary of her death, Lucienne goes looking for her book, and God help anyone who has it in their possession," he said. "She doesn't care who it is. She killed her own damned *mother* to get the book back. This time it ain't gonna be me she finds with it."

The old man opened a door in the back of the kitchen. Ray saw unfinished plaster walls in the room beyond, smelled oil and gasoline. The garage.

"Come on, Visconti, we can make a deal," Ray called after him. "I'm

a good thief when I'm not being set up. You know you could use someone like me on your crew." *Just untie me so I can kill you, you fat piece of shit,*
he thought. "Let me go and tell me what you want me to do."

"What I want you to do?" Visconti said. "You're already doing it.
Ciao, Irish."

The old man closed the door behind him. A few seconds later Ray
heard the automatic garage door open. A car started, then pulled out
into the driveway. The garage door hummed closed, but he could still
hear the car as it drove away.

The clock on the wall said it was five minutes to midnight. Five
minutes to June 13th.

Ray struggled in his ropes but stopped as soon as the coil tightened
around his neck again. He looked down at the book tied to his lap. *Col-
lected Stories and Poems of Edgar Allan Poe.* One of a kind, valuable, and yet
nobody wanted it. He knew the feeling. He'd been a fool to believe the
Mafia guys at Romano's would ever accept some young Irish punk as
one of their own. The clues had been there all along, the way they spoke
down to him and called him names, but he'd believed the lie because he
wanted to.

The story Visconti told him was a lie, too. It had to be. Even if the
old fence believed it himself, he'd already admitted he was superstitious
by nature, and superstitions had nothing to do with the real world. Ray's
grandmother had tossed salt over her shoulder for good luck her whole
life, but she'd still ended up drooling and shitting herself in a nursing
home. Ray never tossed so much as a single grain of salt over his shoulder and he was doing just fine, thank you very much.

Although he would be doing a lot better if he could just get out of
these damned ropes. If he couldn't slip the knots without strangling
himself, his only other option was to break the chair and hope for the
best. He rocked back and forth until the chair's front legs were off the
floor, but he couldn't get it to fall backward. The chair dropped onto its
front legs again. It didn't break, but he winced as the shockwaves set off
the dull throb in his head.

He glanced up at the clock. Two minutes to midnight.

Visconti was just trying to scare him. In about half an hour the fat old fence would probably come back with the guys from Romano's in tow, and they would all have a good laugh at Ray's expense. Depending on how he played his cards, they might just bring him into the crew after all.

Fuck, who was he kidding? Visconti wasn't coming back, and the guys sure as hell weren't going to take him in after setting him up like this. Once Ray got himself free, he would make those assholes pay. He'd go back to Romano's tomorrow night all smiles and handshakes like everything went off without a hitch, but he'd bring his .45 with him, tucked into the back of his pants—

From inside the birdcage the canary let out a peculiar, high-pitched trill. It flapped its wings and flitted from the perch to the floor of the cage, then to the edge of its food bowl, and then back to the perch. All the while, it warbled and fluttered in a panic.

Visconti said the bird never made a sound, and now it wouldn't shut up. Another lie from the fat prick. The bird quieted for a moment, and in the silence Ray heard something else: the soft, muffled sound of scratching.

It came from somewhere behind him. The front door—something was scratching at the front door. A stray cat, probably. That was why the bird was going crazy. The cat wanted in.

But it didn't sound like a cat. The scratches were slow and methodical, the way a person might do it.

He thought of Lucienne's long, black fingernails. He thought of Roderick Usher's dead sister Madeline.

Madman! I tell you that she now stands without the door!

The scratching grew louder, more frenzied.

This is bullshit. It's Visconti. He's back and fucking with me. Probably only drove his car around the block—

The canary went crazy, fluttering all around the birdcage, hurling itself against the bars.

"It's just a story," he muttered under his breath. He rocked in the chair again, trying fruitlessly to break it. "It's just a fucking story."

The panicking canary threw itself against the bars over and over, until finally the birdcage door burst open. Behind Ray, the front door burst open at the same time, as if from a strong, sudden gust of wind.

But there was no wind at his back, only a cool breeze of night air that brought with it a terrible smell . . . Good God, the smell . . .

The bird flew from its cage. Loose in the house for the first time, it circled the kitchen in celebration of its newly unfettered state, then bolted across the living room and out to its freedom—past the lofty and enshrouded figure that stood outside the door.

Every Path Taken

*C*an a human brain continue to function outside the body?"

In her seat in the lecture hall, Emily Bannerman looked up from her laptop, her curiosity piqued by the strangeness of the question one of her classmates had asked.

Professor Vaughan, a bearded, slightly balding man in his late forties with a taste for the argyle sweaters that seemed to be the unofficial faculty uniform at Vermont's Middlewood University, had just wrapped up his lecture. "As an organ, the brain is only three pounds of tissue, but it's responsible for everything that makes you *you.*" As he spoke he aimed his laser pointer like a magician wielding his wand at the SMART board behind him, where a detailed cross-section of a human brain was projected on the screen. "It houses all your memories, everything you've learned, your hopes and dreams, everything you love and hate. In essence, you *are* your brain, and your brain is you."

Next to Emily, her boyfriend Sean thumbed a text message covertly into his phone and hit Send. It appeared silently in a window on the screen of her laptop. *Can I come over again tonight?* She glared at him, annoyed at the intrusion, but he grinned and his gray eyes flashed. Those sharp, inquisitive eyes were the first thing she'd noticed about him, and they were still hard to say no to. She nodded, then forced herself to focus on the notes she'd been taking. She couldn't let herself get distracted. It was important that she pass Professor Vaughan's premed neuroscience class. She'd kept her nose to the grindstone all year, making sure her grades remained good enough to get into a decent medical school after graduation, and she wasn't about to let it slip now.

Professor Vaughan glanced at his watch. "We've got a few minutes left. Are there any questions?"

The students in the lecture hall looked at one another as though daring anyone to delay their escape. No one ever asked questions.

And then she heard it.

"Can a human brain continue to function outside of the body?"

But when Emily looked up from her laptop, Professor Vaughan was still looking expectantly at his students, and the students were still looking around in the hope of being dismissed early. It was as though no one had spoken.

"No questions? All right, then," Professor Vaughan said, switching off the SMART board. "For next time, read chapter six in *Brain, Mind, and Behavior.* You're dismissed."

Emily frowned. She could have sworn she'd heard a voice. A woman's voice.

I can't see anything. Everything is dark.

I try to blink, but I have no eyes.

I try to listen, but I have no ears.

It's as if I don't exist. But I do. I'm here. I'm real.

Where am I? Is anyone else here? These are the questions I want to shout, but I have no mouth.

As a senior faculty member at Middlewood, Professor Vaughan had his own office far from the faculty building the other teachers had to share. It was inside a small stone cottage that sat at the far end of the student parking lot, a private office he'd decorated with shelves of books, framed degrees, and an antique, single-lensed brass microscope from the nineteenth century that Emily thought was beautiful in its simplicity. She felt bad about taking up the entirety of the professor's office hours after the lecture, but no other students came by and Vaughan didn't seem to mind. She'd been taking notes on her laptop all through their discussion but had stopped halfway through when she noticed the door in the wall. Now she couldn't stop looking at it. Every time she looked up from her computer at Professor Vaughan, she found herself sneaking peeks at the door, squinting at it, trying to figure it out.

It was a perfectly ordinary-looking door. There was nothing special about it, except for the fact that she could have sworn it had never been there before. What's more, she couldn't figure out where it could possibly lead. There was nothing on the other side of the wall except the little cottage's stone exterior. If she were to open that door, it would lead directly outside, but even that didn't make sense. There was only one door into this building. There had only ever been one door.

"Miss Bannerman, are you paying attention?"

"Yes, of course," Emily said, turning back to him. What was wrong with her? She needed to focus. Except she was *sure* she'd never seen that door before.

"Good." Professor Vaughan leaned forward, elbows on his desk, fingers laced together. "Anyway, this project I'm talking about could be a very important opportunity for you. You would receive extra credit for it, obviously, but it's also the kind of addition to your C.V. that medical schools find very appealing in candidates. When I was presented with the opportunity of bringing in students from my class, I thought of you immediately. You're one of my brightest pupils, Miss Bannerman. I've seen how hard you work to keep up your GPA. I think you've got a good mind—the right kind of mind for this project. If you're interested, of course."

She was. She'd always had a strong intellectual curiosity, driven since a young age to understand the world around her, how things worked, how things connected. It was why she was pursuing a medical degree. There was so much to learn about the human body, and especially the human mind, which often seemed to her as boundless and infinite as the cosmos itself. And Professor Vaughan was right: this *did* sound like something that could give her an edge when she started sending out applications.

"What exactly is the project?" she asked.

"I can't divulge much at this time," he said. "There's a non-disclosure agreement you'll have to sign, and then I can fill you in. I just need to know if you're interested, and then we can make an appointment to get started."

"I am, absolutely." Her mind sorted through all the exciting possibilities. There was no shortage of topics to study in the field of neurology, or diseases to better understand, from cerebral palsy to autism, Rett syndrome, neurodegeneration . . .

"Excellent," Vaughan said, leaning back in his chair. "However, I must ask you not to mention this to anyone. Best to consider the NDA already in effect, all right?"

"No problem," she said. "I can sign it right now if you want."

"Not yet. I'll contact you when we're ready to begin."

He pushed his chair back and stood up, indicating that their conversation was over. Emily gathered her belongings, rose, and slung her backpack over her shoulder. On the professor's desk was a framed photo showing a pretty brown-haired woman smiling for the camera while two small boys clung shyly to her legs. Vaughan's family, she supposed, although it was hard to imagine her stodgy, sweater-wrapped professor chasing after two little boys—

"Good day, Miss Bannerman," he said, interrupting her thoughts. He was holding the office door open, letting in the cool air from outside.

As she turned to go, her eye caught the door in the wall again.

"Professor," she ventured, "where does that door go?"

He looked at her for what seemed like a beat too long and smiled thinly. "Nowhere. It's just a small closet for the heating pipes. Why?"

"No reason," she said, but she thought his answer was odd. She could imagine an access panel in the wall to reach the pipes, but a door?

"You're a liar!"

Emily straightened. The voice had sounded close, as though it were in the office with them, but nobody else was there.

"Is something the matter, Miss Bannerman?"

"No, everything's fine." She gave a quick smile and hurried out. She'd heard a voice, she was sure of it. The same woman's voice she'd heard in the classroom. The same voice apparently no one else could hear.

I'm cracking up, she thought. She wouldn't be the first premed student to buckle under the pressure. But something about the voice seemed so real.

That night, in her dorm room, with her roommate gone for the night, Sean kissed her passionately and backed her onto her bed. "I've been thinking about this all day," he said.

"Hold on," she told him as he kissed her neck. "I have to tell you something. Professor Vaughan asked me to work with him on a new project. He wouldn't tell me what it is, though."

He looked up at her. "Yeah, he asked me, too. Something about the brain, I think. I'm supposed to drop by his office tomorrow to sign something."

"Tomorrow?" she asked. That was fast. Why hadn't Professor Vaughan asked her to come back tomorrow, too? She felt a little irritated that he'd already made plans for Sean to sign the papers but not her. But then Sean started kissing her again, and any disappointment she felt was quickly forgotten.

What's left of my body if I have no eyes, no ears, no mouth? Do I have any physical form at all?

Now that the shock of finding myself here has passed, I'm starting to remember bits and pieces. The body on the table, the hypodermic needle, that grotesque, inhuman thing hiding in the shadows . . .

Oh, God, this can't be real, can it?

Emily expected Sean to come see her right after his meeting with Professor Vaughan. She was eager to hear all about the mysterious project they would be working on. Even if he'd signed the NDA, she knew she'd get the information out of him eventually. Sean was never very good at keeping things from her. She waited all day, checking her phone for text messages and emails. She ate lunch and dinner alone in the dining hall, waiting for him to show. By nine o'clock that night she sent what had to be her fifteenth text.

where r u? seriously, r u ok?

She stayed awake as long as she could, clutching the phone like a lifeline, but no reply came. She drifted off toward dawn, woke again just a couple of hours later, and immediately checked her phone. Still nothing.

What if he was sick? She imagined Sean in his bed, wrapped in covers, sweating with fever, his phone somewhere out of reach. But a visit to his dorm room revealed a bed that hadn't been slept in, and Sean's roommate hadn't seen him. He hadn't come to her room, and he hadn't returned to his own. So where was he?

In the lecture hall, Emily sat beside Sean's empty seat. Professor Vaughan stood at the front of the hall, reading the students' names off his attendance sheet. Emily glanced around nervously. Was Sean sitting somewhere else? Why would he do that?

Her mind was a thousand miles away when Professor Vaughan called her name. He had to say it twice before she replied, "Here." He checked her name off, then moved on. Emily focused, listening for the name Sean Walsh, both anticipating it and dreading it as Vaughan moved through the alphabet.

"Prisha Vidyarthi."

"Here."

"Jacqueline Wright."

"Here."

Emily stiffened. He'd skipped right past Sean's name. That wasn't something he would do by mistake. Sean had disappeared yesterday, the same day he was supposed to meet with Vaughan, and today the professor had purposely omitted Sean's name while taking attendance. He had to know where Sean was, or what had happened to him.

After class, Emily got stuck in the swell of students exiting the lecture hall. By the time she made it outside, Professor Vaughan was gone. She checked her watch. His office hours didn't start for another hour, but this was too important to wait.

She hurried through the student parking lot to Professor Vaughan's office and was about to knock on the door when his raised voice came from inside, making her pause.

"But you don't *need* another," he said. "You have me, don't you? You promised!"

A harsh, buzzing whisper came in reply, startling her. She took a step backward.

Professor Vaughan's voice came again. "I've done everything you asked. Why do I have to wait?"

More buzzing came in reply, but it sounded different this time. Lower in tone and volume, like a conspiratorial whisper, or a warning. A moment passed, and then the office door opened slightly. Vaughan filled the gap in the doorway, a thin smile creasing his face. He didn't look surprised to see her.

"Hello, Miss Bannerman."

"Oh," she said. Her hand was still lifted in anticipation of knocking, and she lowered it slowly. "How did you know I was—?"

"What can I do for you?" he asked.

"It's about Sean," she said. "I can't find him anywhere, and he won't answer my texts. I know he had an appointment with you yesterday. Did he show up?"

"He did." Professor Vaughan sounded colder than usual, annoyed by her interruption. But what had she interrupted? What was that strange buzzing she'd heard? "Unfortunately, Mr. Walsh had very disappointing news. He told me he was dropping out and returning home immediately. A family emergency."

She blinked in confusion. That wasn't possible. He would have told her. Besides, she'd been to his dorm room and all his belongings were still there. She looked up at Professor Vaughan, who blocked the entrance to his office like a bouncer who didn't want her in the club, and realized he was lying. It wasn't even a very good lie. It was easily disproved, the kind of lie that someone who didn't have much practice at lying would tell.

Another realization struck her then, worse than the last one. Professor Vaughan was lying because he knew something. Because he'd *done* something. Panic made her chest go tight, but she couldn't let on that she knew he was lying.

Despite her efforts, he must have seen it in her face because he opened the door wider and said, "Why don't you come inside?"

"Um, no thanks, I really should get going . . ." She hated how shaky her voice was, how scared she sounded. She wished her feet would move.

"I insist." Professor Vaughan took her by the arm and pulled her inside. He closed the door behind her, and she watched with a lump in her throat as he locked it.

"I was just wondering about Sean, that's all," she said, her voice rising with fear. "It's—it's not important, really."

She felt tears well up in her eyes. He was going to kill her, she was sure of it. He'd killed Sean, and now it was her turn.

"I suppose we can move up the time frame," Professor Vaughan said. "They certainly won't mind a change in schedule."

"What?" She'd half expected him to strangle her, but he walked to his desk instead. "What schedule?"

He opened the desk drawer and pulled out a gun. Emily gasped and froze where she stood. *Oh, God, I was right, he's going to kill me!* Tears welled up again and spilled down her cheeks. She knew she should scream for help, it was the first thing they taught in every self-defense class, but the only sound she could squeeze out was a choked sob. Even if she could scream, who would hear her? They were all the way at the end of the parking lot. He could shoot her right here and no one would know.

"I'm sorry, Miss Bannerman," he said, coming around the desk toward her. "This wasn't the way it was supposed to happen."

She took a step back, her breath hitching in her throat, her hands raised defensively.

"When they first came to me, I was as scared as you are now," he said. "They looked so . . . *inhuman.* But I learned very quickly that they're intelligent, sophisticated. Their knowledge and technology are light-years ahead of ours." He chuckled. "I suppose that's apt, considering how far they traveled to come here. But they're scientists, just like me. It turned out I had no reason to fear them."

Fear who? It sounded like he'd gone crazy. Was that why he'd killed Sean? Was that why he was going to kill her, too? He turned away from her to look at the picture of his family on the desk. She didn't give herself time to think twice. She spun and reached for the lock on the door.

"Don't," Professor Vaughan said.

She flinched, put her hands up, and turned back to him.

"Did I ever tell you what happened to my wife? To my children?" he asked. Emily glanced at the framed photograph, the smiling woman, the two young boys. "It was five years ago. We were driving home after eating dinner in town. I swerved to miss a deer that had wandered into the road, but I lost control of the car." He closed his eyes against some awful memory he was reliving. She thought about knocking the gun out of his hand or trying to grab it, but she didn't have the courage, and then his eyes were open again. "I was the only survivor. I walked away with nothing but a few cuts and bruises. The doctors said I was lucky, but I didn't feel lucky. I went to church every day after the accident, looking for comfort, for answers, but there weren't any. Everyone said it was a miracle that I survived, that it was an act of God, but what kind of god would kill my wife and two innocent children? I decided if something this terrible, this *wrong,* could happen, maybe there was a way to undo it. I read ancient texts that very few people have ever read, tomes filled with powerful, forgotten science and rituals, looking for a way to fix it, but nothing worked. I prayed to gods whose names you've never heard of, but my pleas fell on deaf ears."

He looked at the gun in his hand as though he were contemplating turning it on himself. She got the sense it wasn't the first time.

"And then *they* came, dropping out of the sky like an answer to my prayers. They told me there was a way to change what happened. A way to go back and save them. They told me about a temple at the very center of the universe. Arneth-Zin, the place where all the timelines converge. Within that temple is a sentry, a watcher, someone who's seen all of time unfold, everything that ever happened or will happen. Someone who's studied the pattern of time, who knows where the seams are, and who can open those seams and drop me back in so I can change the course of events. So my family can live. They promised to take me to Arneth-Zin, and in return all I had to do was help them collect specimens to bring back to their world. Human specimens."

Okay, so he really was insane. She could only wonder what he'd done with Sean. Or with his corpse. The thought made her cry again, but Professor Vaughan mistook it for fear and tried to calm her.

"Don't be frightened, Miss Bannerman, they require *living* specimens, not dead ones. This gun is only my insurance policy. I have no intention of using it so long as you don't try to run away. You have nothing to fear from them. They only want to learn. Their scientists and scholars are interested in trading cultural information, but transporting specimens to their world is a problem. Their bodies are perfectly constructed to withstand the cold, airless expanse of space, but our bodies would never survive the trip. Luckily, it's not our bodies that interest them, it's our minds. Our knowledge, our philosophies, our cultural memories. All they need are our brains."

He went back behind the desk and took a syringe out of the drawer. It was already filled with a strange, glowing orange liquid. He pulled the protective cover off the needle with his teeth and spat it out. He came toward her with the syringe in one hand, the gun in the other.

She took a step back, her arms raised in front of her as if she could fend him off. "Don't hurt me. Please."

"I assure you there will be no pain," he said. "They're truly gifted surgeons, unlike anything I've ever seen. Their understanding of neuroscience is centuries ahead of ours. They can remove your brain safely and easily. They can keep your brain alive to transport back to their world, where I'm told if you cooperate with them you will be given a new, artificial body."

She looked desperately for an escape route and saw the door in the wall, the one she'd been so fixated on before. There was no way she could unlock the main door in time, but if the door in the wall wasn't locked it was her only chance. Maybe it really was just a pipe closet and she would only be cornering herself, but she had to try *something*. At the very least, she could put something solid between herself and this raving madman. She sprang for the door and grabbed the handle.

"No, don't!" Professor Vaughan yelled.

She pushed the door open and ran through, but only made it a few steps before the shock of what she saw rooted her in place.

It was a large, brightly lit room, but how could it be here? There was no space in the wall for it, no addition to the outside of the building. She saw an array of strange, humming machines linked by elaborate webs of cords and plugs. On the far wall, shelves were filled with gleaming metal cylinders in neat rows, each about a foot high, their faces marked with three strange, triangular sockets. A vacant space on one shelf marked where a cylinder was missing from the collection.

Sean's naked body lay on a surgical table in the middle of the room. She nearly collapsed at the sight. The top of his head had been removed, his cranium neatly and bloodlessly opened by an instrument far more advanced than a simple bone saw. She let out a scream when she saw his skull was empty, like a hollowed-out fruit.

Behind her, the professor spoke. "I told you I would deliver the smartest minds in my class, and I've kept my end of the bargain. Now take me to Arneth-Zin!"

He wasn't talking to her. There was someone else in the room. She turned slowly. A dark shape stood partially hidden in the shadows behind the open door. It was the size of a man, but nothing else about it resembled one. She saw a segmented, crustacean shell that sported numerous insectoid appendages, which all ended in sharp, pointed pincers. On its back was a pair of thin, batlike wings. Its head was a hideous fleshy mass covered in writhing antennae, which split open and let loose a piercing, angry shriek.

I remember reading about a professor at McGill University in the 1950s who experimented with sensory deprivation. He discovered that prolonged isolation led to anxiety, hallucinations, and madness. I don't know how long I've been here, floating in the dark, but I'm starting to wonder how much time I have left before I lose my mind. Not much longer, I think. It's already taking everything I've got just to stay focused, to keep reminding myself who I am.

But then . . . something happens.

I feel a collision of sorts. I'm jolted, my sense of balance knocked off center. On instinct I put out my hands to brace my fall, but I have no hands and there is nothing to fall against.

The impact does more than send me reeling. It shatters my mind into a blazing white supernova, fracturing my consciousness into innumerable pieces and scattering them to the winds of time. I'm back in Professor Vaughan's lecture hall. I'm back in his office. I'm back in Sean's arms. I'm a little girl. I'm being born. I'm back in every moment of my past, every second of my history, all at once.

It's overwhelming, all of it piling up to crush me under its weight. I'll go mad if I don't find some way to control it. The supernova is still there in my mind, like an anchor, and as I concentrate on the fiery white void I discover I can focus on a single moment instead of all of them at once. I reach through the white, and like a miracle I find myself back in that moment, reliving it, but I still remember. I remember everything.

*   *   *

Emily stood before Professor Vaughan's office door, listening to his voice inside and the harsh, buzzing whisper that came in reply. She understood what those sounds were now. The creature behind the door in the wall. That was how it communicated, making its promises to Professor Vaughan in return for handing over her and Sean. But she'd been given another chance, a do-over, and this time she wouldn't be caught by surprise. She could stop what had happened to her, make it so that it never happened at all. She just had to make sure things went differently this time.

She pounded on the door. She heard the professor whisper to the creature, give it time to disappear back into that impossible room off the side of the building, and then he opened the door.

"Hello, Miss Bannerman."

"*Oh. How did you know I was—?*" She heard the words she'd spoken before, an echo reverberating through time, but this time would be different. This time she wouldn't cry or freeze up. This time she'd have the upper hand.

Emily pushed past Professor Vaughan into his office and walked right to his desk.

"What are you doing?" Vaughan demanded, hurrying after her.

She opened the drawer, pulled out the gun, and pointed it at him. She wanted him dead for what he did to Sean, what he did—or was about to do—to her, but she hesitated. Her heart jackhammered in her chest. She'd never shot anyone before. Could she do it?

He put his hands up, his Adam's apple bobbing at his throat. "Miss Bannerman, whatever it is you think you're doing . . ."

At the sound of his voice, that pompous, condescending way he called her *Miss Bannerman,* she had her answer. She pulled the trigger, and the gun jumped in her hand with a loud bang. Professor Vaughan fell to the floor in a spray of red. She ran to the door in the wall and pushed it open.

The room beyond was just as it had been before, with its strange machinery and shelves full of cylinders, with one missing. She understood those cylinders' dark purpose now. Sean's body was on the surgical table, his head open and empty, his brain removed and housed in the missing cylinder. She thought of him floating in darkness, a bodiless consciousness just as she had been, or still was, and very nearly forgot the creature hiding behind the door. Emily turned just as it emerged from its hiding place, its head splitting open in that terrible shriek. She pulled the trigger, and the shot blew off a chunk of its eyeless, antennae-laden head, revealing spongy, fungoid flesh within. She screamed, not with terror this time but with righteous fury, and pulled the trigger again and again, blowing off more pieces.

She didn't feel the sharp object piercing her from behind, so when the long, pointed tip of a pincer came out of her stomach, she stared at it in confusion. There was a harsh buzzing sound at her back, and she realized another creature was in the room, one she hadn't seen. The gun dropped to the floor. She would have dropped, too, but the pincer through her middle held her upright. It would take a long time to die from this kind of wound, she knew. Long enough for them to harvest her brain, just as they'd done before. She'd failed.

I can see again, though not with my own eyes. Those were left behind on another world. These eyes are artificial, a device with two glass lenses that's plugged into one of the sockets in my cylinder. Through these lenses, I can see the alien world that Professor Vaughan's creatures have brought me to. Through a second attached device, one with a metal disc on top, I can hear them speak to each other. They call themselves Mi-Go, and this strange, technologically advanced planetoid at the edge of our solar system is called Yuggoth. Since I arrived, I've learned Yuggoth is merely an outpost, not their home world. I don't know where their home world is, and I get the sense the Mi-Go haven't seen it in a very long time. Some of them wonder if it still exists.

They communicate in insectlike buzzes and clicks, which the hearing device translates for me. There's nothing poetic about their language. They speak with cold, objective specificity, making no use of allegory or metaphor. Vaughan was right to call them scientists. They're methodical and precise.

I've learned from their conversations that something went wrong on our journey from Earth to Yuggoth. The Mi-Go who was carrying my brain cylinder passed through a spatial anomaly, a disruption in the space-time continuum, and came out the other side insane, or so the others think. When we arrived on Yuggoth, they had to force it into hibernation because it was frightened and confused. It claimed to have

been displaced in time, that it was reliving its many thousands of years of life, expe-
riencing every moment of it simultaneously, although with its present-day memories
and knowledge intact.

But they're wrong; that Mi-Go wasn't insane. It's happening to me, too. I felt
us pass through the anomaly and mistook it for a collision. The anomaly is what
broke me into pieces and scattered me throughout my past. That's how I was given
this second chance.

I have to try again. There has to be a way to change what happened. I concentrate,
reaching into the blazing white supernova in my mind, and I go back.

After Professor Vaughan's office hours, Emily slung her backpack onto
her back and looked at the framed photo on the desk. Vaughan's family.
The ones whose deaths had set him on his insane quest for Arneth-Zin
and its all-seeing watcher. She hated them for dying in that car wreck. If
they'd lived, none of this would have happened. She and Sean would be
fine. They both would have become doctors. Maybe they would have
married and started a family.

Maybe they still could.

"Professor," she asked, just as she had the first time, "where does
that door go?"

"Nowhere," he replied. "It's just a small closet for the heating pipes.
Why?"

"No reason." The words were another echo through time, spoken by a
weaker, more naïve Emily who didn't share her current resolve. It infuriated
her. Professor Vaughan infuriated her. The Mi-Go infuriated her.

"You're a liar!" She hurried to the other side of his desk, opened the
drawer, and pulled out his gun.

"Miss Bannerman, put that down!" Professor Vaughan started toward her.

This time, she didn't hesitate. She took great enjoyment in shooting
the smug bastard. He dropped to the floor in a spray of blood. She
stepped over him and opened the door in the wall. The room beyond
was the same as she remembered, but the surgical table was empty. They
hadn't gotten Sean yet. There was still time.

The Mi-Go wasn't behind the door this time but fussing with some
machinery. It turned toward her in surprise, and she shot its spongy head

to bits. A second Mi-Go moved swiftly toward her from the corner, but she was ready for it this time. She shot it, too—just as a hypodermic needle pierced the side of her neck. Professor Vaughan, his argyle sweater splashed with blood where the bullet had hit him in the shoulder, injected the glowing orange liquid into her veins. She crumpled to floor. Her sight dimmed as she began to lose consciousness, but not before she saw four more Mi-Go loom over her. Together, they lifted her off the floor and brought her over to the surgical table. She'd failed again.

I've refused to answer the Mi-Go's questions about Earth. They don't like that. Their interviews have become more like interrogations, with machines that cause me pain if I resist. I don't know how much longer I can hold out.

I have to keep trying. I must find a way to change the past. I reach through the white.

"In essence, you are your brain, and your brain is you." Standing at the front of the lecture hall, Professor Vaughan glanced at his watch. "We've got a few minutes left. Are there any questions?"

Maybe I can trip him up, Emily thought. If she let him know that she was on to him, maybe it would spook him. Maybe it would be enough to make him call it off. She raised her hand.

"Yes, Miss Bannerman?" Professor Vaughan said.

"Can a human brain continue to function outside of the body?"

Vaughan's face fell. He looked surprised and confused. She had to bite her lip not to smirk in triumph.

"That's an interesting question," he said. "Yes, I suppose a brain could exist independently of the body. It would need to be protected, of course, without the skull to shield it."

"Like in a cylinder of some kind?" she asked.

Vaughan's mouth went tight. She could see his jaw muscles clenching under his skin. "Yes, I suppose that could work. There would be no circulatory system to feed it oxygen, so it would need to be submerged in an oxygenated solution to keep it from starving. But I'm afraid the technology necessary to keep a human brain alive outside the body hasn't been discovered yet."

Bullshit, she thought.

Professor Vaughan glared at her, the surprise on his face melting into suspicion and anger. "Does that answer your question, Miss Bannerman?"

"Perfectly," she said.

"Actually, I'm glad you brought it up. If you'd be so kind as to stay after class for a few minutes, I'd like to discuss it with you further. I know of a special project you might be interested in."

She barked out a laugh. "I don't think so."

Some of the students gasped. Others tried to stifle their laughter.

Sean leaned over in his seat beside her and whispered, "What are you doing?"

Sean! The sight of him alive again, his brain still in his head, made her want to throw her arms around him and never let go.

When they left the lecture hall, Emily noticed Professor Vaughan glaring at her from within the crowd of students. She'd definitely touched a nerve, but would it be enough to change the course of events?

"Try not to piss off the professor, okay?" Sean said. "He emailed me earlier about working with him on the project, and I'm going to do it. I'd be a fool not to."

"Don't," she said, grabbing his arm. "You can't."

"Why not?"

"Just promise me you won't, okay?"

"But this could be something really good for me." He broke away. "I have to get to class. I'll come by tonight."

Emily didn't go to Professor Vaughan's office hours this time. She couldn't stand to see that man again. Instead, she stayed in her dorm room and waited for Sean. The moment he arrived, she blurted out the truth to him. She told him she'd already seen what was going to happen to him, to both of them. She told him about Professor Vaughan and Arneth-Zin and the Mi-Go.

"It sounds like you had one hell of nightmare," he said, sitting on the bed. "But I would be stupid to turn down an opportunity like this just because you had a bad dream."

"It wasn't a dream," she insisted. "It's real. It already happened to us, but now I'm back and I can change it. I can make it so it doesn't happen."

He stared at her like she'd lost her mind. "I don't understand. What do you mean, you're back?"

"Sean, don't go to his office tomorrow," she said. "They'll cut your head open and steal your brain—"

He stood up. "Come on, you can't be serious."

"Come with me. Tonight," she said, her voice growing shrill in desperation. She grabbed his arm. "We'll get in my car and just drive. He won't be able to find us."

"You mean leave school?"

"I don't know how else to keep us safe. I've tried everything else I can think of, I shot him twice, I shot the Mi-Go, but—"

Sean yanked his arm out of her grasp. "Stop it. I don't know if you're on something or if this is some kind of joke, but I'm not in the mood." He opened the door. "I'll see you tomorrow."

Emily chased after him into the hallway. She grabbed his arm and tried to pull him back. "Sean, no! We have to leave! It's the only way!"

"Emily, stop!"

"We can't let them take us!" she shrieked, tugging at him, desperate to pull him back.

"Get off of me!"

He pushed her angrily, hard enough to make her let go of his arm, hard enough to make her fall. She stared up at him from the floor, tears streaming down her face. Up and down the hallway, students came out of their rooms to see what was happening.

"I don't know what's gotten into you, but you're acting crazy!" Sean noticed the other students watching and put up his hands. "You know what? I just can't deal with this right now." He walked away.

"Sean!" she screamed after him. "Sean, promise me you won't go to Professor Vaughan's office tomorrow! Promise me!"

He didn't turn around. She collapsed against the wall, sobbing. She could feel the other students staring, but she didn't care. She'd failed again. Sean would still report to Vaughan's office in the morning. He would still wind up on that surgical table.

She couldn't save him, but maybe she could still save herself. She grabbed her car keys and ran to the student parking lot. Half the lamps were out, leaving wide, dark pools of shadow across the lot. She glanced nervously at Professor Vaughan's stone cottage, but no lights came through the windows. He wasn't there. She hit the unlock button on the key fob, and her car gave a comforting *chirp*. Just as she reached for the driver's side door, someone grabbed her from behind, putting a hand over her mouth to stifle her scream, and pushed her against the car so she couldn't turn around.

Professor Vaughan's voice hissed in her ear, "That was some stunt you pulled in class today, Miss Bannerman. But I promise you, whatever you think you know, the truth is far more extraordinary than you can imagine." She struggled as she felt a hypodermic needle pierce her neck. "Stop fighting, I'm doing you a favor. You have no idea what a unique opportunity I'm giving you. To see an alien world. Experience an alien culture. You should be thanking me."

It's bad enough I'm a victim of Professor Vaughan's obsession and an unwilling subject of the Mi-Go's studies, but to be given the power to change the past and still not save myself from this fate is maddening. It's as though every choice I make brings me to the same end. Every path leads to the Mi-Go. What's the point of being given a second chance if nothing changes?

I miss Sean, whose cylinder is being kept somewhere else. Occasionally, I hear the mechanical voices of other brains speaking in other rooms and wonder if one of them is him. I haven't spoken to him or heard his voice—his real voice—since we were last together at Middlewood.

I wish I'd never gone through that damn anomaly. I wish I'd never been tormented with this useless ability to reshape the past.

Maybe that, at least, is something I can change for the better. One last time, I reach through the white.

She didn't have a plan. She couldn't stop the Mi-Go who carried her brain cylinder from flying through the anomaly. But if she tried hard enough, could she reject the splintering of her mind? If she were prepared for it, could she force her consciousness not to scatter back through her timeline?

She was back in the darkness of the cylinder when she felt the Mi-Go pass through the anomaly again, but she was powerless against it.

Her mind was already splintered, and this time the anomaly only splintered it further, supernova upon supernova, fracture upon fracture, thrusting her backward through her past again, but also forward into a jumbled patchwork of horrific imagery that her mind couldn't—dared not—collate. Each of these splinters fractured again and again, a mosaic of moments from the entirety of her life, until she was everywhere and everywhen, past and future, on Earth and on Yuggoth and then finally—

Somewhere else.

Emily stood upon an arid plain of sand. Before her a stone structure sat half-buried, its timeworn walls decorated with strange, angular carvings. What remained of its massive spires rose toward an alien yellow sky where three moons hung like staring eyes. In the distance she saw enormous towers, the remains of an ancient, deserted city. Scattered among the crumbling buildings were huge, soaring monoliths of black stone, rising high above the towers and emanating a peculiar sense of dread. She found she couldn't look at them long before her discomfort became overwhelming and she had to look away.

She was surprised to discover she was back in her body. Or *a* body. It couldn't be hers. Hers was wherever Professor Vaughan and the Mi-Go had left it on Earth, after pillaging her skull. Or maybe her body was gone, burned or dissolved in acid so there would be no evidence. The body she wore now was solid, real, but it was clearly artificial, something the Mi-Go had constructed to house her brain. She patted her arms, her stomach. It didn't feel like metal or plastic, it felt like flesh, or something close to it.

She didn't know where she was in her timeline. Her future, it seemed. But what was this place?

There was no door in the half-buried structure before her, only an immense archway leading inside, built for someone much bigger than her. If she wanted answers, this looked like a good place to start. She stepped through the archway and found herself in a passage whose walls had been carved with the same strange designs as the exterior. The passage opened onto a titanic chamber, its soaring, vaulted ceiling rising so high that it disappeared into the shadows. At the center of the chamber was a circular dais surrounded by five stalagmites, each a dozen feet tall, bending inward like enormous ribs, and made of the same black stone as the monoliths outside. Atop the dais was an immense throne, hewn from ancient rock, and upon it sat a colossal skeleton. Its massive skull, brown and cracked with the passage of time, resembled a large, smooth boulder. It had no mouth, no eye sockets, no ear holes, just a flat expanse of bone.

A dark, oblong object rested on the throne beside the dead giant. Curious, she pulled herself up onto the throne and sat beside the giant's huge, elongated femur and oddly spiked patella. The object seemed to be a long sliver of that same black stone, and while the giant could have easily held it in one hand, she had to lay it across her lap to examine it. But the moment she touched it, a web of energy burst to life between the five black stalagmites, surrounding her. It took the form of thousands upon thousands of strands, crossing each other to form a grid, and within the countless squares of the grid were moving images. She saw an Earth occupied by lumbering dinosaurs. She saw the raising of the pyramids, the construction of the Brooklyn Bridge, and the continents drowning under massive floods as long-lost islands rose from the ocean's depths. She saw other worlds, too, other forms of life that weren't human or Mi-Go—barrel-shaped creatures with wings like fans, cone-shaped entities with snaking limbs, polyp-like monstrosities that phased in and out of the material plane. She saw civilizations rise and fall on countless worlds. The whole of time played out before her.

She put it together then. All the clues were there. This was Arneth-Zin, the temple at the center of the universe where all the timelines converged. This was where Professor Vaughan had wanted to go so desperately that he'd sold her and Sean to the Mi-Go like lab rats. The dead giant beside her had to be the sentry he'd spoken of. The watcher of Arneth-Zin—blind, deaf, dumb, and long dead. She almost laughed at the irony. It had seen and heard nothing of the timelines that played out in the grid. It couldn't tell anyone its secrets. It couldn't send Professor Vaughan back in time to save his family. Vaughan had destroyed Emily's life, put her through unimaginable horror, for nothing.

She discovered that if she concentrated while touching the shard, she could guide what she saw within the grid. At her command, the grid filled with images from her own life. The choices she'd made. Every path she'd taken. She saw a group of six Mi-Go winging through space, carrying two cylinders, Sean's brain in one, hers in the other. She watched as a burning red ribbon streaked and twisted across space until it struck the Mi-Go carrying her cylinder. The spatial anomaly—the moment that had untethered her consciousness from linear time and ultimately brought her here. She couldn't bring herself to look beyond that. She didn't want to relive her time on Yuggoth. If the Mi-Go had given her a new body, it meant at some point she'd stopped resisting and had cooperated with them. She couldn't watch herself do that.

She watched her family instead, her mother and father and kid sister, none of whom knew what happened to her. She saw them get the news that she'd gone missing, and later, when the authorities gave up the search and declared her dead, her family's grief was so powerful she wanted to cry along with them. But she couldn't. The Mi-Go had built this body for her, and they didn't understand human emotional responses like crying.

She watched Sean's timeline, too, until it became too painful. She couldn't bear to see his empty-skulled corpse on that surgical table again.

She didn't know how much time passed as she sat upon the dead sentry's throne. Days? Weeks? There was a delicious irony in the fact that time had lost meaning for her. Her artificial body didn't age. She didn't need to eat or drink or sleep, so she never had to take her attention off the grid.

Eventually, two Mi-Go entered the temple. One carried a brain cylinder, the other a variety of mechanical equipment. She watched as they placed the cylinder on the floor and hooked the equipment into the three sockets: the lenses for eyes, the metal disc for hearing, and a speaker box for speech. Their job complete, the Mi-Go left.

"Hello?" a scratchy, electronic voice came out of the speaker. Rows of lights blinked on the side of the box in time with the words. "My name is Professor Joseph Vaughan."

Vaughan. So he'd finally gotten his wish. She jumped down from the throne. As soon as she let go of the shard, the web of images between the stalagmites vanished.

"Great sentry of Arneth-Zin, I've come a long way and beg you to have pity on me," Vaughan said. "I beseech you to open the seams of time and let me return to the point where I lost my wife and children.

Please give me the chance to set things right."

She squatted before the cylinder, making sure the lenses could see her face clearly. "You don't recognize me, do you?"

"What—what do you mean?" Even in his artificial electronic voice, she could hear confusion and fear. Good. He deserved to be afraid. "Aren't you the sentry?"

"No," she said. "It's me. Emily Bannerman."

Vaughan said nothing.

"Surely *that* much time hasn't passed," she said.

"I'm sorry, I don't understand," he said. "You know me? We've met?"

Emily let out a bitter laugh. He didn't remember her. That was how little she'd mattered to him. He hadn't cared who she was or what future he was stealing from her when he gave her to the Mi-Go. She'd been nothing but a means to an end. His ticket to Arneth-Zin.

"This can't be happening," he said. "Tell me you understand the pattern of time! Tell me you know where the seams are!"

She shrugged. "I'm as in the dark with this time-travel shit as you are. I can only change my own timeline, not anyone else's."

"You—you can change your timeline?" Vaughan's electronic laughter came through the speaker, an eerie, grating sound. "I knew it, I knew it was possible! You must show me how!"

She supposed she could. She could consult the grid for the whereabouts of the spatial anomaly. He could find a way to pass through it as she did and gain the ability to change his timeline. She could even teach him how to control it so it didn't overwhelm him.

But why would she help the man who'd done this to her?

"Sorry," she said. "If it's any consolation, I know how you feel."

She undid the latches at the top of the cylinder.

"Stop. What are you doing?"

"I understand you better than you think, Professor Vaughan. I know what it's like to have someone you love taken away from you. I know what it's like to carry that terrible emptiness inside. You want nothing more than to be with them again. I can help with that."

She lifted off the lid. Inside, Professor Vaughans's brain was suspended in a thick, viscous liquid.

Vaughan's voice came through the speaker pitched with new hope. "So you *will* show me how?"

"No," she said. "But I can reunite you with your family another way."

She reached into the cylinder and pulled out his slippery, spongy brain. Just three pounds of tissue, as he'd pointed out in the lecture hall a lifetime ago, and yet it housed everything that was Professor Vaughan. She tore it to pieces with her bare hands, throwing chunks of shredded gray matter across the floor until there was nothing left of it. She dumped the solution out of the cylinder, then bashed it and the rest of the equipment against the temple wall until they were mangled and unrecognizable. After that, she felt a lot better.

What she hadn't told Professor Vaughan, what that horrible, selfish man didn't deserve to know, was that she *did* understand the pattern of time. She'd understood it from the moment she discovered that the watcher of Arenth-Zin was blind, deaf, and dumb. The truth was that there *was* no pattern. There were no reasons, no secret designs, no answers to the philosophical questions that plagued man and Mi-Go alike. It didn't matter if you were a student or a professor, a victim or a perpetrator, if you lived your life with love or forgot the names of the people you stepped on as soon as you were done with them; in the end there was only entropy and decay, chaos and tragedy, as though the universe had nothing but disdain for the life that inhabited it. And in an ancient temple on a dead world where all the timelines converged, there was a lone sentry whose job, for reasons that were unknowable, was to stand witness as it all withered and died.

Emily climbed up onto the throne, took hold of the black shard, and watched the grid of time blink back to life. Every path had led her here, guided by that same pitiless universe, as if it had decided Arenth-Zin had been without a watcher long enough.

Why had she been chosen? Was there some kind of intelligence behind it, something beyond even the vast eternity playing out before her, or was she fooling herself into thinking there was any reason at all? Maybe she was nothing more than a leaf blown by random, feckless winds. Did it matter?

It was something she'd have an eternity to ponder.

Spawning Season

I've always been the product of my upbringing. I was born and raised in Jochebed's Cradle, a small fishing village at the southern tip of the peninsula of Virginia's eastern shore. As an adult, work brought me to New York City, but I often felt like an outsider, different from everyone else in ways they couldn't understand. They were at home with hard concrete sidewalks, blaring car horns, pollution, and the constant crush of people. Not me. In the eight years I lived there I came to miss the clean, salty smell of the ocean air. I missed nights that were so quiet all you could hear was the sound of the waves gently lapping at the shore and the boats bumping against the docks. Most of all, I missed Nazareth Hill, the tall cliff on the village shore with a breathtaking view of the ocean. It was where we held our annual Founding Day celebration, marking a history that stretched back to long before the American Revolution. During times of stress, when work was too much and the city felt too oppressive, I imagined I could still feel the soft grass of Nazareth Hill under my bare feet.

I was the last of my family. My older brother, Elijah, died when I was still young. He was ten years older than me, already graduated from high school and working on a trawler when a storm swallowed his boat. We buried an empty casket in the churchyard. There were a lot of empty caskets there. The ocean is unforgiving. It doesn't return those it takes from you. My father died six years after the hurricane that forced us to leave Jochebed's Cradle. By then I was in my senior year of college, which meant he was alone when his heart gave out. I never forgave myself for that, not completely. As for my mother, I had no idea whether she was alive or not. My father raised me on his own.

I wanted nothing more than to be a father myself, partly in tribute to my own, but I wasn't interested in dating. I didn't like the city women, and I didn't want to answer their questions about where I grew up. There were things I didn't tell people about Jochebed's Cradle. Chief among them was the fact that there were no women in the village. We were a community of fathers and sons, grandfathers and uncles, but no mothers, no aunts, no sisters. No wives. I didn't tell people this because I knew what they would say—if there were children, there had to be mothers. But how could I explain to an outsider that my village was different? That *I* was different?

I had no interest in physical intimacy, either. It was better if no one saw what I kept hidden under my clothes. They wouldn't understand.

It was a dream that eventually brought me back to Jochebed's Cradle. Or rather, a sound that came to me in a dream. A long, sustained note, as loud as thunder and as deep as the ocean floor. It shocked me awake in a feverish sweat. I remembered that sound from my youth. I couldn't shake it. Hearing it again roused something in me that wouldn't let go, until all I could think of was going back. I was desperate to see the village again. My vacation time at work was piling up, so I took a few days off and drove south down the coast.

There was an excitement in my blood as I neared Jochebed's Cradle, an anticipation that made my breath grow shallow. I was fifteen when the hurricane blew in from the Atlantic Ocean and we were forced to leave the village. I remembered crying as my father and I drove away, thinking I'd never see my home again. Now I was thirty. I'd spent half my life away from there. I didn't know if anything would be left, or if my memories of a perfect childhood would match the truth of what I found. There was only one road into the village, cutting through a thick forest of red oak. I was surprised to find that the old cement barricade was still there, blocking the road, although the hurricane warning and evacuation order that had been affixed to it were long gone. The barricade was too heavy for me to move, so I parked my car and decided to continue on foot. It was almost sundown, but I'd already come this far. I had to see the village.

The forest that separated Jochebed's Cradle from the rest of Virginia had always felt like a castle wall that protected us from the outside world. We had our boats, and the bounty of the ocean, and the Founding Day celebrations on Nazareth Hill, and we didn't need anything else. As I walked through the woods, my excitement grew. Jochebed's Cradle, my home, waited for me just ahead. Behind me was everything else, superfluous and irrelevant.

When I reached the village, I was shocked to see the damage the hurricane had done. I'd imagined the worst and heard news reports of the devastation up and down the coast, but neither prepared me for the deep sadness that came from seeing the destruction firsthand. Houses stood in ruin, nothing but crumbling piles of timber and brick. Trees had been torn from the ground and left in haphazard deadfalls that blocked off many of the streets. The marina was torn to pieces, the wreckage of fishing boats half-submerged in the water. I could remember a time when the marina had been loud and full of life, the water teeming with boats heading out into the Atlantic or coming back with their nets and holds bursting with fish. Our boats never came back empty. Even when the fishermen of Chincoteague and Hog Island saw their livelihoods dwindle because of pollution and overfishing, the waters we fished stayed clean and bountiful. We never wanted for anything. The ocean took from us, but it gave back in other ways.

I passed the ruins of the tavern, the oldest building in the village, where in the evenings our fathers drank and talked about their day on the water while we children cast make-believe lines from the shore using twigs for rods. Beyond it was the schoolhouse, gone except for the stone foundation covered in grass and weeds. I still remembered the schoolyard rhyme we used to chant while playing intricate games with seashells:

Net the fish and trap the prawn.
Blow the sea horn when it's time to spawn.
Sire your sons without any fuss.
One for the ocean and one for us.

I walked the empty streets accompanied by the ghosts of my past. It was clear that in the fifteen years since the hurricane, no one had come back to rebuild. Jochebed's Cradle had been abandoned and left to rot. My eyes were already stinging with tears from the thought, but when I saw what was left of the house I grew up in, the tears spilled down my cheeks. The second floor, where my father and I slept, where Elijah slept before the ocean took him, was gone. Just gone. Sheared off by the wind and hurled somewhere far away. Behind the house, where the water came up to a small, private beach, I stood in the twilight and looked out at the dark, undulating waves. It was May, still spawning season for many of the fish out there. The female bluefish would be releasing their eggs to drift on the current and be fertilized by the males. Out among the seagrass, the female seahorses would be depositing their eggs into the abdominal brood pouches of the males to be fertilized internally. I took solace in the fact that life went on, if not in Jochebed's Cradle, then at least in the ocean.

How many quiet Sunday afternoons had my father and I taken a rowboat out onto the water, after the chores were done and the fishing boats were docked? The waves sparkled like diamonds in the sun, and as my father rowed I would dip my fingers into the water. Shapes would gather below my hand, dark and misshapen, and my father would point at one that was the same size as me and say, "There he is, Jacob. Your other brother. Your twin."

"*You* were a sire?" I asked him once, astonished at the idea. But of course he had to have been a sire twice, once for Elijah and once for me. And our twins.

"We're all sires when the time comes," he said. "We made a promise, and we always keep our promises."

"How will I know when it's my time?" I asked, but all he said was, "You'll know."

I walked to the village center, still deep in my memories. Nazareth Hill stood tall and unchanged against the darkening sky. The sight of it put a fire in my blood again. I felt intoxicated, giddy, as if I could swim straight across the Atlantic and never get tired.

A twig snapped behind me, where the main road came through the forest. I turned and saw men walking on the road. Their numbers increased as I watched, twenty, thirty, all of them coming toward me. When they were close enough to make out their faces, I recognized many of them as villagers I'd known: Hiram Baskerville, the schoolmaster; Bartholomew Archer, the tavern owner; Josiah Nash, who ran the marina; Ezekiel Page, whose fleet of trucks took the catch to be sold at the Chesapeake fish markets. But the strong and sturdy men I remembered were gray and wrinkled now, slow on their feet. There were others with them, boys as old as fourteen and as young as one. I couldn't believe my eyes, and as the men warmly embraced me in greeting I remained stiff with surprise.

"I don't understand," I said. "What are you doing here?"

Ezekiel looked at me strangely. "Don't you know what day it is?"

"It's Founding Day," Hiram said.

Of course. After so many years away, I'd forgotten the date.

"We come every year," Josiah said. "The village may be no more, but some things haven't changed. A dozen generations ago, the men of Jochebed's Cradle made a deal, and we've always kept up our end."

"But there's no more fishing," I said. "I thought the deal was that if we gave her what she wanted, she would keep our waters full."

"Aye, but the hurricane changed all that," Josiah said. "It's not about the fish anymore. She survived the storm, but her children, the ones in the water, they didn't."

I hung my head. My twin was dead. All our twins were dead. It hurt me as much as losing Elijah had. The ocean is merciless, even to those who dwell in it.

"She calls us back every Founding Day because we made a promise, and we always keep our promises," Josiah said. With a smile he ruffled the hair of the ten-year-old boy next to him. I saw the resemblance in their features. "It's not so bad."

"You heard the call, too, just as we did," Bartholomew said. A one-year-old boy held his age-spotted hand and quietly sucked his thumb. "It's why you came, isn't it, Jacob?"

"I heard it in a dream," I said. "But why now, after all these years?"

"The rest of us are too old," Josiah said. "We can't keep siring year after year."

Bartholomew patted his one-year-old's head. "This one very nearly killed me. My fifth son. I'm not the man I used to be."

"None of us are," came a voice from behind them. The men stepped aside to let through a wizened old man I recognized as Ishmael Dandridge, the mayor. He had to be in his nineties, stooped and skeletal, but he dragged the heavy sea horn behind him, the eight-foot-long spiral tusk of a narwhal. "Come along, it'll be dark soon. And then she'll come."

I followed them without question, taking off my shoes and climbing the slope of Nazareth Hill as I had so many times in my youth. The soft grass on my bare feet felt just as I remembered. The fire in my blood burned stronger. Night had fallen when we reached the top. The tall, sheer cliff that led down to the ocean was hidden in the darkness, but I could hear the waves lapping at the rocks below. I stood in the spot where my father stood before me, and his father before him, in a tradition going back three hundred years. The others stood with me, facing the ocean, their expressions masked by the moonless night. Ishmael handed me the sea horn.

"This is why your blood burns," he told me. "This is why you couldn't think about anything but coming back. It was the same for all of us when it was our time."

The sea horn was even heavier than it looked. I struggled to lift the pointed end to my lips. The ivory tusk was hollow, and when I blew through it the horn emitted a low trumpeting tone. After a few seconds a long, sustained note answered from somewhere out in the ocean, so loud and deep it rattled my bones. The sound from my dream. The calling that summoned me to uphold the bargain. I blew the sea horn again, and this time the response came sooner, and from closer. There was a ruckus below as hundreds of crabs swarmed the beach in a writhing mass, fleeing the ocean. After a third blow of the sea horn I could make out a dark, titanic shape cutting through the waves toward us. The night hid her features, but she glistened from the water. I'd never seen anything so beautiful.

Our mother. Our wife.

I blew the sea horn again, and she returned my call, her massive head swaying in the darkness above, dripping water over us like a baptism. I caught a glimpse of a coronet of bone and a long-ridged snout. The others chanted along with the tones from the sea horn, and in the distance her massive, swaying, serpentine tail broke the surface. Then more broke the surface and I realized they weren't tails, they were limbs, dozens of them.

One wrapped around me, wet and cold but surprisingly gentle as it tightened. Ishmael took the sea horn from me just before she lifted me into the air and brought me closer, closer, until her colossal black form was all I could see.

Many months have passed since that night, and I find myself back in Jochebed's Cradle, sitting on the beach behind the remains of my old house. I always wanted to be a father, to honor my own and to honor the tradition of my village, and now I'm ready. I'm naked, and what I've always kept hidden under my clothes is revealed in the bright moonlight. A seam down the front of my torso that traces a straight line from sternum to pelvis.

The pouch of my stomach is swollen. Inside, my sons are squirming, letting me know it's time. Powerful contractions shake my body until the seam bursts open and both of them spill out. I swaddle one of them in the blanket I brought with me. His name is Aaron, after my father, and I'll teach him to fish as my father taught me, and his father taught him, going back a dozen generations.

Aaron's twin, dark and misshapen, crawls toward the shore. Josiah, Ishmael, and the others stand on either side, protecting him from the hungry crabs that crowd the beach. When he reaches the water, he slips away to be with his mother, and the promise of Jochebed's Cradle is kept.

One for the ocean and one for us.

Six Strikes on a Laboratory Lightning Rod

1

I have to duck to pass through the entrance flaps of the pinstriped tent. Outside, the sounds of the carnival, once full of excitement and laughter, have changed to screams of terror and the thunder of running feet. Inside the tent, ringed by empty wooden bleachers, there is only a charged silence. Across the sawdust-covered floor, a group of men wait clustered like guards before a metal door in the far end of the tent. They give me threatening looks, shouting warnings for me to get out of there. They remind me of barking dogs. I'm too close to the one place I'm not supposed to be—the place no one is supposed to be. The men are ready to stop me before I go any farther. Or they *think* they're ready. The dark cloak that covers my body is already spattered with blood. If they were smart, they would run.

Beyond them, on the other side of that metal door, is the one I've come for.

The men who stand between me and my goal work for the carnival. They are security guards, ostensibly here to keep the crowds in check, but their real job is to prevent the sideshow attractions from leaving. *Freaks*—that's what they call them. The word stings like a barb in my mind. I've been called a freak before, and worse. The methods these men employ are notoriously brutal. Blackmail. Broken limbs. Threats against family members. Carnivals can't make money without their freaks, and money is all they care about.

As for me, I have other concerns.

When they see I'm not leaving, they pick up their makeshift weapons and come at me. Baseball bats. Hammers. Knives. I've fought mobs like this before. I've been fighting them all my long, miserable life. Once they waved torches at me, jabbed me with pitchforks. This mob is no different, their weapons no better.

When the first man reaches me, I snatch the baseball bat out of his hands with one hand and toss it aside. With my other hand I crush his windpipe and toss him aside as easily the bat. The others don't even slow down. They're used to violence. It doesn't faze them.

We have that in common.

They bludgeon me, slash at me with their weapons. The pain means nothing to me. It's an echo of a life before this one. In return, I pull their arms out of their sockets, break their spines, tear their flesh from the bone. The walls of the tent drip with blood. Their shrieks mingle with the screams from outside. Their dead bodies pile at my feet. I hoist a bearded man by the shirt and pull him close. His eyes go wide with horror, and I realize the hood of my cloak has fallen back during the fight. He can see my face. He can see everything.

"Who are you?" he screams.

I hit him hard in the neck, hard enough that I hear the bones snap, and he goes down. I move on to the next, and the next, until the sawdust under my feet is soaked with blood and I'm the only one left standing.

Always, I'm the last left standing.

I pull the hood up over my head and press on toward the metal door at the back of the tent. The bearded man's question echoes in my mind. Who am I?

My name is monster.

My name is creature.

My name is abnormal.

2

It is on one of my rare excursions out of the mountains and into the village under cover of night to scrounge for discarded food and clothing from laundry lines that I see the posters for the traveling carnival that has set up on the outskirts of town. One poster in particular catches my eye. It is a colorful portrait of a new attraction for their sideshow. Even though it is a rough, cartoonish painting, I can see the anguish in his face. He is a prisoner.

I know what it's like to be held against my will. Carried into my prison tied to a log like a pig on a spit. Chained to a big wooden chair in a stone chamber, a mockery of a throne in a king's court. Shackles on my wrists and ankles, and even one around my throat. A single barred window allowing a lone shaft of sunlight inside. How I longed to raise my arms toward it, to stretch my body up to the light, to let it surround and engulf me. To let it release me from this world I never asked to be brought into. Yes, I know what it's like to yearn for freedom.

I know all too well the loneliness of realizing no one is coming to help.

And with a sudden sense of clarity, I know what I must do.

I wait for nightfall before entering the carnival. Nighttime is when the carnival is at its most crowded and I am less likely to be noticed. Still, I can't take the risk of my face being seen. It would cause a panic and I'd never get this close again. To hide the horror of my features, I wear the hooded cloak I found in an abandoned monastery long ago.

Moving through the crowded fairway, I listen for the barkers to guide me toward the sideshow. Around me, parents herd their children from one game of chance to the next. The little ones look happy, their pudgy hands and laughing faces sticky with candy. There was a time when I felt sorry for myself that I didn't have a family of my own, but that time is long gone. I am no one's father and no one's husband, but I suppose you could call me someone's son.

I haven't seen the man who made me in a very long time. My last words to him were generous ones that he did nothing to earn. "You live," I told him. I've regretted those words ever since. When I had the chance, I should have crushed his head between my hands—the hands he gave me. It would be no less than he deserved for bringing me into this hellish world and abandoning me to its corruption and depravity. Who knows, perhaps he's dead now. So many of the people I once knew are dead, but the thought that *he* is among them brings a smirk to my face.

"Oho, and what have we here?" someone says loudly. It is a stout man in a colorful clown costume and makeup, wandering the fairway. "You're a tall drink of water! How's the view of Mars up there? Any sign of Martians?" He honks a bicycle horn at me with one gloved hand.

"Watch out, everyone, we've got a walking lamppost over here!" Another honk.

I keep walking. He follows.

"You look like a tree that lifted itself out of the ground and shook off its leaves!" Honk, honk. "You better be careful all the way up there, pal, you might get struck by lightning!"

I pause a moment, then keep walking.

The clown holds out his hand. He wants to be paid for his insults. I'd pay him just to make him go away, but I don't have any money. I keep walking, and he continues to follow, growing angrier.

"Come on, you piker," he hisses at me, his voice low so no one else will hear. "Pay up." When I don't give him anything, he says, "What's your problem anyway? What's with the monk getup? Maybe I should call you Brother Piker. It's a kinder name than arsehole." He honks the horn again, more aggressively than before, and shoves me.

I couldn't care less about his insults, but the shove bothers me. I've thrown men off of windmills for less. But I keep walking. I can't afford to make a scene and draw attention. The clown veers off with one more angry honk to go bother someone else. He has no idea how lucky he is to walk away. Very few people ever have.

3

I am closer to my destination now. I can hear the barker's voice nearby.

"Come see the monster from the dawn of time! Is it human? Is it animal? Test your mettle against this terrifying sight! Buy your tickets now! The show starts in half an hour! You won't want to miss it!"

The barker stands in front of a huge, pinstriped tent with painted posters all over the sides. They are the same posters I saw in the village. The same anguish is visible in the prisoner's painted eyes. I can feel his despair.

I weave through the milling families on the fairway and make my way to the rear of the tent. A large metal shed stands flush against the canvas wall, but I can only get so close before a chain-link fence blocks my path. That's where they're keeping him for now, before they bring him out into the tent for the paying crowds to scream and gawk at. I could tear through the fence as easily as paper, but the metal shed doesn't have a visible entrance. The only way inside must be through the tent itself.

I am about to turn back to the fairway when someone grabs my hand. I lurch around, caught off-guard, but the touch is a gentle one. A young woman stands beside me in the unmistakable garb of a carnival fortune teller: a scarf over her long, dark hair; big, round earrings; a loose, flowing dress with a pattern of astrological symbols. I've known only one true Romani in my time—an old woman who went by the name Maleva—and I can tell right away this woman's appearance is a costume, nothing more. She is a swindler, like the clown, here only to part people from their money. And yet, the way she holds my hand . . .

Only one other person has ever clasped my hand so gently, with such kindness. Not my maker. Not the one who was meant to be my bride. No, it was a little girl by the shores of a quiet lake, eager to show me how the flowers she'd picked could float on the water. She touched my hand as if I weren't a monster and guided me to sit beside her. It is one of my few happy memories. But then, the accident. I had the mind of a newborn then; I didn't understand that she couldn't float the way her flowers did. How easy it would have been to pluck her out of the lake in time, but my own fear and confusion made me run instead.

Hers is the only death that haunts me. She dwells behind my eyes now, coming to me in my dreams, her and her flowers. When I wake, my cheeks are wet with tears.

This young woman looks up at me with that same fearlessness. It makes me want to stay and luxuriate in her touch.

"Would you like me to read your palm for you, sir?" she asks.

It takes me a moment to find my voice. "No," I say. It is one of the first words I ever learned. I heard it often enough that it stuck, along with other words like *demon* and *beast*.

"Please," she says and gently opens my hand in hers.

I let it happen. I am not ready to pull my hand away. Her touch is like a drug, filling a hole in me I didn't think existed anymore. She brushes her fingertips along the lines of my palm, concentrating on what they tell her.

She frowns and her brow furrows as her fingers gather information.

"Thief," she hisses. "Murderer!"

I have made a terrible mistake allowing it to go this far. She thinks it is my life she sees, but she is reading the palm of an executed criminal, one of many my maker harvested parts from. Although, to be honest, I too am a thief and a killer. The joke is on me if I thought for one second she was truly reading someone else's life.

She pulls away with a disgusted cry, but it's too late for me to run, the trap is sprung. The fortune teller did a good job keeping me distracted, and now, as she recedes into the night, I feel the sharp tip of a knife dig through the fabric of my cloak and into my back.

"Now then," the clown hisses from behind me, "about that money, Brother Piker."

4

I have often wondered who I was before, prior to my first death and my brain ending up in a jar to be studied in a classroom before it was stolen for my maker. Was I a good person? A bad one? What made my brain so worthy of study?

There's no point in pursuing these thoughts. Whatever memories this brain once held are gone now, replaced by new ones. Painted over like an artist unhappy with the first version of a portrait, or perhaps fried out of existence when the lightning crackled and arced down the metal rod and into my flesh.

According to my maker, it took six lightning strikes to initiate my birth. Don't ask me how it worked. In his journal I read phrases such as *sinoatrial node* and *conduction pathways,* but the words didn't mean anything to me. They still don't.

Only one thing stuck out to me in those pages, and it has stayed with me ever since. Lightning's power is raw, primal. Its voltage, temperature, and energy are beyond measure. It has given me something very close to immortality. But according to that same journal, this body of mine only barely withstood those six strikes. Had there been a seventh, it would have destroyed me completely. I would be nothing but ash and burnt meat.

As often as I have wondered about my prior identity, I wonder what would happen if I were struck by lightning now. Would it count as the seventh strike? Would I finally, finally die?

Was it too much of a bother for God to send a seventh bolt of lightning the night of my birth? Was it too much of an inconvenience to spare me from being brought into this wretched world?

5

In the shadows by the chain-link fence, the clown turns me around to show me the knife in his hand. It is small enough to be concealed in his colorful costume. Its blade, though sharp, is only the size of my thumb.

"Now then, friend," he says, "let's see what you've got in those pockets of yours."

Friend. The first word I ever learned to say. What a joke. There are no friends for me among these people.

It angers me that he thinks such a tiny blade could harm me, that I would be afraid of him. I have seen things that would turn him into a gibbering coward: a man who became a bat; another who became a wolf. I should have died a dozen times over—burnt, frozen, buried under falling stones—and yet always, *always* I live!

Rage boils through me, and before he can move I grab his head with both hands. My thumbs dig into his eyes, drawing blood and other, more viscous fluids from his bruised sockets. His screams grow higher in pitch as I crush the life out of him.

The dead girl behind my eyes turns away from the sight.

Whoever I was before, whoever I was when I died, even Hell spat me out.

When his screams fade to nothing, I drop his maimed and bloody corpse at my feet. Immediately, new screams pierce the night. Despite killing the clown in the shadows off the fairway, there were witnesses. People are running, shrieking, trampling over each other to get away. Panicking villagers are a familiar sight to me. If I lowered my hood and showed them my face, I'm sure I'd be a familiar sight to them, too.

There is no more reason to be careful. The fleeing crowd gives me a wide berth as I make my way toward my goal. I have to duck to pass through the entrance flaps of the pinstriped tent.

6

The blood-soaked sawdust squelches under my feet as I approach the metal door at the back of the tent. It is not locked, but I tear the door from its hinges anyway. My blood is on fire. How many men have I killed tonight between the clown and the guards in the tent? I'm sure there will be more before the night is through. I welcome it.

Beyond the door is the interior of the metal shed that is attached to the tent. It is smaller than the tent outside and not as well lit. A tall cylinder of glass stands in the center of the room atop a wheeled wooden platform. Dirty water swirls inside the cylinder, and floating within it is the prisoner I have come for. He has the form of a man, but his body is covered with fishlike scales. His mouth gapes as his gills try to pull what oxygen they can from the murky water. His eyes, big as saucers, plead with me to free him.

Beside the cylinder stands a man whose fine suit and top hat tell me he owns the carnival. He holds a cane in one hand, but strangely, it isn't long enough to touch the floor, and it ends in two copper prongs. His eyes nervously take in the blood that drips down my cloak and paints my hands. Then his gaze darts past me, through the wreckage of the door and into the bloodstained tent beyond, where the floor is carpeted with mangled bodies. As the realization that his guards aren't coming to protect him sinks in, his face changes to an angry sneer. He jabs his oddly short cane at me. Cornered animals never hesitate to strike.

"Stay back," he warns.

I lunge toward him, arms outstretched. With a flick of his thumb on an unseen button, the prongs at the end of his cane jump to life with arcs of electricity. He thrusts them into my chest, and pain explodes through me. The force of it knocks me back. An electric cattle prod. No doubt he has been using the same vile tool to keep his prisoner docile.

I lurch for the carnival owner again, but the cattle prod finds me once more. The shock is like a sword piercing my chest. It drives me to the ground.

On occasion I have taken strength from electricity. It is the seed of my birth, after all, more my true father than my maker ever was. This is different. The electricity from the cattle prod isn't a controlled burst. It is chaotic, potent, as forceful as a lightning bolt. Could this be the seventh strike I have waited for? Could this, at long last, be the end?

I can't let it be. The prisoner must be freed. I couldn't save the little girl, but I can save him. I *have* to save him.

The carnival owner stands over me with a smug laugh. "I suppose you're after my new acquisition. I'm afraid I can't let you take it. I paid a fortune to have it sent to me from the Amazon. I intend to make that money back, and then some." He turns to the shape floating listlessly in the cylinder. "What a specimen. Those features, that musculature. It looks almost human, doesn't it? You'd almost believe it could think or feel. Looking into its eyes, you'd almost believe it had a soul. Oh, yes, people will gladly empty their pockets to see it."

I try to grab him, but he is too quick with the cattle prod. I let out an animalistic cry as the pain lances through me. My whole body shudders. The hood falls back from the cloak, revealing my face. He gasps in surprise and freezes for a moment. It would be the perfect time to strike, but I can't move.

Inside the cylinder, the gilled man's eyes meet my own. Something passes between us. An understanding that, in some way, in the only way that matters, we are alike. Kindred spirits. He begins to pound on the glass with his wide, webbed hands. His fingers end in fearsome claws.

The carnival owner sneers down at me. "Well, well, another freak." He electrocutes me with the cattle prod again. Something is wrong. My heartbeat doesn't feel right. Its rhythm is off. The shape in the cylinder continues to pound on the glass. "Oh, you'll make the children scream, won't you? I could double my money in a single night with you on the stage." The cattle prod comes down on my stomach and I scream. For a moment my heart stops, then twitches fitfully and begrudgingly back into service. "You have to understand, my ugly friend, those of us who are superior have the God-given right to do as we please with those who are inferior. It's the way of the world. The natural order of things." Another jab from the cattle prod, followed by searing pain. It takes my heart longer to resume beating this time. I can hear the shape in the cylinder continue to beat on the glass, but he sounds miles away now. "You understand that I am superior to you, don't you? That your natural place in the world is to serve me? Signal your understanding or you'll get the prod again."

It is hard to catch my breath enough to speak.

"I . . . serve . . . no one."

He thrusts the cattle prod toward me. With all the strength I have left I grab it in my fist before it reaches me, my hand well clear of the dangerous brass prongs at the end.

The smug look on his face melts away.

A moment later the glass cylinder shatters. Water floods the room in an unstoppable wave. The carnival owner is knocked off balance. His top hat falls into the rushing water and is carried out into the tent behind me. I take the opportunity to rise to my feet and yank the cattle prod out of his hand. I turn it around, find the button, and press the brass prongs into the man's chest. The charge blows him backward.

Right into the scale-covered arms of his prisoner, standing before the wreckage of his prison. He grabs the man around the neck with those wide, webbed hands and drags his impressively sharp claws across his throat. Blood spurts from the wound, soaking his fine suit and mixing with the flood at his feet. The carnival owner gives a final gurgle, then falls dead with a splash to the floor.

I catch my new friend before he falls as well. He is weak and growing weaker. I don't know how long he can survive out of the water. Supporting him with one arm, I walk us back out onto the fairway. It is deserted now. The families have fled, and the carnival workers are hiding in their wagons.

Perhaps not *all* of them. A strange chant comes to me on the wind, distantly at first but growing louder. It sounds like an incantation, or a war cry.

"Gooble-gobble, gooble-gobble . . ."

Dark shapes approach, low to the ground. Some are small, adults the size of children. Some are misshapen, with heads that come to a point. Some are legless, pulling themselves with their hands. A limbless man inches forward like a worm, a knife between his teeth. Leading them is a bearded woman no taller than a toddler.

The carnival's last line of defense. It doesn't matter how poorly they have been treated over the years; this is their home, and they think their home is under siege.

My hood is still down. The tiny bearded woman sees me. She sees the scars and sutures and bolts, and she nods, understanding. She waves the others back, calling off the attack.

"One of us," she tells them. "One of us."

They go back in the direction of their wagons. They don't ask me for their freedom. They have their own lives to live, and their own choices to make. So do I. My new friend leans against me, his mouth gasping, his gills trying to suck oxygen from the open air. He is losing strength by the minute. I have to find water for him.

Luckily, I know just the place. A quiet lake not too far away. The spirit of the little girl who died there could use some company.

For years I thought I belonged dead. I yearned to be free of this wretched existence, and each time I opened my eyes again after thinking death had finally claimed me, I felt nothing but disappointment. Now I feel something else, something that lifts the heaviness of my soul. A calling. There are others out there held captive, mistreated by those who call them *freaks* and *inferior*. They feel alone. They think no one is coming to help them. I have a purpose now with which to fill my days before that seventh bolt of lightning finds me.

I pull my friend closer and we start walking.

Whatever Happened
to Solstice Young?

There are times, on dark nights when I'm alone, when the wind blows through the eaves of my house and sounds like a voice whispering my name. A familiar voice. I suppose it should frighten me, and I suppose if I were anyone else it would, but it doesn't. Instead, it gives me a strange kind of comfort.

It's not unusual for me to hear it while staying up late into the night in my living room recliner, grading my students' papers and sipping my evening tonic, a Balvenie DoubleWood on the rocks. If the dean of the university ever found out I drank while grading he would have a conniption, but how does the old saying go? What you don't know can't hurt you? Except I know that's not true. The wind likes to remind me of that.

When it whispers my name, it draws me back to long ago, to that terrible autumn of my youth, so defined by heartache and terror. It began with a simple childhood crush. It began with Solstice Young.

Luminous, with an effervescent smile that could chase the clouds from the sky and the ever-present fragrance of honeysuckle, hibiscus, and lemon—I loved Solstice Young with the wholesome, unconditional love only a child could have for an adult. In the fall of 1983, when the school year was new and the leaves had just started to turn the color of fire and saffron, I was twelve years old and Solstice Young was twenty-two. That ten-year gap might as well have been a chasm of eons, and had she not been the music teacher at my sleepy little town's school I would probably have never laid eyes on her. But I did, I saw her every day for third period, right before lunch, and it felt like a blessing. For a kid who excelled at the art of faking stomach aches to get out of school, that autumn was the only time I can remember actually being excited to go every day.

My love for her bloomed the first day I walked into her classroom, which was one of the smallest in the school. Even in 1983, music classes weren't given much respect. The administration and the school board always seemed on the verge of cutting its funding altogether. They hadn't yet, but in their twisted need to show their contempt they moved the music class to the smallest classroom they could find, a cramped, closet-like room where only half the ceiling lights worked. But somehow Solstice Young made the room feel so much bigger and brighter than it was. She festooned it with all kinds of musical instruments and tacked cardboard album covers to the walls: Fleetwood Mac's *Rumours, Led Zeppelin IV,* David Bowie's *The Rise and Fall of Ziggy Stardust,* Blondie's *Parallel Lines,* Roxy Music's *Avalon,* Duran Duran's *Rio.* We knew what music was back then.

At the time I had never listened to any of those albums, although I knew Keith, my older brother, owned at least one of them. I remembered him coming home with *Rumours* one day, that unforgettable yellow sleeve art burning itself into my mind—a man and a woman holding hands in mid-dance, he with his leg up on a small ottoman, she circling him with her arms outstretched in almost mystical abandon. The man looked like everything I wanted to be when I grew up, dashing and debonair in his boots and vest like a bearded storybook pirate, and the woman—well, there was something about her that was very like the teacher standing at the front of the classroom.

She'd written her name on the chalkboard in a delicate, feminine script—Miss Young, with the *i* in Miss dotted by a smiley face she'd drawn. She wore a white cotton peasant blouse and a long, flowing skirt with a paisley pattern. Her dark blonde hair was long and streaked with highlights, with a single braided strand that hung near her ear. A spray of summery freckles dotted the bridge of her nose and spilled onto her cheeks. Her big blue eyes were bright with the enthusiasm of someone about to teach children for the very first time, the polar opposite of the jaded, tired, permanently annoyed eyes of those who have been teaching for years. I should know. I see those tired eyes in my own mirror quite often.

When Solstice Young smiled, dimples creased her face and it was like the sun was shining right on you. How I loved to make her smile.

When I look back with the mind of a teacher, I can see how she humored us, laughing at all the students' corny jokes even if they weren't funny, and smiling as she listened to countless ridiculous questions and rambling, nonsensical stories. Even mine. But I prefer to remember it differently, to remember her smile as genuine, her heart so big it could encompass the whole class. That's how I want to remember Solstice Young now that she's gone. *If* she's gone.

I was too young at the time to understand what an unusual name Solstice was. I assume now that her parents were Beats or hippies, and given how she dressed and the way she spoke of musicians with the same reverence a preacher would when speaking of Jesus, that was probably the case. I didn't know anything about her except that she wasn't from our little town, where everybody knew everybody. This implied, astonishingly, that she'd *chosen* to come there after graduating from whatever university she attended. It meant she'd *chosen* to teach at my school, and to my feverish, lovesick mind that meant destiny had brought us together. All I cared about, all I lived for, was her attention. Even a table scrap was a meal to me. I raised my hand in class regardless of whether I knew the answer. I volunteered to transcribe notes from sheet music onto the chalkboard for her. I studied extra hard what words like *adagio* and *larghissimo* meant so she would see what a good student I was.

One night in early October, when I was in the family room reading a chapter on Italian Baroque composers, my father came in with a can of beer and shooed me to the far side of the couch. He plopped down where I'd been sitting, picked up the remote, and turned on the local news. There was no point in complaining about the interruption. Nothing came between my father, his post-dinner beer, and the evening news. The house could burn down and he wouldn't get up until the can was empty and the broadcast was over.

I tried to ignore the television, but the word *murder* caught my attention. I looked up from my textbook as the anchor reported that the dead body of a middle-aged woman, one Maisie Talbot of Fox Hill Road, had been found behind the bus station early that morning. Her throat had been torn open by a wild animal. The authorities were urging caution.

"Wild animal my ass," my father muttered, sipping his beer. "I bet it's one of those pit bulls they're always talking about on the news. One killed a kid a few months ago. You ask me, they should all be put down. That's what you do with vicious animals like that."

The next day in class, Solstice Young played Simon & Garfunkel's "The Sound of Silence" for us on the record player. As the haunting opening notes floated through the classroom, she said, "There's something so dark and seductive about the music, don't you think? And that first lyric, 'Hello, darkness, my old friend,' there's a resignation there, a giving up of one's self. But not out of fear. Out of love." She closed her eyes and sang along with the record without an ounce of shyness or timidity, swaying to the music like a charmed snake. "Take my arms that I might reach you," she sang out and hugged herself tight. Her blouse slipped off of one creamy, bare shoulder, but she didn't even care. She was a million miles away, and whatever she was imagining in that moment was hers and hers alone.

Afterward, the other kids laughed in the hallway about it. Even Craig Maberry and Bob Moore, my two best friends, thought it was weird, but not me. I thought it was magical. I felt like I had caught a glimpse of the real Solstice Young, the one no one else saw.

But as much as I wanted to impress her, I couldn't play music. I made such a mess of trying to perform *Hot Cross Buns* on the recorder along with the rest of the class that she had to come to my rescue.

"You've got your finger on the wrong hole," she said, gently moving my hand. "Here, put your finger on this hole instead. That's better, isn't it?"

Then, without warning, her cheeks flushed and she started laughing as if she'd said something funny. It was a different laugh from her normal one. This one was dark and full of secrets, and though I didn't understand what was so funny, the sound of it reached deep inside me and grabbed hold.

I stared at her hand on mine as I played the notes. The warm, perfect feel of it overwhelmed me. Her sleeve pulled back on her arm, and I noticed an angry-looking white scar along the length of her wrist, crisp and straight as if from a razor. The sight of it frightened me, but I forgot it a moment later when she squeezed my hand approvingly. I very nearly fainted. Surely it was a sign, a way of letting me know that she favored me above all the others, that somehow she knew of my love for her and returned it. It didn't matter that she moved on to Billy Mears next and did the same for him; I was still swooning from her attention, still inhaling the mystical fragrance that drifted in her wake like incense.

I didn't know if that combination of honeysuckle, hibiscus, and lemon was a perfume or soap or just her natural scent, but it was like catnip to me. When I smelled it in the hallways of the school I would slow my gait, hoping to catch even a glimpse of her.

Over the next few weeks, during my father's post-dinner beer and evening news sessions, I learned that more dead bodies had been found around town: at the bus station, near the garbage dump, in the alley behind the bars on Quinn Street. The victims were all women, and they'd all had their throats torn open like Maisie Talbot, but the police didn't think it was a wild animal anymore. They were certain now that it was the work of a human being, because all the victims had been drained of blood and no animal could do that, not even the pit bulls my father was so keen on blaming. Night after night I watched the news reports with spellbound awe, until the anchor spoke two words that echoed in my head like a melody I couldn't shake: *serial killer*. It was a term I'd never heard before. Most everyone else back then hadn't, either. It was a new concept the FBI had come up with in the '70s, and the local police had taken it to heart. They determined that a serial killer was targeting women in our town, and recommended all women stay inside after dark until the killer was brought to justice.

During those same weeks I hid my childish adoration of Solstice Young from everybody, including Craig and Bob, but somehow my brother Keith knew. He was two years older than me and attended the same school. He was also the cruelest person I knew. When we passed each other in the hallways at school, he would greet me with a punch in the arm, or stuff me into my locker, all to the delight of his cackling friends. But his favorite brand of torture was to throw my love for Solstice Young in my face every chance he got.

"I saw Miss Young's tits," he told me once, taking obvious pleasure in the shock on my face. We were in his bedroom. He had Pink Floyd's

Wish You Were Here spinning on the turntable and there was still a pungent, herbal odor in the air from the joint I'd seen him toss out the window when I barged in on some business or other. I had surprised and embarrassed him by catching him in the act, and now he wanted to get back at me with these hurtful words.

"Shut up!" I yelled. My anger was quick and possessive. "You did not!"

"I did," he said, a merciless grin on his face. "It was just last week, in the hallway at school. She was rushing somewhere with an armful of books. She dropped one of them, and when she bent down to pick it up I could see right down her blouse. She wasn't wearing *anything* underneath. I saw *everything*. It was all right there on full display. *Everyone* in the hallway saw."

"Shut up!" I yelled again. I shoved him, and forgetting whatever business had brought me to his room, I ran into my bedroom and slammed the door. I threw myself onto the bed and cried into my pillow. I didn't know why I was crying, except that it felt as though my brother's story had sullied Solstice Young somehow, abused her in some way she didn't deserve, as if she were no different from the lewd naked women in the magazines Keith kept hidden under his bed. But she *was* different. She was special, and the way Keith had talked about her made everything feel thorny and wrong and ruined.

October was nearing its end. The foliage was gone, leaving behind bare trees like skeletal, grasping hands. The grass faded to a lifeless brown. The air turned cold and bitter, and on some days it would sting your face if you didn't wrap up in a scarf. The hothouse bloom of summer was long dead, and everything was about to change.

On Saturdays, Craig, Bob, and I liked nothing more than to watch old black-and-white horror movies together and then run around in the yard pretending we were being chased by Dracula or the Mummy or the Wolf Man. Craig could run faster than any of us, faster than anyone. That boy could run like the wind. On days when our parents let us wander, we liked to go to the old cemetery on the edge of town. It wasn't in use anymore, and as far as we knew no one but us ever went there. There was even a chain on the gate, but it was too long to do any good. All we needed to do was push the gate open wide enough to slip inside. The gravestones were mossy and chipped, so old you couldn't even read the names and dates on them anymore. The grass and weeds were so overgrown they blocked your view sometimes, so that you'd push aside some tall weeds and find yourself staring at a stone angel whose face had worn away to nothing. It was the perfect setting for us to horse around in, laughing and shrieking and hiding from Frankenstein's lurching, stiff-armed monster.

But our favorite part of the old cemetery was the moldering, abandoned chapel that stood amid the graves. Its wooden walls had rotted through and were covered with clinging brown weeds. Its roof had collapsed in places, and the spire had partially crumbled to leave only a twisted, mold-black arm that reached yearningly toward the sky. The three of us would watch the chapel from behind a row of graves, knowing the front door had fallen off its hinges ages ago and daring each other to go in. We were too scared to do it, of course, but it was enough just to imagine what the inside of the chapel looked like—dark, dusty pews draped with sheets of cobwebs; the altar probably smashed to pieces by beer-fueled older boys or else made home to families of mice, or better yet, thousands of crawling, chittering insects; empty holes where the stained-glass windows had been, looming like the black eye sockets of a skull.

The sun sets early in October, and by the time we started back from the old cemetery it was already dusk. When we reached Main Street, we stopped to point and laugh at the young couple we saw kissing against the brick wall of an antiques shop. My laughter died away when I saw that the woman whose back was pressed to the wall and whose lips were pressed so passionately to someone else's was Solstice Young. My chest tightened and my stomach dropped to my feet. The man she was kissing was a little older than her, with dark hair and a stubbly jaw. He was dressed in jeans and a leather jacket over a Black Sabbath concert T-shirt. As he slid his hand up from her waist to twine his fingers in her hair, I saw he wore a big gold ring in the shape of an upside-down pentagram, that most metal of symbols. He looked exactly like the kind of guy parents didn't want their daughters dating, and so of course Solstice

Young, who marched to the beat of her own drum, was kissing him right in front of everybody. Right in front of me.

The man ended the kiss and began to pull away. She bit his bottom lip and pulled it with her teeth. When she let go, she looked at him with a devilish smile that seared itself into my mind. It bored down deep in me and awoke something I'd only ever felt before when sneaking peeks at Keith's hidden magazines. But even that delicious, furtive pressure had been only a shadow of the urgency I felt now in every beat of my heart. I watched, rapt and envious, as she took the man's hand and led him down the sidewalk.

"Who was that with Miss Young?" I asked, watching them vanish into the darkening twilight.

"That must be her boyfriend," Craig said. "I heard her talk about him before."

"When?" I demanded, prickly and defensive.

"Remember when I had to stay late at school for detention?" Craig said. I did. He'd hidden a piece of chalk inside Mr. Palmer's eraser so that it drew a line across the chalkboard when he tried to erase a geometry lesson. Mr. Palmer had been so angry he hurled the chalk across the room, shattering it against the far wall. Snotty little Jessica McCrum ratted Craig out and he got a detention. I felt bad for him having to be there with all the druggies, dopers, space cadets, and juvenile delinquents, but we all agreed the practical joke with the chalk had been so funny it was worth it. "When they let us out of the detention room, Miss Young was talking to Miss Nugent in the hallway. She said she met a guy who was new in town like her. I guess they've been going out for a while now."

Miss Young had a boyfriend! I railed furiously against the idea, tried to tell myself she didn't really like him, but I'd seen the way she looked at him. You couldn't fake that kind of longing. Believe me, I knew.

I went into a funk. I didn't want to get out of bed the next day, but it was Sunday and my parents dragged me to church. I didn't want to get out of bed on Monday, either. The idea of seeing Solstice Young was too much to handle, but my parents made me get up and go to school. I considered skipping music class, but once I smelled that familiar fragrance outside her classroom it lured me in, filling my head with promises that she wasn't dating that guy after all, that it was all a misunderstanding, that she was still . . .

Still what? Mine? But she wasn't. She never had been. I knew that, I wasn't crazy. I was just a pimply-faced kid and she was in her twenties. What did I think was going to happen? That we'd get married and live happily ever after as in some stupid story? I paused in front of the door as cold, hard reality weighed down on me, snapping my heart in half under its burden. Then I took a deep breath and forced myself to enter the classroom.

The first thing I noticed was that she looked different. Tired, paler, with bags under her eyes as if she hadn't slept all weekend. I tried to feel indifferent about it, but instead I felt bristly and resentful. Even at twelve years old, I could think of things that a boyfriend and girlfriend did together that would cause them not to get enough sleep. She was spacy and uncoordinated throughout the class, forgetting what she was talking about, writing the wrong word on the chalkboard, telling us to read a chapter we'd already read. I supposed her mind was elsewhere. I supposed this was what love did to people.

It went on like this for several days. We moved up from playing *Hot Cross Buns* on the recorder to playing *When the Saints Come Marching In*, but I was still hopeless. It didn't help that I was distracted by jealousy. Solstice Young had to correct my fingers again, and like a trained dog my heart leapt to attention in her presence, but this time when she touched my hand her skin felt cold and clammy. As she moved my finger from the wrong hole to the right one—there was no laughter from her this time—her sleeve pulled back to reveal the scary white scar on her wrist again . . . and something else. There was another scar on her wrist, pink enough to still be new, only this one was in the shape of a crescent. It reminded me of the mark I'd left on Keith's arm when I was little and he was too rough with me and I bit him.

She leaned over to get a better look at my hands, and the neck of her blouse fell open. Remembering Keith's story and how bad it had made me feel, I looked away quickly, but not before I saw it. A second crescent-shaped scar on the swell of her breast. I thought feverishly of Solstice Young with her boyfriend's bottom lip between her teeth

Biting . . .

and the same urgent feeling I'd felt on Main Street came rushing back a hundredfold, an unbelievable pressure screaming for release. I thought I would go mad from it.

Every day she looked a little worse, her rosy skin turning white as paper, the brightness dulling in her eyes. Her hair turned limp and stringy. Sometimes she seemed barely strong enough to lift the textbook. But instead of feeling sorry or concerned for her, I grew angrier. This, I decided, was her punishment for betraying me. I wince now when I think about it, my white-hot rage that she had chosen, reasonably and correctly, a man of her own age over a mooning child, but a broken heart clouds the mind and at twelve years old I didn't know any better. The changes came over Solstice Young so gradually that nobody else at school noticed, only me. She was my world, and I saw everything. If she needed help, if she needed someone to see what was happening and do something about it, then I failed her. That's something I have to live with.

But I don't think she did. I don't think she wanted that at all.

Eventually, Solstice Young stopped coming to school. We had a substitute music teacher, Mrs. Hanson, a stern harpy who always seemed angry to be there and whose pinched face and resentful sneer cured me of any further schoolboy crushes on teachers. No one knew what had happened to Solstice Young, not even the other teachers. With a killer on the loose everyone feared the worst, though no one said it out loud. I went into a funk even deeper and darker than before. Nothing mattered. The world could stop turning and fall into the sun for all I cared. Solstice Young was dead—I was sure of it. Craig and Bob tried to get me to come play with them, but I refused. All I wanted was the safety of my bed and the comfort of my tear-stained pillow. Finally my parents told me it was either go play with my friends or be forced to see a psychiatrist, so I went with Craig and Bob, grudgingly, to the old cemetery on the edge of town.

This time, when we dared each other to go inside the chapel, I didn't chicken out. I ran right in, not caring what I would find, not even caring if I died in a roof collapse or at the hands of the serial killer. Neither fate awaited me. The interior of the chapel looked as I had imagined it, full of dust and cobwebs and water damage from the holes in the roof. I was surprised, however, to find a thin metal cross still standing on the altar, badly rusted but upright. The sight of it brought my simmering anger to a boil. There was nothing good in this world. The cross was a lie. *Everything* was a lie. I picked up a rock from the floor, and with an angry shout I threw it at the cross. The rock knocked it off the altar, and the cross broke apart on the floor with a loud crash.

The sound brought my friends running. I don't remember what happened after that. My fury was too overwhelming. I found out later from Craig and Bob that I had fought them and shouted curses at them. They had to run and get my brother Keith, who came and dragged me out of there. I don't recall anything between throwing the rock and being at home again, listening to my parents whisper frantically about whether I was developing a nervous condition.

But as the days passed, they never found Solstice Young's body the way they did the other victims. This was a balm of sorts for my anguish. It meant there was a chance she hadn't died at the hands of a serial killer, that her final moments hadn't been filled with fear, a thought that had tormented me to the point of utter devastation. It left hope alive that she had simply skipped town with her boyfriend to establish a new life, safe and happy, somewhere else. That thought stung me with a fresh pang of possessiveness, but at least it meant she was alive. I could be happy for her, if nothing else.

The murders grew more frequent. The police found more bodies every day, and not just women anymore. Men and children had been added to the roster. "Children!" my mother had wailed, nearly collapsing in horror at the news. "What kind of a monster would kill children?" No one had an answer for that. Perhaps if they had, things would have turned out differently. As it was, it was only a matter of time, in a town that small, before the killer struck someone close to me. When you're a child, you think bad things only happen to people on the news. You think it can't touch you, but it can, and there's no way to prepare for it. It flattened me, pounded me into the earth like a hammer, when they found Craig Maberry's bloodless body in the woods near the school.

Poor Craig. Always the class clown, he'd been given a detention again, this time for making faces in Spanish class. It was hardly fair: he was only trying to make Abby Berger laugh because she was so scared about the killer; but rules were rules. It was early November and the sun had already set when detention let out. The police reckoned the killer got him on the walk home from school.

I was inconsolable. If the earth had opened up under my feet to swallow me, I wouldn't have fought it. I was a zombie at Craig's funeral. I couldn't look at anyone, not even Bob, who was just as shellshocked as I was. It was a closed-casket service. They couldn't reconstruct Craig's neck well enough to display the body.

The town put a curfew in place. No one was allowed outside after dark unless it was an emergency. But once Bob and I had recovered from the shock of Craig's death, we didn't let that stop us from coming up with a plan to honor our fallen friend. In secret, whispered phone calls we decided we would go to the old cemetery and write in chalk on the inside of the cemetery wall, where only the brave and the intrepid would see it, *Never forget: Craig Maberry was here first.* There was no way our parents would let us do this, of course. They hadn't been letting us do *anything* lately. So it would have to be done at night, after they'd gone to bed. It meant breaking curfew, but that didn't matter to us nearly as much as honoring Craig. With the fearless bravado of the young, which others might call foolishness, we agreed to sneak out of our houses at midnight and meet at the cemetery gates.

When the time came, I clambered down the trellis on the side of our house with a pocketful of chalk and ran full-speed through the empty streets toward the cemetery. It was freezing out, the coldest night of the fall so far, and my panting breath turned to clouds of vapor before me. A strange, chilled fog wound through the streets and clung to the lampposts, diffusing their light into an eerie haze. When I passed the brick-walled antiques shop on Main Street, I thought suddenly of Solstice Young, and my heart ached at her absence. At the cemetery gates I waited for ten minutes, shivering in the cold, but Bob didn't show. I figured he'd either chickened out or had been caught by his parents. But I was determined to complete our mission, with or without him.

Inside the cemetery, the fog enveloped the gravestones and turned them into dark, huddled shapes like a crowd of ghoulish onlookers. I was about to pull the chalk from my pocket when the sound of the chain clanking against the gate stopped me. I turned, thinking Bob had joined me after all, but the figure I saw through the veil of fog was too tall, the size of an adult. It was covered head to foot with gray funeral shrouds that made it almost indistinguishable from the haze around it. I ducked down behind a tombstone in terror, then peeked over the top. I held my breath so the vapor wouldn't give me away. No clouds of breath came from the shrouded figure, but they issued from a second shape that emerged from the mist beside it.

Bob.

Now I knew why he hadn't shown up. The shrouded figure had caught him. I wanted to signal Bob, let him know I was here, but I was too scared. I didn't want the figure to see me. But something was wrong with Bob. He wasn't trying to get away. His face was slack and expressionless. His eyes stared blankly into the fog. The shrouded figure reached over to put a hand on Bob's back, and something glimmered on one of its pale fingers. A ring—one I'd seen before. A gold ring with an upside-down pentagram.

Bob was passive and compliant as the shrouded figure guided him into the old chapel. I released my breath and the vapor burst out of my mouth in a heavy cloud. For a moment I was too terrified to move, but I had to. It was Bob. I had to try to help him somehow.

I followed them, but it was like a dream. My feet wouldn't move as quickly as I wanted, and the cold, impenetrable fog was a wall holding me back. When I finally reached the chapel, I stayed just outside the doorway and peeked in. A thick odor of decay hung in the air. The shrouded figure was leading Bob toward the far end of the chapel where, to my horror, I saw a second figure waiting. This one was covered in gray funeral shrouds, too, but was smaller and slighter than the first. The taller one passed Bob wordlessly over to the smaller one. Bob's expression never changed, not even when the second figure stroked his face, pushed his head to the side, and bent its cowled head to his neck. I heard the sound of teeth ripping into tender flesh. Too terrified to move, I looked away, unable to watch, but I could still hear it. The slurping, sucking sound. I put a knuckle between my teeth and bit down. It was the only way to stop myself from screaming.

When the sound stopped, I dared to look again. Bob's lifeless body lay on the floor, his throat torn and glistening, his eyes open and sightless. I know there was no way I could have helped him—I would have died, too; but the crushing guilt I felt upon seeing him like that has never left me. I watched as the second figure approached the first, and their shrouded faces met in a horrible kiss. The taller one took the smaller's arm, lifted its upturned wrist to its mouth, and I heard the awful sounds again.

This time I didn't look away. A charge ran through me. Not of terror, but of something else, something carnal, as one shrouded figure bit the wrist of the other

Biting . . .

and drank from it, as if to share in the taking of Bob's blood.

The smaller figure suddenly turned its shrouded head toward the doorway where I stood. It was too dark to see inside the shroud, but the chill that came over me told me *it* had seen *me*. I turned and ran.

My mother had wanted to know what kind of a monster would kill children. I knew the answer now. Even through the confusion and the fear, I knew. Of course I did. How many old movies had I watched on a Saturday afternoon in which undead creatures rose from their graves to feast upon the blood of the living and turn a chosen few into creatures like themselves? But I'd never thought they were real, just actors who wore long capes and spoke with Eastern European accents—not *this,* not real creatures who could come to my town and kill people I knew. I ran, and when I remembered the cross that had stood tall and proud on the chapel's altar before I broke it, the cross that could have stopped or hindered these creatures if the stories were true, I was overcome with a despairing shame. My own careless rage had created a sanctuary for them. I'd given them a safe place to hide. Me.

I ran all the way home, climbed up the trellis, locked the window behind me, and the bedroom door too, for good measure. I spent the rest of the night with the covers drawn up to my neck, sobbing for Bob and staring at the window. I waited for the shrouded figures to appear, convinced they had followed me home, but they never came. After an eternity, the sun rose again.

In the morning I told my parents I was going to stay home from school, and because they thought I was still in mourning they didn't argue. After my father left for work, and after my mother left to run errands with my assurance that I would be fine at home alone for an hour, I sneaked out of the house again. I returned to the old cemetery, but this time I went through the woods. It took longer, but I couldn't risk being seen on Main Street carrying a can of gasoline from our garage. My father's words echoed through my head like a drumbeat: *They should all be put down. That's what you do with vicious animals like that.*

I knew enough about these creatures to understand what had to be done, and since I was the one who had inadvertently given them a place to hide, it was up to me to do it. I marched into the old chapel, confident I would be safe in the light of day while the creatures slept in their hidden spots, and poured gasoline on everything, pausing only to note that Bob's body was gone. Standing in the doorway, I pulled from my pocket a book of matches I'd taken from the kitchen. I lit one, used it to light all the other matches still in the book, and threw the blazing matchbook into the chapel. It had been a dry autumn, and with the help of the gasoline the old wood went up fast. I didn't stick around to watch it burn. I couldn't risk getting caught. I ran and made it back home before my mother returned.

When my father turned on the news that night, I heard the chapel had burned to the ground. The police blamed teenage hooligans inspired to vandalism by heavy metal music, that all-purpose bugaboo of the 1980s, but no one was ever arrested for it. No one ever came to question me. I wasn't even on their suspect list. I never told anyone what I'd done, or why. When my parents told me Bob had been killed, that his body had been found discarded in a corner of the cemetery, I had to pretend I didn't already know and cry all over again. I did a pretty good job of it.

The murders stopped after that. The townsfolk theorized that the killer had moved away, or had died and was lying in the morgue without anyone being any the wiser. I grew up, graduated high school, and left town to attend a university where, inspired by my memories of Solstice Young, I studied to be a teacher. When I graduated, I focused on getting a job teaching at the college level. I wanted older students. I didn't want any twelve-year-olds mooning over me the way I had over her. It would have been unbearable.

Along the way I met women of my own age, but no relationship lasted long. None of them measured up to my memories of Solstice Young. She was never far from my mind, even as the gulf of time between my childhood and adulthood stretched wider. Whenever the mood hit me, which was frequently, I would search for her name in newspapers, phone books, and, later, on the Internet, confident that any Solstice Young I found would be her. After all, how many Solstice Youngs could there be in the world? But I never found anything. I never found out what became of her. On dark nights when I'm alone—and I'm always alone now, because no love runs as deep as first love—and the wind whispers through the eaves like a beckoning voice, I tell myself I still don't know. But I do. I do.

They say smell is the strongest sense that is tied to memory, and I have generally found this to be true. The scent of fresh-cut grass reminds me of Saturday afternoons spent running from imaginary monsters in the backyard with Craig Maberry and Bob Moore. (Had we known there were real monsters to run from, how foolish we would have felt.) The odor of dry, dusty earth brings back memories of our secret playground, where we would run shrieking with laughter through the tombstones. When I followed Bob and the shrouded figure into the chapel all those years ago, I smelled the stench of decay in the air, but I smelled something else, too, beneath it. The fragrance of honeysuckle, hibiscus, and lemon.

It makes me think about how there were two of those creatures in the chapel, not one. It makes me wonder who Craig, the boy who could outrun anyone, might have seen coming for him out of the woods the night he died. Someone he would have recognized. Someone he wouldn't have run from. A familiar face within the shroud.

They say what you don't know can't hurt you, but it can, and there are still so many important things I don't know. Was Solstice Young's boyfriend, he of the upside-down pentagram ring, the start of it all? I suppose if I were cursed to undeath for all eternity, I would want her by my side forever, too. She had that effect on people. Or was it possible they were turned by a third creature I never found?

I wonder sometimes if she was an innocent victim, or if it was a choice she made. Despite her sunny exterior, there was a darkness to Solstice Young that I had been blind to as a child. She was a woman of contradictions, just like her name. After all, a solstice could be the longest day, or the longest night.

And then there's the biggest question of all: Were they in the chapel when I burnt it down? I didn't dare go back to look for bones. The murders stopped, it's true, but that didn't mean they were dead. Creatures like them aren't tied to a single location, a single town. They might have moved on.

The reason I wonder is that on some nights it's not just the familiar voice on the wind whispering my name that catches my attention. There's a familiar scent, too, a fragrance that slips tantalizingly between the window and its frame. It brings back memories of a young woman I thought had burned as brightly as the sun, but who had felt such despair that she had once dragged a razor down her wrist, who had stood before the class with her eyes closed and spoken unashamedly of how seductive the darkness was, and who might have given herself over to it in the end; a young woman I had loved so completely that I could forgive her anything. And whenever I smell it—*hello, darkness, my old friend*—I open the window and invite it in.

Daughter of Echidna

1

In the car, Mom clenches her teeth, making the muscles of her jaw contract under the skin. Her grip is tight on the steering wheel. Kenna looks the other way, out the passenger-side window. Today is Sarah Lieberman's birthday, and although Kenna doesn't really want to go to her party, Mom insists on taking her there anyway.

"It's important to have friends," Mom says as Kenna keeps her eyes out the window. She can't look at Mom's angry, grinding jaw. She doesn't like how it makes her feel.

"Sarah and I haven't been friends since fourth grade," Kenna reminds her, as if Mom ought to know all the ins and outs of her life at school, even though whenever she asks how Kenna's day went, the answer is always the same: fine. She's in sixth grade now. That's two whole grades since she and Sarah used to insist on sitting next to each other in class, playing together during recess, having sleepovers. She doesn't remember how it ended, only that it did.

"She invited you to her birthday party, didn't she?" Mom asks. It's not a real question, so Kenna doesn't answer. "That means she's still your friend. She wants you there."

Kenna sits in silence, playing with one coppery red ringlet above her ear. What if Sarah only wants her at the party to pick on her? What if everyone there makes fun of her the whole time? She's not sure that's something Sarah would do, but then again, she's not sure it isn't. A person can change a lot between fourth grade and sixth.

"It's important to have people you can talk to," Mom says. "I wish I did."

Kenna thinks she's going to add *when I was your age,* but she stops there. Does Mom not have any friends? Kenna thinks back, but she can't remember meeting any. Sometimes Dad says Mom doesn't need anyone but him, which ought to sound romantic but doesn't.

Kenna looks at Mom, who looks more sad than angry now. In a way, that's better. Sad feels safer than angry. But Kenna knows she's not getting out of going to Sarah's party. It sometimes seems like Mom wants her out of the house as much as possible. Kenna was signed up for gymnastics, Little League, *and* drama workshop. It's too much. She told Mom that, but it didn't change anything. Frankly, she's surprised she even has time to go to Sarah's stupid birthday party.

Mom drops her off in front of the Lieberman house and tells her not to forget to give Sarah the birthday card they bought at the drug store. Kenna waves goodbye with the sparkly red birthday card enve-lope, as if to say *I know, stop babying me.* She presses the doorbell. Mom's car idles at the curb. She won't leave until Kenna's inside. It's a safety thing. It's also really embarrassing. Kenna hopes the other girls don't see. Finally the door opens and Sarah's mom, Mrs. Lieberman, greets her warmly and ushers her inside, letting her know the others are in the kitchen. Kenna hears Mom drive away as the front door closes behind her and has a moment of low-grade panic. There's no escape now.

Mrs. Lieberman brings her into the kitchen, where Sarah and four other girls are sitting around the table. Kenna recognizes two of the girls from school. She doesn't know the other two and figures they must be from Sarah's temple. (That's what they call their church, isn't it? A tem-ple?) There's a big cake in the middle of the table with Elsa and Anna from *Frozen* painted in icing and a sparkling candle on top in the shape of the number 11. Even though she doesn't want to be there, Kenna is relieved she didn't miss the candle being blown out. That's the most important part of a birthday party.

"Hey, Sarah," she says awkwardly from the kitchen doorway.

Sarah squeals Kenna's name and comes over to give her a big hug, and just like that, it's like they're best friends again. Kenna sits at the table with the others, and Sarah blows out the candle. Mrs. Lieberman serves cake to everyone. Kenna gets half of Anna's face in her icing, which she finds hilarious, and everyone laughs along with her. Sarah opens the cards everyone brought, including Kenna's, though she almost forgot to hand hers over. (Later, when she tells Mom about the party, she'll leave that part out.) Then, when Sarah is ready to open her parents' presents, her dad, Mr. Lieberman, comes into the kitchen in a blue dress shirt, his sleeves rolled up along his hairy arms to his elbows, and a plain black skullcap on his head. He puts one arm around Mrs. Lieberman, and even though his touch is gentle, not rough, Kenna can't help but flinch right there at the table. Sarah's parents kiss. Kenna's parents would *never* kiss in front of other people. They don't even kiss in front of her.

The other girls laugh behind their hands, but it's not because of the kiss. It's because they saw Kenna flinch and now they think she's weird. Her face burns with humiliation. She was right. They're all making fun of her. That's the reason she was invited after all. They were just waiting for the right moment. She should never have come. She fumes silently and wills her tears to stay away while Sarah opens her presents.

Afterward, the children are ushered outside to play in the backyard. It's warm and sunny, and everyone's shadow is twice as big as they are. Kenna wishes she had a springtime birthday like Sarah, but hers is in February, the coldest, darkest month. No one wants to come to a birthday party in February. For this reason and so many others, Kenna believes her life is cursed.

The girls are supposed to stay in the backyard, but there's a new house being built in the empty lot next door that Sarah wants to explore, so of course they all have to. The other girls run off, squealing and laughing. Kenna hangs back. She's the odd one out.

The other girls run around a wooden beam that will one day be part of the new house, circling it like sharks. Kenna watches and kicks at the dirt. Her foot hits something that feels like a stone, but when she looks down, she sees it's got an odd shape. She digs it free of the earth.

It's a small statue of a woman's body. Her arms and head are missing, which reminds Kenna of some famous old museum statue. She rubs her thumb over it, brushing away the dirt and feeling the two small bumps of the headless woman's breasts, the subtle folds of the gown she's wearing. Where did it come from? Did one of the other girls drop it? Remembering how they laughed at her, she tucks the statue into her pocket. When the girls are called back inside, she doesn't tell anyone what she found.

Sarah's big furry collie is named Hamantaschen, which draws laughter from the girls from temple but not from Kenna, who doesn't get it and feels left out yet again. She spends the remaining half hour before Mom is scheduled to pick her up watching Sarah and the others try to get Hamantaschen to sit. They yell "Sit! Sit! Sit!" until the dog finally sits, bending to their will.

When Mom arrives to take her home, Kenna says goodbye to Sarah and the others, but they're too preoccupied with Hamantaschen to do more than mutter and wave. On the drive home, Mom is quieter than before. There's a red bruise like a ring around her wrist. Was it there before? Kenna can't tell. She's losing track of which bruises are new.

She doesn't tell Mom about the little stone statue in her pocket. It's hers, and she likes having a secret no one else knows about. A *good* secret for a change.

2

It's after nine, which means lights out, but Kenna's up, hiding under her covers behind her closed bedroom door and reading by the beam of a flashlight. It's a book for school, but this time it's interesting enough that she *wants* to read it. An encyclopedia of Greek mythology.

Her favorite Greek myth is Theseus and the Minotaur, but even though she's tempted to skip ahead to it, she promised herself she would read the book in order. Tonight's chapter is on Echidna, one of the oldest gods. She had the upper body of a beautiful woman and the lower body of a fearsome serpent. She was immortal, unable to grow old or die, and Kenna, completely enthralled by the idea, imagines Echidna is still around somewhere, sleeping under a bridge or hiding in a drain pipe, marveling at the wonders of the modern world.

Dad's raised voice comes from down the hall outside her bedroom. Kenna freezes. Mom's lowered voice warns Dad that he'll wake Kenna. She wishes she were asleep. She knows the sound of a fight when she hears it.

"I told you I didn't want her hanging around with those people," Dad yells. He won't keep his voice down, no matter how much Mom asks. He never does.

Kenna doesn't like the way he says *those people*, as if there's something wrong with Sarah's family just because they're different. Even though she and Sarah are probably on the outs forever now, Kenna feels the urge to defend her, to tell Dad he's wrong. But she knows better than to *ever* tell Dad he's wrong.

She switches off the flashlight. She feels safer in the dark.

"It's important for her to have friends," Mom answers. She's angry too, and forgets to keep her voice down.

"She can have all the friends she wants, just not *them!* How many times do I have to tell you? They're not like us. You can't trust them."

"Who she makes friends with isn't up to you," Mom says.

A pit opens in Kenna's stomach. Mom has made a terrible mistake. She talked back to Dad. Kenna hears the hard, familiar sound of a hand smacking skin. However, this time the shouts and screams are followed by a sound she hasn't heard before, something heavy thumping and rolling. It reminds her of the sound her rubber ball made when it bounced down the stairs.

She pushes the book and the flashlight out of the bed, hoping both of them land on the rug quietly enough not to be heard, and wraps herself in the covers. She knows better than to leave her bedroom now, or even to look as if she's awake if Dad checks in on her. She won't close her eyes, though, not unless she hears him twisting the doorknob, then she'll pretend to be asleep until he leaves. She stares out into the darkness of her bedroom. The little statue she found in the dirt behind Sarah's house stands on the bedside table, where she put it when she got home. In the dark, it looks like a miniature cemetery monument.

Mom's pained cries come from the foot of the stairs, followed by Dad's footsteps stomping down to her. He tells her to stop being so dramatic, that she'll be fine, then makes a phone call. He tells whoever is on the other end to send an ambulance.

"My wife tripped and fell down the stairs," he says.

Kenna stares at the statue, concentrates on it, until there's nothing else, nothing but the armless, headless woman, until it's as if Kenna is not in her bedroom anymore, not even in the same house, as if she doesn't exist.

3

Kenna hates the hospital. She has been there before and hates the antiseptic smell and the way something she can't see is always beeping. She hates the moans of misery and pain that come from the rooms she and Dad pass as they walk down the hallway toward Mom's room.

Dad stops in front of the men's bathroom. "Go ahead, Kenna. I'll be right behind you. I just need to pee." He hands over the bouquet of flowers he bought in the little shop downstairs. "Give these to Mom, okay? Make sure she knows they're from me."

He disappears into the bathroom. Kenna hopes he gets lost in there and never comes out.

She walks to Mom's room, and there she is, in bed with an IV drip in one arm and a brace on the other. Kenna pauses at the door, frightened at how banged-up she looks. One lip is cut, one eye bruised. Kenna grips the bouquet harder, crinkling the plastic wrapper. Mom is in the hospital because of her. She wouldn't be there, wouldn't even be hurt, if she didn't take Kenna to Sarah's party—a party Kenna didn't even want to be at. She wants to cry. She wants to beg for forgiveness. She feels as if her body isn't big enough to contain what she's feeling and she's going to explode.

What if Mom never recovers? What if this time she never comes home?

A nurse passes behind her in the hallway. "In or out, dear," she says, and keeps walking.

Kenna finally steps into the room. She puts the flowers on the bedside table, next to a pill bottle full of little brown tablets. She picks it up, looks at the label. *Anzemet 100mg, take once daily, antinausea.* Kenna removes her backpack full of schoolbooks and puts it on the floor, trying not to be too loud. Mom is doped up on painkillers, but her sleepy eyes open as if she can sense Kenna's presence. Those eyes used to be bright, sharp, even mischievous sometimes when she thought Kenna wouldn't notice, but now her eyes look dull and flat. The eyes of a barnyard animal unaware of what's happening to it.

"Hey, Mom," Kenna says. "How are you feeling?"

Mom smiles weakly. When she speaks, her voice is slow and slurred. "I'm okay, baby."

But she's not; it's so clear she's not. Kenna chokes back a sob. "This is all my fault."

Mom's eyes shift to her again. There's more of her in them this time, a glimmer of awareness. "Kenna, no . . ."

"If you hadn't . . . taken me . . . to Sarah's party," she says through her tears, sucking in gulps of air.

"No," Mom says again. "It's not your fault. It's mine."

Kenna wipes her eyes, feeling a sudden flush of anger at Mom. "Why would you say that? How is it *your* fault?"

Mom blinks slowly, surfing a wave of morphine. She drops deep, nearly into sleep.

"If you don't keep the viper happy, you'll find his fangs in your throat," Mom mumbles.

It's drugged-out gibberish, but it's also not. She's talking about Dad. She thinks appeasing him is the best way to avoid his wrath. Don't talk back and you won't wind up in the hospital. But she's wrong. Mom has tried again and again.

Kenna blinks and finds herself in the small bathroom adjoining Mom's hospital room. She puts a hand on the wall's safety railing to steady herself. What is she doing in there? The toilet is empty. The sink is dry. Why did she come in there? *When* did she come in there? She turns to the door and sees her backpack leaning against it. Why would she bring her backpack into the bathroom?

She opens the bathroom door and peeks out into Mom's hospital room. Dad is there now, sitting on the edge of the bed and smiling down at Mom as if he's not the one who put her here. How much time has passed? Why can't she remember? Kenna walks over to the side of the bed and puts down her backpack. No one gives her a funny look or asks what she was doing. No one seems to notice anything wrong at all.

"When can I take you out of here, baby?" Dad asks Mom.

Mom smiles and blinks sleepily. "Soon."

"Not soon enough," he says. He kisses her hand, the one that's not in a cast. "Did Kenna tell you the flowers are from me?"

Mom looks at the flowers on the bedside table. Kenna freezes, a deer in the woods hoping the hunter won't see her. She didn't tell Mom anything about the flowers. If Dad finds out she didn't relay his message, he'll be mad. Kenna will get a smack on the face for it when they get home. He only uses an open hand on the face, so it won't leave a mark people can see. Dad's doctor said he's not supposed to let himself get worked up because of his heart, but he does anyway. He gets worked up into an uncontrollable, violent anger, and then they get blamed for it.

"Yes, she told me," Mom says, and Kenna breathes again. "The flowers are beautiful. Thank you, my handsome man." Mom puts her good hand on Dad's cheek, keeping the viper happy.

4

After visiting Mom, Dad drops Kenna off at school. She hops out of the car and doesn't say goodbye. She's too angry.

She missed first period, but she's in time for history class. The lesson is about the Trojan Horse. Even something that looks nice or pretty can have something dangerous hidden inside it, so you shouldn't judge things by what's on the outside. Kenna is only half-listening. The more she thinks about Mom blaming herself for being in the hospital, the angrier she gets. It's not Mom's fault. It's not Kenna's fault, either, really. It's Dad's fault.

At lunch, Sarah Lieberman invites Kenna to sit with her. Maybe she wants to smooth things over after what happened at her birthday party, but Kenna spends the entire period quietly fuming, so nothing comes of it. Probably their friendship is over forever now, but Kenna can't find it in herself to care. She has other things on her mind.

At her locker she hoists her backpack over one shoulder. Something rattles inside it. She thinks of a rattlesnake and its tail. She thinks of a viper and its fangs.

Dad picks her up after school. She rides silently as they pick up a pizza for dinner. Back home, the symphony of silence continues, the only sounds coming from crinkly paper napkins and Dad's loud sips from his beer bottle at the dinner table. If Mom were there, she'd tell him he shouldn't drink because of his medication, but she's not, so he's making the most of it.

Kenna breaks the silence. "When is Mom coming home?"

"When the doctors let her," he answers.

He takes a bite of his pizza slice, the gooey cheese hanging off the crust like worms. Kenna puts her own slice down, half-eaten. She's not hungry anymore.

"How did she fall down the stairs?" The words are out of her mouth before she can stop them. She feels very brave and very scared at the same time.

He looks up at her from his plate. His eyes are hot like lava, like laser beams. Why did she ask that? She's already shaking. She hides her hands under the table.

Dad takes another bite of pizza like a lion tearing the flesh off an antelope carcass. "Your mother fell down the stairs because she's clumsy and stupid," he says. "You'd be smart not to be like her."

Kenna gets the message. She doesn't ask any more questions.

When nine o'clock comes, it's lights out again, but she stays up reading her encyclopedia of Greek mythology. She can hear Dad watching TV in the living room downstairs, the clink of his second or third beer bottle as he puts it down after each swig. She tunes everything out so she can concentrate, holding the flashlight over the chapter about Echidna she started last night.

Echidna was married to Typhon, a fire-breathing monster so terrible and fearsome that even Zeus and the other gods were afraid of him. His legs were coils of deadly vipers, and he stood as tall as the sky, with huge wings that could blot out the sun. His head was surrounded by a mane of hundreds of snakeheads. Kenna can't imagine why Echidna would marry someone so awful. Even worse, they had children together, which Kenna knows means they *did it*. All their children were as terrible as Typhon, which was how Echidna came to be known as the Mother of Monsters. She gave birth to Cerberus and the Hydra, the Chimera and the Sphinx, and three daughters called the Gorgons.

A loud crash comes from the kitchen, followed by Dad exclaiming, "Ah, shit! Damn it!"

Kenna knows it's not safe to leave her room, but it sounded bad. She creeps out of her bedroom and down the stairs to see what happened. Her father is crouched on the kitchen floor over the pieces of a broken beer bottle. The pill bottle of his heart medication stands by the sink like a sentinel, watching with eyes of chalk-white tablets.

"Dad, are you okay?" she asks.

"I'm fine. Go back to bed," he says, picking up shards of glass and putting them in his palm. He flinches and sucks air between his teeth. Bright red drops of blood drip from his fingertip and splash on the kitchen floor.

"Your finger!" Kenna says, moving toward him.

He turns angrily to her and raises his other hand as if he's going to smack her. "I said go back to bed, goddamn it!"

She runs up the stairs and back to her room. She pulls the covers up to her chin. And then, suddenly, she's back in the hallway outside the kitchen, only everything is dark now. The kitchen light is off and Dad is not there anymore. She hears him snoring upstairs. Kenna touches the wall to make sure it's real, feels the texture of the wallpaper under her fingertips. This isn't a dream. How did she get there? Was she sleepwalking?

She hurries back to her bedroom. The digital clock by her bed reads 1:30 A.M. She gets under the covers and stares into the dark of her room. Bathed in light from the clock, the little statue on her bedside table looks different. It didn't have arms before, she's sure it didn't, but now it does. Slender, graceful arms, and hands with sharp talons for fingers.

5

The next day the hospital lets Mom come home. Kenna is already home from school when she's discharged, so when Dad drives to pick Mom up, Kenna waits alone, pacing the living room nervously. When the door finally opens and Dad helps Mom inside, Kenna runs to greet her. She still has the brace on her wrist, but the bruises on her face have faded.

"Mom, you're home!" Kenna says, giving her a big hug.

"Easy, baby, easy. I'm still sore." She wraps her good arm around her and squeezes her tight.

"Kenna, don't bother your mother," Dad says. "She's still healing up."

Because of you, she thinks angrily. Everyone believes the lie that Mom tripped and fell down the stairs, even the doctors at the hospital, but Kenna knows the truth. It was Dad. Either he hit her so hard she was knocked down the stairs, or he pushed her, threw her down the steps the way he does with the garbage bags out front sometimes. As if she's garbage too.

"But you're okay now, aren't you, Mom?" Kenna asks.

"I'm fine, I'm fine," she says, but she turns away rather than look her daughter in the eye. "I should sit down. I'm still a little nauseous from the painkillers. They were supposed to give me something for that, but I think they forgot."

Kenna frowns. She's sure she saw a bottle of antinausea medicine in Mom's hospital room. Didn't she?

"It's time for me to take another painkiller, too," Mom says.

If she needs a painkiller, it means she's still in pain. Anger at Dad swells in Kenna's chest, but she pushes it down. She's getting good at pushing it down, even though she knows it's going to need to go somewhere eventually.

For the rest of that night and all the next day, her parents act like a normal family. No voices are raised, no one gets smacked, there's no screaming or crying or trips to the hospital. But this is the pattern every time. After a blowup, things get quiet again, sometimes for weeks, sometimes only for a day or two, before the next one. When she was little, Kenna used to hope during each quiet period that it was over for good, that Dad wouldn't hit either of them ever again, but she isn't a naïve little kid now. She's eleven, and she knows the quiet can't be trusted.

It breaks on the third day. Dad wants to have a beer with dinner. Mom tells him he shouldn't because of his medication. He waves off her concerns and pops the bottle top.

"Did you take your pills while I was gone?" she asks.

"Of course I did," he says. "Stop nagging me."

She stands up, pushing away from the table with her good arm. "Where are they? I'll go get them now. You're supposed to take them with food."

"Leave it alone," he says.

Kenna slumps low in her chair, ponders the benefits of becoming invisible. The fuse has been lit. Whether it's a long fuse or a short one depends on what happens next.

"Are they in the bathroom?" Mom asks. She starts out of the dining room.

"I said leave it alone!" Dad is on his feet, face red, eyes like a bull ready to charge. He points at Mom's empty chair at the table. "Just sit down!" She doesn't move, locks eyes with him. "Sit down! Sit *down!* Sit *down!*"

Kenna thinks of the girls at Sarah Lieberman's party trying to make Hamantaschen sit. And just like the dog, Mom gives in and returns to her seat. It's the safest course of action, but what Kenna feels isn't relief; it's shame. She's ashamed of her mother for sitting like a dog.

It occurs to her that this will never end. She and Mom will never be safe.

Dad gets up, storms up the stairs, then stomps back down with his pill bottle. He opens it, shakes a brown tablet into his hand, pops it in his mouth, and swallows it down with a swig of beer.

"There," he says. "Happy now? I took my fucking pill."

Kenna retreats to her bedroom after dinner and reads the encyclopedia of Greek mythology. Despite her promise to herself, she skips ahead from Echidna, the Mother of Monsters, to read about her three daughters, the Gorgons. The picture shows them as winged women with fearsome boarlike tusks, sharp brass talons on their hands and feet, and snakes for hair. The word *Gorgon* comes from the Greek word *gorgos,* which means *grim and dreadful,* and that definitely matches the picture.

The eldest of the Gorgon sisters was Stheno, whose name meant *strong and forceful,* and who had red snakes on her head, which makes Kenna think of her own coppery hair. The second born was Euryale, whose name meant *far-roaming,* and whose snakes were muddy brown in color. The youngest of the three was Medusa, the only one Kenna has heard of before. Her name meant *to protect and rule over,* like a queen, and her snakes were green as emeralds. All three sisters could turn men to stone with just a look.

She closes the book and wonders what it would be like to turn someone to stone. The sounds of Mom and Dad arguing seep through her bedroom wall. She imagines herself staring at Dad so hard, he turns into a statue. Staring at him so hard, he dies. Then it would be only her and Mom. Then they would be safe.

She lies down to go to sleep, slides her hands under her pillow the way she always does. Her fingers touch something that shouldn't be there. It's small and hard, like plastic.

When Kenna opens her eyes, she's standing in her parents' bedroom at the side of the bed. Mom and Dad are lying back-to-back, curled away from each other. Kenna slaps a hand over her own mouth so she won't make a sound. How did she get there? Is she sleepwalking again? It hasn't happened since Mom came home. She thought it was over.

She tiptoes to the door. Dad stirs in bed behind her, and she freezes. If he finds her in their room in the middle of night, she'll get hit for sure. He mutters something. Her name? Something from his dream? She waits, still as a statue. When she hears him snoring again, she sneaks quickly out of their room and back into her own.

Her bright digital clock reads 1:30 A.M., just like before.

The statue on the bedside table has grown stone wings from its back.

6

The next day, Saturday, Kenna spends moping around her room and napping. She feels tired all the time now. Maybe it's from the sleepwalking. She writes a letter in her notebook to Sarah Lieberman, saying she still wants to be friends, but the memory of the girls at the party yelling at Hamantaschen to sit makes her angry again, so she rips it up and throws it away. Who is she kidding? No one wants to be friends with someone who's angry all the time.

No one wants to play with a broken toy.

Dinner is a horror show. Her parents argue the whole time. Dad gets so red in the face, he looks like a cartoon devil. He threatens to hit Mom, who flinches just as Kenna did at the party. Kenna watches it all from a thousand miles away, from another planet. She eats quickly, then goes back to her room and continues reading about the Gorgons in her encyclopedia of Greek mythology.

(This is the last night she will read from the book. After tonight, it will be covered with blood, its pages stuck together, unreadable.)

The Gorgons were supposed to be monsters—they were the daughters of Echidna, the Mother of Monsters, after all—but Kenna is surprised to learn that all three sisters were actually sworn protectors of the Temple of the Oracle. The chapter goes on to explain that in ancient Greece the face of a Gorgon was considered a symbol of protection. It appeared on shields and armor carried into battle. It appeared on women's shelters to let women know they would be safe there.

Kenna is confused. Why are the Gorgons considered monsters if they're actually protectors? Is it because of the way they look? Is it because they're protectors of women? The Gorgons don't strike Kenna as monsters at all. They strike her as heroes.

Lying on her back, she closes the book, clutches it to her chest, and closes her eyes. She is not sure how long she sleeps, but she is woken by the sound of arguing coming from the kitchen downstairs. Dad is yelling, using words she hasn't heard him use in a long time: *cunt, bitch, harpy*. He's worked up now, and there's no stopping him. She wonders what he's so mad about. Did Mom say something? Did she talk back? It doesn't matter. She might not have said anything at all. Kenna pulls the pillow around her ears to drown out the noise. Something rattles and rolls out from under the pillow to land on the rug. She refuses to look, refuses even to open her eyes, but then she hears something crash downstairs. A plate? A glass?

She leaves her room and creeps downstairs to see what's happening. It's only when she reaches the bottom of the steps that she realizes she's still clutching the book to her chest. She doesn't want to let go of it now. It's the shield she will carry into battle. Gripping the book tighter, she makes her way to the kitchen and gets there just in time to see Dad shove Mom. Mom stumbles, her back slamming into the edge of the kitchen counter, and then she falls. Tears squeeze from her eyes as she sits on the floor and cradles the brace on her wrist.

Mom murmurs to herself between sobs. "I promised myself I wouldn't let this happen again."

"Oh, you promised yourself, did you?" Dad mocks her. "Stop your blubbering and get up off your ass. You're making a spectacle of yourself."

She glares up at him with hard, furious eyes. "You son of a bitch . . ."

He pulls back his arm like he's going to smack her. "What did you say?"

"Stay away from her!" Without thinking, Kenna runs into the kitchen. She pushes Dad away from Mom, putting her shoulder into it against his considerable weight. Her whole body feels as if it's on fire.

"Kenna, no!" Mom yells.

Dad stumbles and catches his hip on the edge of the kitchen counter. He falls, splayed out like a scarecrow, face down on the linoleum. He turns over and stares up at her with eyes full of wild rage.

"Are you out of your damn mind?"

Kenna freezes, paralyzed and trembling with fear. She raised her voice to Dad. She fought back. She knows what's coming next.

Dad smacks her across the face. It's a hard blow, the hardest he's ever given her, and when she reels back, she tastes blood in her mouth. It spills from her lip to spatter across the book in her hands.

"Greg, that's enough!" Mom says, struggling to stand.

He hits Kenna again. Her mouth is full of blood. The book is covered in red. It drops to the floor with a heavy slap.

"That's *enough!*" Mom screams. "Stop it!"

"I'll say when it's enough!" Dad roars. His face is purple. Veins pop in his neck and temple. He pauses. His face scrunches up. "Fu—" He tries to swear, but he's out of breath. He drops to his knees and clutches his chest.

Kenna is on all fours, spitting blood on the kitchen floor. Did Dad knock one of her teeth loose? Mom rushes over to her, puts her arms around her.

"Oh, baby, are you all right?"

Kenna can't answer. There's too much blood in her mouth.

"My—my pills. Get my pills." Dad sounds desperate, a drowning man grasping for a life preserver that's just out of reach.

Mom lets go of Kenna. Straightens up.

"Don't," Kenna says, but Mom is already running up the steps two at a time to get Dad's medication.

Kenna drops from all fours to lie curled on her side. She swallows blood until her mouth is clear. Dad collapses on the floor in front of her. Face to face, they stare at each other in silence. She wills him to die. He reads it in her eyes.

He knows she has killed him.

Kenna smiles a bloody-toothed grin.

Mom runs back into the kitchen with his pills, pops open the pill bottle, and shakes out a pile of brown tablets into her palm. "What are these?" she screams. "These aren't your pills! Greg, these aren't your pills!"

Kenna gets up. She picks up the blood-spattered book and carries it with her back upstairs to her room. She closes the door behind her.

On the floor, next to the bed, is the plastic pill bottle that rolled out from under her pillow. She picks it up. The label reads, *Anzemet 100mg, take once daily, antinausea.* Mom's pills from the hospital.

Kenna understands now. The forgotten memories come back to her. She takes the pill bottle off the bedside table in Mom's hospital room. She is in the kitchen after Dad has finished cleaning up the broken beer bottle and gone to bed, retrieving his pill bottle from where he left it by the sink and switching the contents of the two bottles, knowing he is careless and would never notice the difference in color between his chalk-white heart pills and Mom's brown anti-nausea pills.

Kenna sees herself standing in her parents' bedroom in the dark, watching over Mom. Protecting her.

Mom's voice becomes hysterical downstairs. She calls for an ambulance, but Kenna knows it won't arrive in time. Dad has gone too many days without taking the right pills. She looks at the clock. Once more, it's 1:30 A.M. At last she understands the significance of that time, why it kept repeating again and again.

It's the hour when her father dies.

Next to the clock, the little stone statue is complete. Arms, wings, and now a head. A woman's head with boarlike tusks and writhing snakes for hair.

Kenna smiles. She's not afraid. This is no monster.

In fact, she's beautiful.

The Fifth Horseman

1

He thought of them as "the Four Horsemen"—four of his fellow professors at the small Northeastern university where he taught. They were an inseparable unit, looking for all the world like those apocalyptic figures of legend as they walked shoulder to shoulder from their offices at one end of the campus to their classrooms at the other. In the faculty lounge they sat together, clumped closely around a table like mussels on a wave-washed rock. Out on the quad they spoke in hushed tones to each other, their backs to the rest of the world, a closed circle. Dunbar Brooks wouldn't have minded the Four Horsemen so much, might not even have noticed them in the first place, if it weren't for the fact that Yvonne was one of them.

Dunbar taught English Lit, a mix of both classic and modern authors—Irving and Ishiguro, Lawrence and LaValle, Wilde and Foster Wallace—a syllabus that mirrored his own voracious, indiscriminate reading habits growing up in a house full of books. He'd never been a kid whose parents had to tell him to stop watching TV and go read, although occasionally, on nice summer days, they'd had to take a book out of his hands and shoo him outside to get some fresh air. Dunbar had grown up idolizing his father, who loved books as much as he did, and as a child he'd learned two important things from him. The first was that books were like keys; they opened doorways in the mind that could expand the horizons of imagination and intellect. Every year, with each new class, he cherished the opportunity to share those keys with his students.

The other thing he'd learned was to mind his own business. It helped him keep his cool every time a new campus security officer stopped him to ask what he was doing here, or when he visited his white

136

colleagues at their homes and saw the neighbors peeking out from behind their curtains, phones in their hands. He'd been pulled over by police while driving the speed limit in his own neighborhood; eyeballed by
townies the few times he stopped for an after-work drink at the local
bar; and followed by store security guards while dressed in a suit and tie,
shoes shined to a high polish as if he were the world's most upscale
shoplifter. None of it had escalated, thankfully, which was a miracle he
credited to heeding his old man's advice.

*You mind where your own feet go, Dunbar, and don't concern yourself with what
other people step in.*

But the Four Horsemen were a different matter, because Yvonne
Turner, comparative religion professor, was one of them, and had been
ever since she and Dunbar broke up four months ago. Or maybe since
before then and he simply hadn't known. But in the time since they split,
the change in Yvonne was noticeable. She'd been so outgoing when they
were together, an unapologetic extrovert with a bright smile and a warm
hug for everyone. Now she seemed reticent, withdrawn, caught up in
something he worried was snuffing out the parts of her that he'd fallen
in love with.

Horseman number two was Colin Zebrowski, philosophy professor
and the man Yvonne had started dating a month after she broke up with
Dunbar. Colin's office was directly across the hall from his own in the
faculty office building, and after a few awkward instances of watching
Yvonne swing by to pick up Colin for their evening plans, Dunbar now
kept his office door closed, even when he was inside. This had confused
a few of his students, who were used to the faculty's open-door policy
during office hours, but he figured if they were smart enough to get into
the university they were damn well smart enough to learn how to knock.

Horseman number three was Peter Salazar, linguistics professor.
Back in his native Belize, Peter's work had won him an award from the
Latin American Linguistic Society, which he'd leveraged into a teaching
position in the U.S. He'd started at the university at the same time Dunbar had and was the first friend Dunbar had made among the faculty.
Their friendship hadn't lasted, although there was no momentous event
like his breakup with Yvonne to mark before and after. Peter had simply

drifted away over time, drawn like the others into the gravitational pull of Rick Brannigan.

Anthropology professor and stealer of people from Dunbar's life, Rick Brannigan was the fourth Horseman and their ostensible ringleader. He was a large man, tall and wide, a human barricade in a trilby and long black coat. He was pompous and overbearing, the kind of man who loved to hear himself talk. He'd been at the university longer than any of them; Dunbar guessed he was in his sixties, a good two decades older than himself, although he couldn't be sure. There was something youthful in the size and sturdiness of Rick's frame, but something older in his eyes. Not just the crow's feet that wrinkled their corners, or the skull-like dark circles from decades of living on a teacher's minimal sleep schedule, but a jaundice to the whites of his eyes that spoke of long years spent in dark, gritty caves; hot, dusty plains; and cramped, smoke-filled puddlejumpers. His parents had been famous anthropologists back in the day, the kind who used to be quoted in magazines or interviewed on the news whenever some new ruin was found. Rumor had it Rick spent most of his childhood living with them among the indigenous peoples of South America. Apparently, his ties to that continent were still strong, because Rick had chosen to spend the whole of February break there— the only time Dunbar had ever seen the Four Horseman reduced to three.

But on the last night of the break, Rick Brannigan returned to campus, and the quadrumvirate was made whole again. Dunbar was walking to his car in the faculty parking lot when he saw Rick pull in, although not in his usual Nissan four-door. Rick arrived in a rental truck instead, accompanied by four workmen in paint-spattered jeans and puffy winter coats. Dunbar paused beside his car and watched the workmen unload an oblong wooden crate from the back of the truck. With their breath steaming the cold evening air, they placed it on a pallet truck and followed Rick to the faculty office building. As Rick held the door open for them, the workmen struggled to lift the crate off the pallet truck and carry it inside. Even from the parking lot, Dunbar could hear Rick bellow at them in his imperious lecture-hall voice.

"Gently! The contents are fragile and extremely important!"

Dunbar didn't envy the workmen. Not only did they have to deal with that pompous ass, but Rick's office was on the second floor and the crate looked heavy as hell. He got in his car and drove home.

2

Dunbar's father may have cautioned him to keep his nose clean, but that advice hadn't saved his own life. Michael Brooks had been a fixture at the town library for over forty years, working his way up from an after-school job to earning a master's degree in library science, eventually becoming senior librarian at the same branch where he'd started. There, he gave back to the community by launching a popular after-school program for high school students with nowhere to go while their parents were at work, and a weekend storytelling hour that packed the library with restless toddlers and grateful, overwhelmed parents.

That all came to an end because his car had a busted taillight. Later, when Dunbar read the deposition, he learned that the police officer who'd pulled his father over, Officer Benjamin Purcell, already had his hand on the butt of his gun when he approached the vehicle. Purcell testified that he'd been expecting trouble, and when asked why he replied that after four years on the force you could just tell when someone was likely to be a problem. Dunbar found it plenty easy to read between the lines.

It was night, it was raining, and his father had just wanted to get home after a long day. The last act of Michael Brooks's life had been to reach for his registration in the glove compartment. There was a grand jury proceeding, but as far as Dunbar was concerned it was a farce. Officer Purcell maintained that Michael Brooks had reached for the glove compartment too fast, causing him to fear for his life. Imagine that. Killed by a police officer not for failing to comply, but for complying too quickly.

Because the shooting was deemed justified, Michael Brooks's life insurance company decided he must have been killed during the commission of a crime and withheld payment while their legal team looked for morality clauses and loopholes that would permit them to void the policy. Dunbar, then in his early twenties, had to drop out of grad school to save enough money to help his mother bury his old man. In the end, the insurance company failed to find its loophole and the payout finally arrived a year later, around the same time that Officer Purcell was promoted to detective.

3

Overnight, a winter snowfall had blanketed the campus. Not the usual heavy Northeastern snowstorm this time, Dunbar noted with relief, just enough to coat the dead grass on the quad. It crunched crisply under his shoes as he made his way to the faculty lounge. Rick Brannigan's TA, a grad student named Liv, stood outside the building, hugging herself against the cold and drawing furiously on a cigarette. She was as pale as the snow around her in a white sweater and faded jeans, her short dark hair the only slash of color, like a single brushstroke on a blank canvas.

"Hey, Professor Brooks," Liv said. She threw the cigarette butt into the snow and immediately lit another.

"Everything all right, Liv?" Dunbar asked.

"Oh, I'm just going out of my fucking mind, that's all." She puffed on the second cigarette. A small, blue tattoo flashed on the inside of her wrist, but the cuff of her sweater covered it again before he could see what it was. "Professor Brannigan won't come out of his office and he expects me to cover his classes for him. I'm fine covering maybe one or two classes, but not a whole week's worth. I have my own schoolwork to do, you know?" She exhaled a long stream of smoky breath, dragonish in the winter chill. "Sorry, Professor Brooks. I'm just stressed. I don't mean to lay all this on you."

Dunbar frowned. A week had passed since he saw Rick in the parking lot, but now that he thought about it he realized he hadn't seen him since. "What do you mean he won't come out of his office?"

Liv shrugged and squinted into the distance, where the sun glowed mutely behind a gray layer of clouds. "He practically lives in there. When I need to talk to him about his classes, he'll only do it by email, and even then he doesn't answer half the time. I only saw him outside his office once since he got back, but he was so distracted he would have walked right by me if I hadn't stopped him. He's completely obsessed with whatever he brought back from South America."

He thought back to the wooden crate Rick's workmen had carried to the faculty office building. "What did he bring back with him?"

"Who knows? But it's all he cares about now." Liv tossed the second cigarette butt, which landed beside the first with uncanny precision. She didn't light a third. "I gotta run to cover another class. I might as well tell the students not to come anymore if the professor can't be bothered to." She violently ground the butts into the snow with her shoe, then marched away from the building, the steam of her breath trailing after her like locomotive smoke.

Inside, the faculty lounge was packed with professors seeking a refuge from the cold. They crowded the small tables and couches and huddled around the coffee maker. Dunbar poured himself a cup and scanned the room for a free place to sit. He spotted Yvonne sitting alone at a small, two-person table near the windows, going over a stack of papers with a red pen. Instinctively he peered around the lounge for the rest of the Horsemen, who never seemed to be far from one another, but Yvonne was on her own. Strange. Had the Four Horsemen split up while Rick was away, or was that just wishful thinking?

He pondered joining her. They hadn't had a real, civil conversation in the four months since they broke up, just a few terse hellos and passing head nods. But they were both adults, weren't they? Maybe it was time to put the past behind them and move forward as professional colleagues, if nothing else. It was worth a shot.

He walked over to her table. "Hi, Yvonne. Mind if I join you?"

She looked up at him, and his heart stopped. That still happened on occasion. Despite the lingering pain from the breakup, there were still times when he found himself bowled over by her. Her eyes were darker than his coffee, and deep enough to fall into if he wasn't careful. She had stopped wearing wigs a couple of months ago, and her short, natural hair only made her more beautiful.

"Do whatever you want, Dunbar," she said.

Yvonne pulled the papers closer to her, making room for him. He was a little disappointed that she wasn't surprised to see him or curious about why he wanted to sit with her, but he sat.

"Student papers?" he asked, and immediately winced. He was an idiot. What else would they be?

"Yes, from my Advanced Seminar in Comparative Religion."

So far, her answers had been clipped, brusque. Dunbar attempted to power through, peeking at the title of the paper in her hand.

"Rastafarianism, Ganja, and the Meaning of Life." He laughed. "You've got to be kidding me. How big a pothead is this student?"

There was a time when Yvonne would have laughed with him, but now she just glanced up at him sharply, annoyed at the distraction. *This was a mistake,* he thought. He shouldn't have said anything. He shouldn't have sat with her.

"She's actually one of my more promising students, and she doesn't smoke pot," she said. "At least, that's what she keeps telling me."

A partial smile curled the corners of her lips, and for a moment Dunbar saw the old Yvonne sitting across from him. He missed her sly humor. But then, he missed a lot about her. Those Sunday mornings they spent in bed doing the crossword puzzle and drinking coffee, *good* coffee that put the faculty lounge's sludge to shame, until finally the newspaper would be tossed aside and their hands would roam each other's bodies like nomads. He still remembered how smooth her skin was . . .

He took a quick sip of coffee before any more memories could ambush him.

"So what does this promising student have to say?" he asked. "Is smoking *ganja* the meaning of life, or does it just mellow you out so much that you don't care?"

She grinned at his joke but didn't look up from the paper.

Encouraged, he continued, "Or maybe life has no meaning and we should all just smoke up while we can."

Her smile faded, and he realized he'd taken it too far, walked right into quicksand.

"You haven't changed, Dunbar. That was always the difference between you and me. I believe life has meaning, that everything happens for a reason. But you were always too angry to see that."

"I was never angry with you," he said. "Not when we were together."

"Not with me," she said. "With God, because of what happened to your father."

That was Dunbar's off switch. Whatever pleasure he'd felt at briefly reconnecting with her instantly shut down. This argument was an old road for them, and he didn't want to go down it again.

"I saw Liv outside," he said, changing the subject. "She's wound so tight about covering for Rick she's liable to snap in half. What's going on with him? Why isn't he teaching his classes?"

Yvonne's hand went to the gold cross around her neck, sliding it back and forth on its thin gold chain, a nervous tic she'd never been good at hiding.

"It's nothing to be concerned about," she said.

She wasn't going to win any Oscars for her performance. But his father had warned him about poking his nose into other people's affairs, so he put up his hands and said, "Okay."

The door opened, letting in a blast of cold air, and Colin Zebrowski lurched into the faculty lounge encased in a puffy parka. He rubbed his hands together for warmth, spotted Yvonne, and made his way to their table.

"Hey there," Colin said. Yvonne immediately let go of her necklace. Colin kissed her on the forehead, then smiled thinly at Dunbar. "How's it going, Dunbar? Everything good?"

"Sure, Colin." He forced himself to smile back. None of them would be winning any Oscars.

"We better get going, hon," Colin said. "We have to prepare for that thing tonight."

"Yes, of course." Yvonne stood from her chair.

That thing tonight. How purposely, painfully vague. It was like watching two theatre students try improv for the first time, afraid of boxing themselves in with specifics. But of course why should they tell him anything? He wasn't a part of Yvonne's life anymore. He was an outsider now, practically a stranger, and only fools told strangers their business.

Colin walked back to the door to wait for Yvonne while she got her belongings together. When she opened her bag to stuff her papers in, Dunbar noticed a book inside. Out of habit, he read its title before she zipped the bag closed again: *Death, Ritual, and Belief among the Nazca by Jason and Maureen Brannigan.* He shook his head. The authors' surname

was no coincidence. Jason and Maureen Brannigan were Rick Brannigan's late parents, the famous anthropologists. Why was Yvonne carrying a copy of their book? It was bad enough Rick put it on his syllabus
every year, forcing his students to buy it so that the royalties he'd inher-
ited would keep coming in, but was he making his friends buy it now,
too? Dunbar wouldn't put it past him.

He didn't recognize the word *Nazca* and filed it away for later.

"Off to the Lodge with the other Freemasons, I take it?" he asked
Yvonne.

She seemed genuinely amused by that. "We're not a secret society,
Dunbar. What is it you think we do, exactly?"

"I honestly don't know." He glanced at the faculty lounge door,
where Colin waited, watching them closely. Weirdly closely, as if he were
trying to eavesdrop. Dunbar could feel the conversation speeding toward another line he shouldn't cross, but he couldn't stop himself, or
maybe he didn't want to. "I don't understand how Rick has a hold on
you as he does on the others."

"Rick doesn't have a *hold* on me, Dunbar. I make my own choices,
and so do Colin and Peter," she said. "You know what the four of us do
when we're together? We talk. We have long, intellectually stimulating
conversations about philosophy and religion. We discuss different ideas
from all over the world about God and life and meaning, except unlike
you we take the subject seriously."

"I thought you had the Bible for that." He regretted the remark as
soon as he said it. He was hurting and wanted her to hurt, too, wanted
to remind her that she'd deemed him unworthy as a partner because he
didn't share her unquestioning faith, but it was like a backfiring gun. It
hurt only him, reopening the wound.

"I honestly don't know who you're angrier with, Dunbar, me or
God," she said. "But maybe it's time you stopped looking for someone
to blame and started looking for some meaning, too. If not in the Bible,
then in some other religious text or teaching. Even I know God is bigger
than a single book."

He scoffed. "No, thanks. God is either too busy laughing His ass
off or He straight up doesn't give a damn about us. I don't expect there

to be any more meaning to life than that."

"See what I mean about you not taking the subject seriously?" She put her bag over her shoulder. "If you don't open yourself to possibilities, Dunbar, you'll never find any answers."

He watched her walk out of the lounge with Colin. Talking with her had been a mistake. He wasn't ready, and he was starting to doubt he ever would be.

4

Dunbar stayed late in his office that night, reading student papers on Marlowe's *Doctor Faustus*. Every year it was the same. When discussing how Faustus' obsession with acquiring knowledge leads him to make a deal with the Devil, his students always—*always*—complained they just couldn't buy that a scholar as brilliant and learned as Faustus would make such a stupid, shortsighted mistake. Their naïveté was amusing. They didn't know it yet, but by the time they were Dunbar's age they would make hundreds of stupid, shortsighted mistakes. Thousands. It was called being human.

Steam banged its way out of the radiators, and water sloshed through the ancient, exposed pipes that crisscrossed the ceiling like webbing. His office might be noisy, but it was warm enough that he was reluctant to go back out into the winter chill. He glanced at the time on his phone and was surprised to see it was nearly midnight. Damn. He hadn't meant to stay so late. He didn't like driving home at such a late hour. It made him nervous.

Officer Purcell's gun emerging from the rain-soaked dark, aiming through the open driver's side window . . .

He shook off the image. He hadn't thought of his father's death in a while, a realization that both comforted him with its normalcy and speared him with guilt, as though he were a bad son for having gotten on with his life. On the occasions when he could look at it dispassionately through the lens of his professor brain, it was interesting what could bring it all back to him—a scene in a novel where a father says goodbye to his son; a scene in a film where someone drives a lonely stretch of road at night. Of course, it was a given that certain things had to be avoided altogether. TV cop shows were a prime example. He couldn't stomach the way they depicted the police as flawless angels, men and women of a higher calling who never did the wrong thing or made the wrong choice.

Dunbar left the papers on his desk so he could pick up where he left off in the morning, grabbed his winter coat off the peg on the door, and shrugged it on. He was just locking the door behind himself when he heard voices whispering in the stairwell, the stamp of feet on cement steps. Who else was here this late? Last year some students had snuck into the building to play a joke on their film professor, replacing all the classic movie posters in his office with posters for pornographic films. Were they trying something like that again?

He walked quietly to the end of the hall, where he could peek around the corner into the open stairwell. They weren't students. Yvonne and Colin were climbing the stairs, and following behind them was Horseman number three, his old friend Peter Salazar. They were heading up to the second floor, presumably to pay a visit to the newly hermitlike Rick Brannigan in his office. Dunbar stayed out of sight until they left the stairwell, and then exited the building. He'd already made a fool of himself in front of Yvonne once today; he didn't need to give an encore performance.

When he got home, he poured himself a glass of Scotch and drank it down. After his debacle in the faculty lounge, the wound was still raw. Luckily, alcohol was a time-tested salve. He poured himself a second glass, sat down in front of his computer, and looked up the word *Nazca*.

It turned out they were an indigenous civilization that had populated the southern coast of Peru between the years 100 B.C. and A.D. 800. (*Before Christ* and *Anno Domini*—Jesus, he couldn't get away from God today.) The Nazca worshipped nature gods in the form of a killer whale, he read, as well as a leopardlike cat and a strange serpentine creature. But after reading about their bizarre burial practices, which included burying the dead with their heads cut off and replaced with jars that had a human head painted on them, he was too creeped out to continue and shut the computer down.

He finished off the Scotch in his glass. If Yvonne's "long, intellectually stimulating conversations" with Rick, Colin, and Peter were about freaky-ass shit like headless burials, the Four Horsemen deserved each other.

5

Dunbar returned to the faculty office building at 6 A.M. the next morning. He hadn't planned on getting to work so early as to be the first one there, but he'd slept fitfully. Nightmares had plagued him in which he and Yvonne were being chased by shadowy figures with jars for heads. In the dream they were still together, still lovers, holding hands as they ran. He woke feeling mournful and unsettled, and hadn't been able to fall back asleep.

He unlocked the front door of the faculty office building and entered, but he paused in front of his office. The door to Colin's office, directly across from his, was slightly open. It was dark inside, but through the gap he could see the silhouette of the porcelain owl Colin kept on his desk. He'd told Dunbar once that it was actually a cookie jar, though he didn't use it as one. He just liked owls. Whatever.

But Dunbar could see something else through the gap in the door too, an odd shape, long and thin, that floated in the air near the desk. He blinked, thinking it was a trick of the shadows, but the shape remained. He nudged the door open a little farther. The light from the hallway spilled into the room.

Colin hung from a rope tied to the exposed ceiling pipes. Beneath his feet a chair lay on its side. His eyes were open and bloodshot, his tongue swollen between his lips, his pale face now dark and splotchy from burst capillaries.

"Jesus!"

Dunbar ran into the room and grabbed Colin's legs, pushing upward, trying to counteract the noose's stranglehold, but it was too late. Colin's body was cold. He'd been dead for hours. And yet the door to the building had been locked when Dunbar arrived. Did that mean Colin had been here all night? Had he never left after Dunbar saw him in the stairwell with Yvonne and Peter?

He called 911, and the police came quickly, accompanied by an ambulance. Cops blocked the entrance to the building so no one else could get in, while EMTs gently cut Colin down, examined his body, and rolled him away. More cops poked around the room, barking questions at Dunbar, making him repeat himself, informing him curtly that he couldn't leave until the detective arrived.

So Dunbar waited, eyeing the guns at their hips nervously, until the detective finally showed up, a short, balding white man who introduced himself as Detective Napolitano.

"And you are?" the detective asked.

"Dunbar Brooks. I found the body."

"Dunbar Brooks," Napolitano repeated. "Dunbar's an unusual first name."

"My parents named me after Paul Laurence Dunbar, a writer in the late nineteenth century."

"Oh, yeah? What did he write?"

"Poetry. Novels. A play," he said. "My parents loved to read, and I think they hoped I would become a writer. I didn't, but I teach English Lit, so I suppose that's close enough."

Shit, he was babbling.

"Can't say I've heard of this Paul Laurence Dunbar," Napolitano said. "Where'd he come from, Ireland? He sounds Irish."

"No, he was American. His parents were slaves from Kentucky."

"Huh." The detective dropped the subject and moved on. "Did you touch the body, Professor Brooks?"

"Yes. As I told the officers, I tried to get Colin down before I realized he was dead."

Napolitano nodded. "Did you know Mr. Zebrowski?"

"Not very well."

"Did he ever show any signs of depression? Ever talk about offing himself?"

Offing himself. Classy.

"I really don't know," Dunbar said. "As I said, I didn't know him well."

"But you knew him well enough to touch the body, right? Most people leave the bodies of dead strangers alone."

Dunbar crossed his arms defensively; then straightened them again. Appearing uncooperative in a room full of police was a bad idea. "I was just trying to help. I wasn't thinking about anything else."

Detective Napolitano's hand dropped to his side, where his gun was holstered. Dunbar went cold, but the detective only pulled a business card out of his pants pocket and handed it to him.

"Call me if you remember anything that might be important," Napolitano said. "Even if you didn't know him well."

Dunbar was all too happy to leave Colin's office. In the hallway he paused to steady himself. All those cops in the room, their well-oiled guns resting at their hips.

It was unlikely anyone had informed Yvonne yet. She would be devastated. Such horrible news should come from a friend, but he didn't know if it was his place to tell her, given their history and how terribly his attempt at a conversation had gone yesterday. Still, he didn't want it to come from a stranger like Detective Napolitano. That would only make it worse.

Yvonne didn't have classes or office hours today, he knew. He thought about calling her at home but decided this wasn't the kind of thing you could tell someone over the phone. It had to be done in person. Dunbar left the faculty office building and skirted around the crowd of gawking students and professors outside. The cops on crowd duty glared at him, wondering who he was.

It didn't take him long to drive to Yvonne's house. He still knew the way by heart.

No one answered when he rang the bell. He knocked, but there was no response. It was still early, which meant there was a good chance she was asleep. Normally that would have been enough to make him turn around, but he knew Yvonne. She would be furious if he waited instead of telling her right away. On a whim, he tried the doorknob and found it unlocked. That was odd. Yvonne had grown up in a bad neighborhood; she'd learned from an early age to always lock the door at night. He pushed it open slowly, calling Yvonne's name as he stepped inside.

It wasn't a large house; the salaries of university professors didn't buy large houses. But everything inside looked just as he remembered. There was the living-room couch. How many times had they sat entwined on it, streaming movies on her TV? Yvonne hated horror movies, he recalled. She didn't scream or jump when she got scared—she cried, as if the idea of a teenager ripped apart by a monster was so un-thinkably tragic it demanded tears. There was the kitchen. How many meals had they cooked together, chopping vegetables and seasoning fish while they commiserated about some new boneheaded university policy or traded stories about their students? And there was the bedroom. He had memories of that room, too.

He paused. The bedroom door was closed, but not all the way.

"Yvonne?" he called softly. "It's Dunbar. I'm sorry, I know this is weird, but it couldn't wait."

He knocked gingerly on the door, which swung open under his knuckles. Yvonne was sprawled across the bed, but something was wrong. She was on top of the covers and wearing the same clothes as yesterday. His gaze flitted to the bedside table, where a lidless, translu-cent orange pill bottle stood beside the alarm clock.

"Yvonne!"

He ran to the bed and shook her, tried to wake her, but she was already cold, her lips pale. Her blew into her mouth, performed chest compressions, but he couldn't revive her. She was gone, and all he could think about was their stupid argument yesterday, how he'd tried so hard to hurt her. Why couldn't he have been kinder? He'd always held onto a kernel of hope that they would find their way back to each other, that their split was only temporary, but now . . .

He took a deep breath, steadying himself. There would be time for selfish thoughts later. He looked at the label on the bottle: eszopiclone, prescription sleeping pills. Yvonne had trouble sleeping sometimes, he remembered, and had come to rely on pills to get a solid eight hours. The fulfillment date on the label was only a week ago, but the bottle was empty. She'd purposely overdosed. Killed herself, just like Colin.

He looked down at her again, in horror, in regret, in grief, and was overcome with the nagging thought that something was missing. Then he realized what it was—the gold cross she always wore around her neck was gone. He found it on the floor, below one outstretched hand, as though she'd been holding it when she died. He picked it up. The chain was broken, snapped in half at the back.

6

Dunbar sat on Yvonne's couch, facing the TV they had watched so many times together, and waited for the police to arrive. It had taken everything he had not to break down, to keep it together long enough to call 911. Now, waiting for the police to arrive with Yvonne's body lying in the next room, all he felt was numb. He looked at the gold cross in his hand. It hadn't simply belonged to Yvonne, it had been as much a part of her as her hands, her feet. She'd worn it every day, even to bed. She never took it off. Why had it been on the floor instead of around her neck where it belonged?

The door burst open, shattering the heavy, melancholy silence into which he'd fallen. Four uniformed police officers barged into the house, their radios squawking, their boots tracking dirt from outside onto the rug, which Yvonne would have hated. Dunbar rose from the couch to meet them, but before he was fully on his feet, before he was fully aware of what was happening, he found himself staring down the barrels of four handguns.

"Hold it right there," one officer said. "Let us see your hands."

Ever since his father's murder, he'd wondered what it would feel like to have a cop point a gun at him. It was worse than he'd imagined.

"Your *hands*," the officer said again, louder. "What's the matter, you don't speak English?"

Dunbar put up his hands. "My name—my name is Dunbar Brooks. I'm the one who called you—"

"Sir, I'm going to need you to calm down," the officer interrupted.

He thought he *was* calm, but then he realized he was hyperventilating. He wasn't in control of himself, but he needed to be. More than anything, with four police officers pointing their guns at him, he needed to be calm and in control.

"Sorry, officer," he said, keeping his hands up. "I'm calm."

The officer holstered his gun, and the other three followed his lead.

"I got this," the officer told the others. "You go check the body. Dispatch said it was in the bedroom."

The other three officers moved down the hall to the bedroom, but Dunbar kept his eyes on the man in front of him, who was removing a pair of handcuffs from his belt.

"Turn around and put your hands behind your back."

Dunbar stared at him, uncomprehending. What was happening?

"Are you going to make me repeat myself again? Buddy, I'm trying to be patient with you, but you're getting on my last nerve. Let's go. Turn around."

Dunbar, in a daze, turned around and put his hands behind him.

"What have we got here?" The officer yanked Yvonne's necklace out of his hand. Dunbar had forgotten he was still holding it. He felt the officer snap the cold metal cuffs around his wrists, then tighten them until they bit into his skin.

"Is this really necessary?" he asked.

"Sir, I told you, you're going to need to calm down."

Officer Purcell's gun coming out of the dark and the rain, pointing through the car window . . .

Dunbar took a deep breath and let it out slowly.

The officer ordered him to sit on the couch, then took a quick, cursory statement from him. Yvonne's gold cross dangled from his hand as he jotted notes in his notebook. When they were done, the officer informed him he wouldn't be going anywhere until the detective arrived.

Fifteen minutes later, Detective Napolitano finally showed up, stepping through the door with a takeout cup of coffee in his hand. The coffee was steaming, still hot, and Dunbar realized that while he'd been handcuffed on the couch like a criminal, the detective had stopped for coffee.

"Mr. Brooks," Napolitano said, coming over to him. "Imagine my surprise finding you at two crime scenes today."

Dunbar didn't know if the detective was being sarcastic, and frankly he didn't care. He just wanted to leave. "Can you let me out of these cuffs, Detective?"

Napolitano nodded, put down his coffee, took out his key ring, flipped slowly through his keys until he found the right one, then unlocked the cuffs and pulled them off. Dunbar rubbed the sore skin of his wrists where the metal had left a raw mark.

"Thank you, Detective." Dunbar stood up, forcing the humiliation down deep where the detective and the police officers wouldn't see it.

The officer who'd cuffed Dunbar briefed Napolitano while the other three moved through the house like invaders, guns at their hips, taking photos and jotting things in their notebooks. A sticker on the cover of one cop's notebook read: *Hate the police? Next time you're in trouble, call a CRACKHEAD!*

"So tell me what you were doing here, Mr. Brooks," Napolitano said.

"I came here to tell Yvonne what happened," he said. "She and Colin were dating. I found her body and called it in."

He waited for Napolitano to apologize for the way the officers had treated him. He kept waiting.

"I thought you didn't know Mr. Zebrowski very well, but suddenly you know who he was dating?" the detective asked.

Dunbar suppressed a heavy sigh. "I knew Yvonne, not him."

"So what do you think happened? Some kind of suicide pact between lovebirds?"

Dunbar shook his head. "I can't imagine Yvonne taking part in something like that. She's a—she *was* a religious woman."

"Not religious enough to keep from swallowing a whole bottle of sleeping pills, I guess."

Dunbar stiffened. He didn't like Napolitano talking about her that way. It was disrespectful, but he knew better than to argue with a cop. It would only end with him in cuffs again.

"Did you find a note?" the detective asked him.

"No."

"Strange. There wasn't a note in Mr. Zebrowski's office, either. Suicides usually like to let people know why they're doing it. One last chance to say *fuck you* to the world." Detective Napolitano held up a small plastic evidence bag. Inside it was Yvonne's necklace. "I'm told you were holding this when the officers arrived."

"It belonged to Yvonne."

"Are you in the habit of stealing jewelry from dead bodies, Mr. Brooks?"

"What? No. I found it on the bedroom floor, but it shouldn't have been there. She would never have taken it off. It meant something to her."

Napolitano put the bag in his pocket. "Sounds like you two were close."

"We used to be. We dated for a couple of years."

"Did she say anything to you about being depressed? About wanting to end her life?"

"No. We don't talk as much as we used to. *Didn't* talk as much, I mean." He sighed. He still couldn't believe she was gone. "If you want to know what was going on with her, talk to Rick Brannigan. Aside from Colin Zebrowski, he was her closest friend."

Napolitano nodded. "Did she leave you for Mr. Zebrowski?"

"What?" The question took him by surprise, so much that he thought he'd misheard. "No. She started seeing him about a month after we broke up."

"A month, huh? That's not very long."

"If you say so."

"She was probably already thinking about him before you broke up. Happens all the time. Some women are never satisfied with what they've got. They're always looking for something else." Dunbar wanted to punch Napolitano in the mouth. The detective looked at his notes again. "You told the officer who took your statement that the front door was unlocked when you got here?"

"That's right."

"Huh," Napolitano said. "So I'm not going to find out you still have a key to this place? Some other way you might have gotten in?"

There were implications in the detective's question that made him not want to answer, but he looked at the raw marks on his wrists and swallowed his pride. "No, I don't have a key anymore. I gave it back to her when we broke up."

Napolitano nodded. "Suicides don't like the idea of not being found. That could be why her door was open, and why Mr. Zebrowski left his office door open, too. Strange, isn't it? They're in such a hurry to go, but they don't want to be left all alone. Did you know that? About suicides leaving their doors open?"

"No, I didn't."

"It's in just about every article on the subject," Napolitano said. "You ever research that kind of thing? For work or anything else?"

More implications. "No."

"Huh." Napolitano pulled the small evidence bag out of his pocket again and held it up so that they could both see the cross inside. "I'm going to find your prints all over this necklace now that you've touched it, aren't I?"

"I guess so."

"Just like your prints are on Mr. Zebrowski's body because, as you put it, you were just trying to help."

Here we go, Dunbar thought.

"Tell me, Professor Brooks," Napolitano said. "Just between you and me, did it bother you how quickly your ex-girlfriend took up with Mr. Zebrowski? Someone whose office is right across from yours, so you'd have to see them together all the time—your ex with a *white* guy?"

Dunbar didn't know which insult made him feel sicker—that Napolitano thought Yvonne was so shallow she would jump at the first chance to leave him for a white man, or that the detective thought the hurt Dunbar felt had anything to do with the color of Colin's skin. He clenched his hands but caught himself and forced them to loosen up. He didn't have the luxury of anger.

"Am I free to go, detective?"

Napolitano shrugged. "I don't see why not. Just don't go far. We may need to talk again."

7

Dunbar canceled his classes and took the rest of the day off. He managed to keep it together until he got home. He didn't have time to take off his suit and tie before he fell onto his bed and the floodgates opened. He wept to release the humiliation of being handcuffed by the police, and the terror he'd felt that they were going to do him the way they did his old man. And when that passed, he wept for Yvonne, drawing tears from a seemingly bottomless reservoir of grief. Her death was an affront, an impossibility. The world without Yvonne Turner in it didn't make sense. He knew every inch of her body, as she'd known his, and now the body he'd made love to was cold and dead. How could someone with whom he'd shared so much be gone?

He'd felt incomplete without her ever since the breakup. Had she felt incomplete, too, in some way? Was that why she'd done it?

The idea of a suicide pact with Colin was absurd. Yvonne was a grown woman, the smartest person he knew, with numerous degrees and tenure at a prestigious university, not some love-struck, codependent teenager with a *Romeo and Juliet* fixation. Even when he'd seen her at her worst, when her beloved mother died and she was at her most despondent, she'd never mentioned any suicidal thoughts. Yvonne had thrown herself into religious observance instead, turning to her Christianity to get through her grief. She'd always been a holiday churchgoer, but after her mother was buried she started attending every Sunday, putting an end to their lazy mornings of crossword puzzles in bed. Soon after, she was going twice a week, and not long after that the arguments began.

Yvonne insisted that people's ability to love one another was a reflection of the love their creator had for them, while Dunbar countered that if people were made in God's image, then their inclination toward injustice was a reflection of God's own apathy, His lack of compassion. On and on it went until Yvonne broke things off with him. She decided she would rather be with someone who shared her beliefs. Someone like Colin, it turned out. That was one thing Detective Napolitano got right. The speed with which she'd taken up with someone else *had* hurt him. He wondered for the hundredth time whether Yvonne had already started to drift into Rick's circle before the breakup, and if that was how she'd met and fallen in love with Colin, but there were no answers there. There were no answers anywhere.

The tears came again. He cried until he was exhausted, and then he slept. His dreams were tortured and feverish, filled with gaping emptiness and unappeasable yearning. When he woke it was dark out, and something Detective Napolitano had told him kept repeating in his mind: they hadn't found a suicide note in Colin's office. But maybe they hadn't known where to look. They'd probably searched the drawers, shelves, and trash can, but they didn't know the porcelain owl on Colin's desk was really a cookie jar. They didn't know it could open.

He wondered if he should just butt out and let the police do their work. It was what his father would have cautioned him to do. But he didn't trust Napolitano to do the job properly. It was clear from their last encounter that the detective suspected him of being involved in Colin and Yvonne's deaths, and that meant Napolitano was looking in the wrong place.

But there was more to it than that. The need to know why Yvonne killed herself was overwhelming, and the more he thought about it, the more it seemed as if the answer might be tied to why Colin had done it, too.

He forced himself to eat something, then waited until it was late enough that he would be able return to campus and enter Colin's office unseen. He drove there in the dark, alone, too focused on his mission to think about his father and Officer Purcell this time.

When he arrived, the faculty office building was on fire.

8

Dunbar stood by his car in the student parking lot, a safe distance away, watching as fire trucks surrounded the building and firefighters worked to put out the blaze. Two suicides, and now a fire. Were they connected or a coincidence?

He caught movement in the corner of his eye and saw someone run into the woods at the edge of the parking lot. It was Peter Salazar, the linguistics professor and one of the Four Horsemen. The *Two* Horsemen now, some caustic part of his brain chimed in. Dunbar chased after him.

"Peter! Wait!"

He plunged into the woods, shoving branches aside, his shoes crunching the thin layer of snow that coated the forest floor. He followed Peter deeper into the trees, calling his name again. Finally, Peter turned, pulling a gun out of his coat pocket.

"Get back!" Peter yelled.

Dunbar froze and put up his hands. It was the second time he'd had a gun pointed at him, but no less terrifying than the first. He fought through the fear to find his voice.

"Peter, it's me. It's Dunbar."

"Dunbar?" Peter lowered the gun, his face in shadow. "What are you doing here? You shouldn't be here."

Dunbar dropped his hands slowly. He noticed Peter had lowered the gun but still had his finger on the trigger. "What the hell's going on, Peter?"

"I had to burn it," Peter said. "I waited, though. You'll tell them that, won't you? I waited a long time to make sure everyone was out of the building and no one would be hurt. I should have left right after, but I had to see it burn. I had to be sure."

"Wait, *you* set the fire?"

"It had to be destroyed," he insisted.

Dunbar took a step forward. "Peter . . ."

He lifted the gun again. "Don't. Just—just stay where you are."

Dunbar stopped again. He tried to keep his breathing calm, but the opening at the end of the gun barrel stared at him like an angry eye, a black hole into infinity. "Peter, we used to be friends and now you're pointing a gun at me."

"I'm sorry, Dunbar," Peter said, though he didn't lower the gun again. "This has nothing to do with you. Just go before it's too late."

"It's already too late," he said. "Yvonne and Colin are dead. They killed themselves."

"I figured." Peter nodded sadly. "We should never have done it, but we'd been talking about it for so long we couldn't stop ourselves. We should have left it alone."

"Should have left *what* alone?"

"That thing Rick brought back from South America," Peter said. "The body."

Dunbar blinked. "Rick brought back a *body?*"

"It was a mummy, probably hundreds of years old, still inside its sarcophagus. Rick bought it from a religious cult on an island off the coast of Peru, some offshoot of the Nazca that dates back a thousand years," Peter said. "But once the plan was in place for Rick to buy it, we started having second thoughts. Colin was concerned because it was against international law, but Rick told us not to worry about that; he could pay off the local police, the pilots, and the customs officials. I thought it was, at the very least, problematic to take this important religious and historic artifact away from the indigenous people of a third-world country. It made us no better than the colonialists. Yvonne was the only one who didn't have any reservations. She supported the idea from the start."

"Yvonne?" Dunbar asked, surprised. "Why?"

"She wanted to know the truth," Peter said. "But it's like the old saying—if you're going to ask questions, you'd better be prepared for the answers." He laughed crazily. "This cult in Peru, their big thing is prophecy and divination, only they like to use the dead as oracles. I don't mean Ouija board bullshit, I mean actual dead bodies. Rick said the ritual was real, he'd seen it when he was a child living among them with his parents, and he wanted to try it himself. We all did, back when it was just empty talk. But then he brought the mummy back here, and it was too late to say no after all the money and effort he put into it." Peter was barreling on now like a runaway train, a sinner consumed with the need to confess. "Once it was safely in his office, he told us there were things he had to do to prepare the body first, things that were going to take time. I didn't ask, I didn't want to know, but last night he was finally ready. When we got there, he'd cleared out all the furniture in his office; there was only the sarcophagus sitting open in the middle of the room. The mummy inside was horrible, a withered, twisted, misshapen thing. Rick had us sit in a circle around it and put on blindfolds. He said the ritual wouldn't work if we . . . if we *saw.*"

"You were going to use the mummy as an oracle?" Dunbar said. "You can't be serious."

"I wish I were joking," Peter said. "We sat there, blindfolded like idiots, while Rick played that goddamn tape recorder of his."

Dunbar knew the recorder Peter meant. Rick had never trusted digital media to capture his cultural recordings. He still used the big, bulky tape recorder he'd had since the eighties, so old it was held together with duct tape and pure force of will.

"He'd recorded the cult's ritual, their chanting," Peter continued.

"You're going to think I'm crazy, but as soon as it started playing the lights began to flicker. I could see it around the edges of my blindfold. But that's not the worst part. I *heard* it, Dunbar. I heard it move in the sarcophagus."

A chill crawled up Dunbar's back. "That's not possible, Peter."

"I thought the same thing, but I had to see, I had to know for sure. I tore off my blindfold." Peter was breathing harder now, the blood draining from his face. "I saw it—I saw it *sit up*. Oh, God, that thing's face! I can't get it out of my head! I screamed, and—everything stopped. The lights went back to normal, and the mummy fell back into the sarcophagus and didn't move again." He swallowed, his Adam's apple bobbing at his throat as he seemed to come back to himself. "Rick was furious. I've never seen him so angry. I thought he was going to kick me out, but I begged him to let me stay. Now that I saw it was real, I had to know what it would tell us. So we tried once more, without peeking, and it worked. It *worked*, Dunbar!"

"That's not possible," he said again. "The dead don't come back."

"We asked it questions—the big questions, the ones everyone wants to know. What is the meaning of life? Do we have a purpose? Think of it, Dunbar. The *mysterium tremendum*—the profound mysteries, revealed at last."

The moon shifted then, or maybe the smoke from the fire did, and the moonlight fell on them. Peter's tawny complexion reflected it so that he practically glowed. Dunbar knew it had the opposite effect on him, turning him dark and glistening. In the distance, the firefighters sprayed their hoses at the inferno. Peter stared at the fire through the trees.

"When it was over, when the mummy was back in its box and we had the answers to our questions, we went insane," he said. "There's no other word for it. We screamed like lunatics. Rick clawed at his own face. Yvonne was sobbing. We couldn't get out of that room fast enough. We couldn't even look at each other. But I knew Colin was going to hang himself as soon as he took the rope that had been tied around the sarcophagus in transit."

"And you didn't *stop* him?" Dunbar said.

"Why would I stop him?" Peter said. "I don't blame him or Yvonne for what they did. It was the only rational response."

"There's nothing rational about any of this." Dunbar took another step toward him. "Peter, just give me the gun."

Peter shook his head, keeping the gun pointed at him. "I told you to stay back."

Dunbar mustered the courage to take another step forward. "You're in enough trouble, Peter. You don't want to add murder on top of arson. But I can help you. I can talk to the police."

"You don't get it, Dunbar," Peter said. "You didn't hear what it told us. When you ask questions you're not supposed to ask, you get answers you're not supposed to know. You can't understand. You should pray that you never do."

He put the gun in his mouth and pulled the trigger.

9

Dunbar sat in his car outside Rick Brannigan's house. The anthropology professor hadn't been hard to find; his address was right there in the faculty directory. His house was surprisingly large, an old Victorian in a nice part of town. Dunbar knew Rick came from money, but between the sizable house and his apparent ability to pay off every official between here and Peru for the crate's safe passage, he'd never imagined how much.

Finding Colin and Yvonne's bodies had been terrible enough, but seeing Peter kill himself was shocking. His ears still rang with the echo of the gunshot. How long had he stood gaping in horror at Peter's body before he finally came to his senses? He couldn't say. He'd pulled out his cell phone to call the police but stopped himself. He'd had enough guns pointed at him already. On top of that, if Napolitano found him standing over yet another dead body he could guess how that would play out. He briefly considered calling the Dean, or even Liv, but he couldn't risk it circling back to him. He left the woods, drove to the one gas station he knew that still had a pay phone, and made an anonymous call to 911. In the end, that was the best he could for the man who'd been his very first friend among the faculty.

Dunbar watched Rick's windows for any sign of movement inside.

He felt numb, off-kilter, but also furious. He didn't believe Peter's story of ancient cult rituals and oracular mummies with answers so terrible it had driven them to take their own lives. No, whatever the real reason for their deaths was, Rick was responsible; he was sure of it. He'd never liked Rick. Something about him had always seemed overly charismatic and controlling, like a Svengali—or a cult leader. He had lured Peter, Colin, and Yvonne into his orbit, and now the three of them were dead.

What had gone down in Rick's office? How had he convinced them to kill themselves? Dunbar planned to find out. He'd get a confession out of the bastard one way or another, even if he had to beat it out of him.

There was no movement in the windows, either upstairs or down. It was two o'clock in the morning; Rick was probably asleep.

His father's advice came back to him and made him want to turn around, to let it go and hope the police found Rick on their own, but now that felt like cowardice. He kept seeing Yvonne dead on her bed, Peter with a hole blown through the top of his head on the forest floor, Colin swinging from the ceiling pipes. Rick had to be stopped.

Sorry, Dad, he thought. *Not this time.*

Dunbar left his car and walked up the flagstone path that cut through the well-manicured lawn, then up the steps to the porch. He glanced over his shoulder. The odds of Rick's neighbors being awake at this hour were slim, but he was still nervous. The last thing he needed was for someone to call the police and report a black man prowling around an affluent white neighborhood in the middle of the night.

He tried the door. Surprisingly, it was unlocked. Napolitano had told him suicides didn't like the idea of not being found, but Dunbar put the thought from his mind. Rick wasn't dead. Rick was behind it all.

He entered the house and walked through the dark foyer. In the dining room, the light was on and the table was cluttered end to end with papers and books, a telltale sign that this was the home of a teacher whose classes were in session. Amid the mess he spotted Rick's big, clunky tape recorder, old and edged with silver duct tape. Had Rick really recorded some native population's religious ceremony, perhaps as part of an elaborate hoax to play on Yvonne and the others? Or did the tape only hold some dry lecture Rick had recorded; some band he enjoyed? Curious, he reached for the recorder, his finger brushing the blocky, square Play button.

A voice from the next room called, "I was wondering when you'd come, Dunbar."

He left the tape recorder and moved into the living room, where Rick's bulky form reclined in a big wingback chair. Angry red scratches marred his plump cheeks. Peter said Rick had scratched himself in his madness after the ritual, but it could just as easily have been someone else. It could just as easily have been Yvonne.

"They're dead, Rick!" Dunbar said, stalking toward him.

"Sit," Rick told him calmly, indicating the chair across from him.

"I'm not your fucking dog. Did you hear what I said?"

Rick stood. He was holding a long, thin object that Dunbar didn't recognize until he thumbed open the blade. A straight razor. "I really must insist you sit."

Dunbar stopped where he was, halfway between the two chairs, wishing he'd taken Peter's gun with him. Could he wrestle the razor out of Rick's grasp? He doubted it. Rick was bigger than him, probably stronger too, and could carve him up before he managed to pry the razor from his beefy hand. Dunbar backed up slowly and sat. "They're all dead, Rick. Yvonne, Colin, Peter. What did you do to them?"

"Do to them?" Rick scoffed, sitting down again. "Nothing. We did it together. We're all guilty. By the way, that detective came to see me. Napolitano. I assume it was you who gave him my name. He won't be bothering us anymore."

Dunbar sat forward. "What did you do?"

"I'm not some dime-store gangster, Dunbar," Rick asked. "I didn't hurt him, if that's what you're thinking. I fed him a story about Colin going off his meds and killing himself in a fit of depression, and how Yvonne was so heartbroken she took her own life. It's a ridiculous fiction, one you would hardly deem worthy of teaching in your literature class, but it was what the detective wanted to hear. He'd already convinced himself it was something along those lines. All I did was agree with him."

"Closing the case was that easy, huh?" Dunbar said.

"I'm a professor at a prestigious university. The police afforded me a certain amount of credibility and respect. I'm sure they did the same for you."

"Not exactly," Dunbar said. "Things are going to get a lot more complicated once the police hear what Peter did. They'll have more questions, and you can be damn sure I'll send them your way again."

"Peter's dead, you already mentioned it," Rick said. "I assume he killed himself like the others."

"Not before he burned down the faculty office building."

Rick shook his head. "That idiot. It wasn't even there anymore. He burned down the building for nothing."

"*What* wasn't there anymore?" Dunbar pressed. "What was in your office, Rick?"

"You mean you don't know?"

"Peter told me some bullshit about a ritual involving a mummy coming alive and answering questions. I want to know what *really* happened."

"Is it really so hard to believe what he told you?" Rick asked. "Every civilization that mummifies its dead does so for the same reason—to preserve the body so that the deceased's spirit can eventually return to it. Many years ago, when I was a child, my parents introduced me to a cult that lived on an island near Peru. They call themselves the *Interrogadores*. Their ancestors split off from the Nazca a long time ago. You see, the Nazca mutilated their dead to prevent them from coming back, even going so far as to hack off their heads and replace them with painted jars, but the *Interrogadores* didn't see the point in that. They *wanted* their dead to come back. The body I purchased from them was over two hundred years old, and yet it was mummified so perfectly that it remained as viable a vessel for its spirit as when it was alive."

Dunbar shook his head. "The dead don't come back, Rick. It just doesn't happen. Believe me, there were plenty of times when I wished it did."

"And yet every religion around the world tells us that the spirit lives on after death," Rick said. "The *Interrogadores* believe the dead are granted knowledge on the other side, that every truth is revealed to them, every secret, every answer. Isn't that a good enough reason to call them back, so they can share those secrets?"

"You're talking about necromancy," Dunbar said. "You don't really believe in that shit, do you?"

"Do you believe in God, Dunbar?"

The question only angered him further. "That's none of your business."

"Yvonne believed. She believed fervently, right up until last night in my office, when she was faced with a truth that made her tear the cross from her own neck. I, on the other hand, was always a skeptic. I thought, if God exists, how could there be so much horror in the world? How could He let repressive regimes flourish while men of conscience are tortured and imprisoned? How could He allow bombs to fall on schools in wartime, on hospitals and orphanages? How could He let children starve, or the innocent be executed?"

Officer Purcell's gun looming in the dark, the flash of its muzzle in the rain . . .

Dunbar shook his head, trying to shake the image loose, but this time it wouldn't budge. It wouldn't be ignored.

"If you could ask, wouldn't you want to know why?" Rick said. "Wouldn't you *demand* to know the reason for all this suffering?"

"What . . . what was the answer?"

Rick shook his head sadly. "In this case, Dunbar, ignorance really is bliss."

Dunbar got to his feet. "Bullshit, Rick. This is all bullshit!"

"Is it? Why don't you take a look at what's in the other room, if you're so convinced?" Rick pointed to the first door in the hallway off the living room.

"What's in there?" Dunbar said.

"The truth, if you really want to know it."

Dunbar stalked to the door. "Don't move, Rick. Stay right here."

"Don't worry," he said. "I'm not going anywhere."

Dunbar opened the door. Beyond was a small guest room comprised of a bed and some modest furniture. On the floor was a small clay sarcophagus, chipped and weathered by time, its paint long since faded. The lid was made of ragged, thatched straw—old, but not as old as the rest. He approached the sarcophagus slowly, took hold of the lid, and lifted it.

The mummy inside was as horrible as Peter had described. It hadn't been buried prostrate like the Egyptian mummies he'd seen in museums, but rather it was curled into a fetal ball, its knees up to its chest, its arms crossed. Its thin brown skin reminded him of dry paper. Its face was a gnarled mask of desiccation and rot, empty sockets and jutting teeth. The flesh at its joints had been lubricated with oil, he saw, and ceremonial markings had been drawn on its body in red paint, including a strange serpentine creature on its chest. Was this part of the preparations Rick had locked himself in his office for a week to carry out? Was it true, then? Everything Peter had told him, everything Rick said—was it all true?

He put the cover back on the sarcophagus and returned to the living room. "Rick," he said, but then he stopped.

Rick was slumped in the chair, the open straight razor still in his hand. Blood rimmed the blade, and stained the front of his shirt below the gash in his throat.

The last of the Four Horsemen was dead.

10

Dunbar sat on the edge of the bed in Rick's guest room, the sarcophagus before him, its thatched straw cover removed and set aside. The old, battered tape recorder rested on his knees.

He thought about his father driving alone on that rainy night so many years ago, just wanting to get home, and how he must have felt when he saw the sirens in the rearview mirror. He thought about how loud the crack of Officer Purcell's gun must have sounded in the night, and wondered if his father, reaching for his registration in the glove compartment, even knew what was happening before he died. He thought about how God allowed so much injustice in the world, so many wrongs that were never set right. Was there a reason for all their suffering, some meaning behind it as Yvonne had believed, or was it all just indifference? Was it all just cruelty?

He pressed Play. The sound that came out of the big speaker at the top of the recorder reminded him of the Tuvan throat singers he'd heard in a PBS documentary, more a sustained tone than a chant. Then, just as Peter had described, the lights began to flicker. Dunbar took off his necktie and tied it around his head as a blindfold. The voices continued to emanate from the tape recorder, the reverberation growing so powerful it shook his bones.

It occurred to him that, in doing this, he had become one of them. The fifth Horseman. It also occurred to him that there was a good chance he might share the same fate they had for their curiosity. But it was worth the risk. He had to know.

He heard the creak of old bones, the papery rustle of dry flesh, the hollow slap of an ossified foot upon the floor. The floorboards creaked. Slow, dragging footsteps came closer. Dunbar's heart pounded in his throat. He wanted to tear off the blindfold to see what was happening, but he didn't dare risk spoiling the ritual the way Peter had.

The hairs on his arms stood up. The stench of oil and earth overwhelmed him. He sensed a presence before him, looming over him, waiting.

He asked his question.

Cold breath, dusty and ancient, caressed his ear as the mummy began to whisper.

Companion

To Lawrence Greenberg, the soft murmur of the ventilator in the corner of the hospital room sounded like a whispered secret. Inside the machine, mechanical billows pumped air through tubes into Lawrence's father's lungs. Harold Greenberg didn't look much like himself as he lay in the hospital bed, eyes closed, a bandage covering one side of his head and half his brow. He'd always been talkative, intellectually curious, with eyes that sparkled with the need to learn and understand. Now he looked empty, a beach ball leaking air.

"Have you come to any decisions, Mr. Greenberg?" Dr. Janisse asked, standing at the foot of the bed. It was the same question he'd asked Lawrence every day for nearly three weeks.

"No," Lawrence said. The same answer.

"You know how I feel about it."

"I do."

"Your father has been hooked up to artificial life support for almost a month. He no longer has any brain functions and can't breathe without the ventilator."

"I know." Lawrence looked over at his father. How was it possible that a man who had devoted himself to studying history in order to understand the world around him could become nothing more than a sack of flesh and bone in a hospital bed?

"He will never regain consciousness," Dr. Janisse said. "It's not fair to keep him like this. To him *or* to you."

Lawrence knew the doctor was right. He should pull the plug. As his father's healthcare proxy, the decision was his to make. His father wouldn't want to go on like this. But his chest kept rising and falling, and though Lawrence was aware it was the work of ventilator breathing for him, it looked too much as if he were alive.

What if Dr. Janisse was wrong? What if Lawrence made the decision to take his father off life support right when he was about to regain consciousness? What if all he needed was another week, another day, another *minute?*

"Please, just think about it," Dr. Janisse said before leaving the room.

Lawrence looked at his father again. He'd been here every day, sitting at his father's bedside in this stark, impersonal room in one of New York City's best hospitals, but there had been no change. His father hadn't regained consciousness in the three weeks since he fell down the stairs of his home. It was just an accident, a slip of his foot, and yet it robbed Harold Greenberg of everything he was. It robbed him of his intelligence, his wit, and yes, even his occasional, annoying stubbornness. It had robbed Lawrence, too—of his father, the only family he had left. How could something so small create such monumental, terrible ripples?

On the bed, his father's chest rose and fell, rose and fell.

Lawrence left the hospital room. In the hallway that led to the elevator, everything smelled like floor cleaner and Windex, but it wasn't enough to hide the stench of illness and age, of stale, lingering death all around him. His heart pounded. His breath grew short. He had to get out of here. He jogged to the elevator and jabbed the lobby button until the doors closed. Downstairs, as he approached the front door, he was so intent on escape that he almost didn't hear someone call his name.

It was Kira, the woman who worked behind the front desk where visitors checked in. They'd seen each other almost every day these past weeks, and for some reason she'd taken a liking to him.

"Mr. Greenberg!" she called again. She got up from behind the desk and approached him. She was pretty, with curly hair and a kind smile. She carried a small metal cookie tin, which she held out to him for an awkward moment until he took it from her. "I made more of those strawberry jam sugar cookies for you, since you mentioned you liked the last batch. These should be even better." Her expression changed from happy to concerned. "Has there been any change with your father?"

He shook his head. He lifted the cookie tin in a meager show of appreciation and said, "Thanks." Then he turned and walked to the exit.

In the glass of the revolving door he caught Kira's reflection. She looked disappointed, as though she wanted him to stay and talk with her a little longer. He couldn't imagine why.

Lawrence caught the 6 train downtown toward his apartment on the Lower East Side. One perk—if you could call it that—of spending time with his father at the hospital after work was that rush hour was over by the time he got to the subway, and the trains were significantly less crowded, which he liked. He didn't enjoy being around other people. He found an empty seat with ease, and immediately his eyelids began to droop. He hadn't realized how tired he was. How tired he'd been for weeks now. He let them close, and fell instantly asleep, his chin bobbing against his chest with motion of the train.

He dreams of space, a vast and infinite field of stars, and burning through the darkness between those stars are twin beams of light. They flash in succession, first one then the other, flash-flash, flash-flash, like the rhythm of a heartbeat . . .

Lawrence opened his eyes, unsure how long he'd been asleep. His neck and chest were beaded with sweat despite the cool air inside the train, as if he'd been in a feverish sleep. When he looked up, he saw the train had pulled into a station. Just as the subway doors slid closed, he realized it was at the Brooklyn Bridge–City Hall station, the last stop on the downtown 6. He jumped to his feet and ran to the door with an anxious moan, hoping they would open again, hoping someone would see he was still on the train, but instead, the train lurched forward, moving into a dark tunnel. No one was supposed to stay on the train after the last stop. If they found him here, would he get in trouble?

The lights flickered. He heard the loud screech of the metal wheels as the train began to turn in a long arc, making its way along a subterranean loop that would take it back to the Brooklyn Bridge–City Hall stop, albeit on the uptown track. Outside the windows, the darkness of the tunnel grew lighter, giving way to an unexpected sight.

It was an old, abandoned subway station, right in the middle of the loop. A few globe-shaped fixtures burned dimly on the tiled wall. Old chandeliers hung from tall, vaulted ceilings, and stained-glass mosaic skylights were illuminated by the streetlights above. Lawrence moved closer to the train window to take it all in.

"I know this place," he whispered to himself.

His father, the historian, had told him there were nearly a dozen ghost stations in the New York City subway system. Some were old stations that had been abandoned; others were planned new stations whose construction had never been completed. He remembered now that when he was young, he and his father had stayed on the 6 train past the last stop, just as he'd done now, so his father could show him this very sight. It was the old City Hall station, which had opened at the turn of the twentieth century as the very first subway station in the city and closed some forty years later. The childlike wonder he'd felt seeing it back then washed over him again now. It was breathtaking.

At the center of the platform was a tiled archway with the words CITY HALL spelled out across the top. Beneath it was the foot of a staircase that led upward into darkness.

Standing at the foot the stairs was a man, his back to the train.

Lawrence squinted, trying to get a better look. Probably it was an MTA worker, or a homeless person seeking shelter.

As the train rolled by, the figure turned to watch it go.

Lawrence reeled back from the window.

Even in the half-light outside the train, there was no mistaking what he saw. *Who* he saw. Staring back at him from the platform of the old, abandoned subway station was his father.

The train pulled away and the windows went dark again. Lawrence couldn't move. He stared through the window at nothing, breathing hard. How could his father be here? It wasn't possible. Lawrence had just left him at the hospital.

The train completed its loop and rolled back into the Brooklyn Bridge–City Hall station on the uptown track. As soon as the doors opened, Lawrence raced up the stairs, across the mezzanine level above the tracks, and down the other stairs to the downtown platform just as another train was just pulling in. He weaved through the disembarking passengers and onto the train. Like last time, the doors closed without anyone telling him he had to get out because it was the last stop. The train started back through the same looping tunnel as before.

The abandoned station appeared again, but his father was gone. The platform was empty.

The train completed its loop to the uptown track and opened its doors to passengers. Lawrence stayed on, continuing to ride uptown. He exited at the Bleecker Street stop and walked to his apartment. There he found he had no appetite for dinner. He put on the television but couldn't pay attention to whatever was playing.

Had he really seen his father?

He'd fallen asleep on the train, hadn't he? He must have been dreaming. It was the only thing that made sense.

And yet, he could have *sworn* it was him.

He leaned back on the couch, lost in his memories. Harold Greenberg had loved history, but more than that, he'd loved taking Lawrence fishing on the big country lake where they summered in Lawrence's youth. They went out on a metal rowboat, which either came with the cabin they rented or belonged to his father, Lawrence couldn't quite recall, although he remembered all too well how hot the boat's metal benches got under the summer sun and the red burns on the backs of his thighs. One of Lawrence's favorite memories was being out on the lake while his father showed him how to bait a hook.

"Listen carefully, Larry—*Lawrence*," he'd said, correcting himself. Lawrence never liked the name Larry. He always thought of himself as a Lawrence. His father tried to honor that wish, but sometimes he slipped up. He got the sense his father always wanted a son who was less fussy, not so tightly wound. The kind of boy who went by Larry. "If it's bass you're looking for, you want to use worms like nightcrawlers," his father went on. "If it's swordfish, you want to use squid or mackerel. It's all about fishing with the right bait."

In Lawrence's memory, his father was healthy and vibrant, not the gray and withered thing rotting in a hospital bed. But when he'd seen him—or *thought* he saw him—on the subway platform he'd looked healthy again, as if he were the same able-bodied man who'd taught him to fish. It could only mean it was a dream after all. The father he remembered was gone. He wasn't coming back.

The TV programs that played in the background had switched over to the news. Lawrence watched as his eyelids grew heavy again. Someone was interviewing an astronomer about a new pulsar that had been spotted by NASA's space telescope.

"A pulsar begins with a neutron star, which is basically what's left of a star after a massive supernova," the astronomer said. "A neutron star no longer actively generates heat, but what some of them do—most of them, in fact—is emit twin beams of radiation from their poles. The star spins very quickly, and as it does so, the beams sweep across space like the light from a lighthouse. When we observe this phenomenon from Earth, it looks as if the star is pulsing every few seconds, like a light turning on and off, on and off. That's how they got the name pulsars."

Lawrence grabbed a blanket off the couch and put it over himself. Just a few more minutes, he promised himself, and then he would go to the bedroom. But he couldn't keep his eyelids from drooping.

"Yet you and your team found something different about this pulsar, didn't you?" the reporter asked.

"That's right. This pulsar has a companion," the astronomer said. "This second object, whatever it is, circles around the pulsar at immense speed, but for all intents and purposes it's invisible to us. We only know it's there because it's interfering with the pulsar beams that the telescope is picking up."

"So what *is* this invisible companion?"

"We don't know yet, but there are two likely possibilities. The first is that it's a very small black hole, small enough to allow the pulsar beams' light to escape its gravity. The second is that it's another neutron star. It's not unusual for two neutron stars to fall into mutual orbit. They gradually spiral inward toward each other until they merge."

Lawrence finally let his eyes close all the way. He never made it to the bedroom.

He dreams he's rising into a dark expanse, floating prone on his back, and before him, impossibly, coming closer through the darkness, he sees himself. Lawrence Greenberg, reflected. He reaches out, and so does the other. Their forefingers touch, a strange mirror of Michelangelo's Creation of Man . . .

His alarm clock woke him. He felt sluggish as he showered and got ready for work, oddly drained of energy despite sleeping through the night. Perhaps the situation with his father was weighing on him even more than he thought.

No, "situation" was too vague a word. Too easy. What it came down to was a *decision*. One only he could make. But how was he supposed to decide whether his father lived or died? It was unconscionably cruel to put such a monumental, irreversible choice in his hands. It was unforgivable. If only someone else, anyone else, could make this decision instead. But there was no one. Only him.

Walking to the subway stop, he noticed the moon was still visible in the bright morning sky, round and white. The sight made everything feel off-kilter, illusory, as if he were still dreaming. When he got to the office, he passed the day as he always did, with his head down, doing what was expected of him and nothing else. He'd watched coworkers come and go, seen them get promoted to better titles and greater responsibilities, but that wasn't what he wanted. He just wanted to get through the day without being noticed.

The window near his desk offered him an unobstructed view of the moon's daytime visit. Because it was a double-paned window, there was a reflection of the moon on the inner pane, causing it to look as though a second moon, identical to the first, hung beside it in the sky.

After work, Lawrence went back to the hospital. His father was in his bed, unchanged from how he'd looked the day before, or the day before that. Still, when one of the nurses on the floor came by to check on him, Lawrence couldn't help asking her if his father had left the hospital last night.

She smiled at him. She thought he was joking. "Oh, yeah, he just popped out for a drink before hitting the clubs, like he does every night."

Lawrence sank in his chair. It was wishful thinking that what he'd seen was real. And yet, it had *felt* so real. He could remember everything about it in a way one couldn't with dreams—the feel of his hands against the greasy window glass, his knees on the hard plastic seats, the faint whiff of urine and spilled coffee that permeated the subway car.

The look on his father's face that seemed to say, *Come find me.*

It all felt concrete, undeniable despite its impossibility.

His father was in his hospital bed and hadn't left. What had Lawrence seen? His father's soul? His ghost? Normally, he didn't believe in such things, but he couldn't shake the sense that what he'd experienced was his father reaching out to him, trying to tell him something.

Either that or he was crazy.

There was only one way to find out.

Lawrence hurried from the hospital room to the elevator. When the doors opened, Dr. Janisse stepped out of the elevator, momentarily blocking Lawrence's way.

"Oh, Mr. Greenberg, good evening," the doctor said. "I'll be checking in on your father shortly, but I was wondering if you've finally made any decisions about next steps?"

Without answering, Lawrence pushed past him into the elevator and jabbed the button for the lobby. Dr. Janisse watched him in confusion as the doors slid closed. When Lawrence reached the lobby, he jetted out of the elevator toward the front door.

"Mr. Greenberg!" Kira called excitedly, standing up from behind the desk. "How were the cookies? I used a little less sugar this time, and I wondered if you could taste—"

Lawrence hurried past her and through the revolving door, his own determined face reflected in the glass before him. Out on the street, he made his way to the downtown 6 train and purposely skipped his usual stop to stay on the train all the way to the end. When the other passengers emptied out, he remained, staring at the doors as if he could will them to close quickly. Finally they did, and the train rolled into the dark tunnel to begin its loop.

The darkness brightened again as the train passed into the old City Hall station. Lawrence knelt on the seats again, his face and hands on the glass, peering into the dim light. As he passed the central stairway, he saw his father there. Strong, healthy, upright, he stood facing the tracks, looking directly through the train window as if he'd been expecting Lawrence.

Whatever this was, whatever was happening, Lawrence was convinced now more than ever that his father had something to tell him. What was it? To keep him on life support? To let him die? Lawrence had to know.

The train passed the abandoned station too quickly, and his father was gone before Lawrence was ready, leaving only a yearning ache in his chest. He stood by the doors until the train pulled into the Brooklyn Bridge–City Hall station again. He jumped out onto the uptown plat-form, his feet already moving before the doors were even fully open, and ran up the stairs. He crossed the mezzanine and raced down the steps to the downtown platform.

The digital sign hanging from the ceiling told him the next down-town 6 train would arrive in twelve minutes. That would give him enough time. He only hoped he knew what he was doing.

A narrow ledge extended beyond the end of the platform, running alongside a row of MTA storage rooms on one side and parallel to the tracks one the other. The entrance to the ledge was blocked by a small swinging barrier warning that no unauthorized people were allowed past that point, but the barrier wasn't locked. It swung open easily on its hinges. Lawrence glanced back nervously, but no one on the platform was looking at him. Even if they were aware of what he was doing, they didn't say anything. Everyone minded their own business in New York City, a fact he'd never been more grateful for.

Lawrence walked along the narrow ledge until there was no more ledge to walk, only the tracks below. He took a deep breath. He couldn't believe he was really doing this. It was a test, he realized. His father was asking him to be brave. For once in his life, for his father, the man who'd meant everything to him, he could be brave.

He lowered himself onto the tracks. Beyond the reach of the sta-tion's lights, the tunnel was dark enough that he had to use the flashlight on his cell phone to light his way. He started walking. He knew enough to avoid the third rail, where deadly amounts of electricity powered the trains. A smoky, metallic odor permeated the tunnel, and everything seemed to be coated in a thick layer of soot and dirt, but he kept walking, following the tracks.

It was, indeed, the bravest thing he'd ever done, and also the crazi-est. He was nearly hyperventilating with nervousness. He wasn't worried that another train would come barreling down the tracks before he reached safety, even though he often glanced behind him just to be sure. What really worried him was getting caught. No one was supposed to be on the tracks. How would he explain his actions? *I'm sorry, officer, I thought I saw my comatose, brain-dead father in the old City Hall station.* They would laugh him right into a jail cell. Or a padded one. Would he lose his job if he went to prison? Would the hospital decide in his absence to pull the plug on his father without him? Maybe that would be for the best. At least it would take the decision out of his hands.

But his father wasn't in the hospital, was he? Not the part of him that mattered, not the part of him that was and always would be Lawrence's father.

When he reached the abandoned station, he pulled himself up onto the platform. Somehow, the lights were brighter now. The tiles along the walls reflected the light from the chandeliers, which glowed the way they must have back when the station was in use. He glanced down the length of the platform and saw a shape waiting at the base of the stairs beneath the archway.

"Dad!" he called.

Lawrence hurried toward him. Ahead, his father turned and began climbing the stairs. When Lawrence got there, he looked up the staircase and caught a glimpse of his father at the landing above, turning to the right. Lawrence followed.

"Dad, wait!" he shouted.

He ran up the stairs, his footfalls echoing through the empty station. He reached the top, heart pounding, and turned right. Several yards ahead, he saw his father enter an arched chamber. He followed him inside.

The small chamber was lined with the same ceramic tiles he'd seen on the platform walls downstairs. His father was nowhere to be seen, but there was a strange dark patch covering most of one wall. Its asymmetrical shape and rich, glistening darkness reminded him of an oil slick, but it was pulsing light, on and off, on and off, like someone was flipping a switch. The light was coming from *within* it.

"Dad?" he said, approaching the dark patch.

If there was light inside it, it had to be a hole, not just a dark liquid on the wall, despite what it looked like. He reached out with one hand. His fingers touched what felt like a thin membrane, then passed through into the darkness.

At the same time, another hand reached out of the darkness to one side of him. It was his own hand. He recognized it right away, the cut on the knuckle of his thumb, the hangnail on his ring finger. He pulled his hand back, and the other hand retreated. He stared at his fingers, flexed them. His whole hand tingled as if it had fallen asleep. Light pulsed through the darkness, on and off, on and off, a hypnotic rhythm. He put his hand in again, feeling that strange membrane open for him, and this time he reached deeper. More of his own arm reached out again.

He wondered if he was dreaming. Whatever this was, it wasn't something that belonged in the waking world. He pulled his arm out, watching the other retreat as he did, and then closed his eyes and pinched himself as hard as he could.

When he opened his eyes again, he wasn't in bed at home, as he thought he might be. Instead, he was still here, standing before a strange hole in the wall of a forgotten subway station.

What *was* this thing? And where was his father? He'd seen him enter this room, yet he had disappeared. The only answer was that his father had gone through the hole ahead of him. It was part of the test. He expected Lawrence to follow.

He took a deep breath and stepped through. The membrane wrapped around him, pressing against his face and chest for a moment, then gave way.

Lawrence found himself floating in quiet, endless darkness. The space was airless, yet he felt no need to breathe. Before him, like a lone beacon in a sea of velvety black, was the pulsar. It hovered impossibly close, its beams of bright radiation blasting outward into the dark, bathing him in bright, bleaching light as they swept over him with each rotation of the star.

The darkness was thick as wet cement. He was a fly in amber. It took what felt like hours just to turn his head. Finally he faced the hole he'd come through. Beyond it, a man identical to himself looked back at him from inside the tiled chamber.

The tingling he'd felt in his hand now covered his entire body. The darkness seemed to be dissolving him, bits of himself bleeding outward like streamers into the void. The process was very, very slow, unraveling him by millimeters, yet it was also painless. To be undone so gently came almost as a relief.

Through the hole, Lawrence watched himself, his double, his complement, walk away.

Two years later, Larry Greenberg returned to the abandoned subway station. So much had happened since he'd last stood in the small tiled chamber, it was like a whirlwind. He'd decided to let Harold Greenberg die in peace—a decision Dr. Janisse was very happy to hear. Larry was there when they took him off life support to hold his hand and say goodbye. He struck up a conversation with Kira at the hospital's front desk and asked her out for coffee. It went well, and the next week they went out to dinner, and the week after that it was dinner and a Broadway show. Eventually he left his apartment on the Lower East Side and moved with her to an apartment they bought together on the Upper West Side. Thanks to the inheritance from his father and the promotion he received at work, Larry and Kira were able to afford the wedding of their dreams.

The black spot was still on the wall where he'd left it, pulsing with light. He sensed only the slightest bit of Lawrence remaining in the darkness beyond, a distant echo of loneliness and regret. He stood there until the last spark of Lawrence finally snuffed out.

Larry walked back down the stairs to the old platform, and then onto the tracks that led back to the Brooklyn Bridge–City Hall station. He had to get home soon. Kira was pregnant and her back was killing her. Larry was in charge of dinner, as he probably he would be until the baby came. It wouldn't be long now. They were having a boy.

He hoisted himself up onto the platform and walked to the uptown train, brushing his hands clean. He looked forward to the day when he could take his son out in a boat and teach him how to fish. It was all about using the right bait.

General Slocum's Gold

1

On August 2, 1870, Emperor Napoleon III of France sent his troops to the southern German city of Saarbrücken. Heinrich Schumacher stood shoulder to shoulder with his fellow German infantrymen, watching the French army crest the hill on the outskirts of the city. The sound of their heavy boots trampling the dirt was like thunder. The Franco-Prussian War had been building for months, but the French incursion would be the match that lit the powder keg. He raised his rifle and waited for the order to fire.

2

The rope is knotted tight around my wrists. Carson has me tied to the chair in my tiny Chinatown studio apartment. He waves his .38 in my face, and for a moment I've got nowhere to look but into the empty black O of the barrel. If I can get loose, get the gloves off my hands, I can end this now. But with the gun pointed at me I have to stay still. I don't want him to know I'm working the knot.

"Check the dresser," Carson tells the thug he brought with him, a thick-necked meathead with a black trench coat, crew cut, and scar on his left cheek. Central Casting henchman. I don't know much about Carson except this: he's not one for originality.

"What's it look like?" the thug asks.

"It's a map," Carson says, annoyed. "A piece of paper with lines on it. How hard can it be to recognize a fucking map?"

Whitey only gave me the map this afternoon. It's not a good sign that Carson already knows about it. He's new to the game, a low-level thief who hasn't made a name for himself yet. Five years ago, before I got sent upriver, I'd never even heard of him. He thinks this is his chance to make a big splash; if he rips off a top-level player like Whitey, it'll be his shortcut up the ladder. It's as good as suicide, but I guess the promise of untold millions in gold can make a man crazy.

Gold. Even now, in 2007, the word is enough to tempt even the most jaded thief. Buried treasure, Whitey called it when he first approached me about the heist; right here in New York, right under everyone's nose on an island in the East River. It sounded like a *Treasure Island* pipe dream to me, but Whitey had proof. He had a map.

But if a bottom-feeder like Carson knows about the map, odds are the rest of New York's criminal underworld does too. And that's a problem.

Carson lowers the gun so it's pointed at my chest. He stoops down to look me in the eye. "Hey, Sackett," he says, "how was Rikers? I hear things can get pretty brutal in there."

I don't answer. I'm still trying to work the knot.

"Especially the showers," Carson continues. "You make any boyfriends while you were upriver?"

"Why?" I ask. "You jealous?"

Carson grins coldly. "Don't make me put a slug in your head. Not yet." His pale blue eyes leave mine for a moment to look at the gun in his hand. "There's plenty of time for that later."

Carson's thug finishes rooting through the top drawer of my dresser. Threadbare white socks and Fruit of the Loom briefs lie piled at his feet. He tosses the empty drawer onto the floor and pulls opens the next one.

"This would go a lot faster if you'd just tell us where it is," Carson says. "I might even leave here with all my bullets if you cooperate."

It's easy to tell when someone's lying. They look away for a second, as if they're tracking a mouse running across the floor. Sometimes they swallow in the middle of their sentence. Carson does both.

As long as he doesn't know where the map is, I'm useful. He'll keep me alive.

The ropes are loosening. I can twist my right wrist more than I could a minute ago.

The meathead dumps the second drawer onto the floor. Sweaters, T-shirts, a pair of jeans I never wear. He pulls open the next one.

"Tell you what," Carson says. "You give me the map and I'll put you on my team. I could use someone with your experience."

Third drawer: a spare set of sheets that hasn't been washed in years and four crusty old towels. The thug is getting visibly annoyed. He wants to hit someone, break some legs, dislocate some shoulders. He hasn't been trained to search through dresser drawers for a piece of paper.

"This is a one-time offer, Sackett. Weigh your options." Carson holds both his hands out as if he's the Scales of Justice. He tips his gun hand down. "Death." He tips the other one down. "A cut of the gold. The answer seems obvious, doesn't it?"

His thug digs into the fourth and final dresser drawer. I can feel the rope sliding down my wrist. Almost there.

"But maybe your brains turned to mush in Rikers, huh? Maybe you don't know a good thing when you hear it?"

The thug dumps the last drawer on the floor. Leather gloves. Dozens of them. Lucky for me Carson doesn't know why I have so many. He's too new to the game to know about my hands, what I can do with them.

"The guy's got some kind of leather kink," the thug says, toeing through the pile with his shoe.

"Or maybe he doesn't like germs," Carson says, and I find myself staring down the barrel of his .38 again. "Is that it, Sackett? You the Howard Hughes type? What scares you more, the bullet in the chamber or me sneezing on you?" He turns to the thug. "Turn this place upside down. Find the fucking map."

I twist my wrist one last time. The rope slips free. I grab it so it doesn't fall to the floor.

I'm out of the chair like lightning. I've got Carson in a chokehold before he knows what's happening. With my left arm I catch his neck in the crook of my elbow, with my right I grab his gun hand. The thug turns, gapes, reaches into his coat. I force Carson's trigger finger with my own and a crimson flower blossoms on the thug's neck. He drops with a heavy thud.

Carson gags, choking. His Adam's apple bobs against my bicep. I bring up my knee, bang his wrist against it, and the gun drops out of his hand. I let go of his neck and lower Carson to the floor. I don't want him to pass out. I want him to be awake for this. He gasps for air, coughs, glares at me as if he wishes he could kill me with a look.

I lean over him and shake my head. "Carson, Carson, Carson," I say. He sits up fast and lunges for the gun, but I push him back down and kick the gun away. It skitters across the scuffed linoleum floor and into the nest of dust bunnies under the bed.

"You're dead, Sackett," he says. "There won't be enough of you left . . ." He coughs, unable to finish the sentence.

I take off my black leather gloves, one finger at a time.

"You should've done your homework, Carson."

I let the gloves drop to the floor. The air feels cool on my fingers. They're not used to being uncovered.

"You should always know your target. Everything about them." I lay my palms flat on his chest. Carson looks up at me with wide eyes. Now he knows what my hands can do. He feels it happening.

I close my eyes. Behind my eyelids I see the pale, hairy skin beneath his shirt. I look deeper, at the red-and-white muscle and yellow flab under his skin. I go deeper still, looking past the bone, and there it is: Carson's heart, red and brown and veined with fatty white. It's beating fast. He's scared. He's not sure what's going on, but he can feel it, he knows I'm rooting around inside him with just my hands on his chest.

I force my will down through my arms. It flows like water in a drainpipe, into my hands, into Carson's chest. It's a weird, slippery feeling I've never gotten used to. It feels as if my head has been hollowed out, my empty skull buzzing with a thousand bees.

But it's worse for Carson. I wonder if he can feel me squeezing his heart. I watch it slow, spasm, then finally stop. His body tenses, then goes slack. I pull my will out of him and open my eyes. He's dead, his head tipped to the side, eyes wide, mouth open. It's the same look of surprise I see every time. I slip my gloves back on.

In the bathroom I switch on the light, a fluorescent that flickers overhead and tints everything a pale green. I pull open the shower curtain. If Carson's thug had made it to the bathroom, and if he'd bothered to check the shower, maybe he would have seen the one pristine white tile among all the grimy, moldy ones on the wall. Maybe he would have thought it odd.

I press one side of the tile, and it swings open on a hidden hinge. Lying in the hole on the other side is a long black tube with a shoulder strap. A poster carrier. Inside is Whitey's map. I snatch it out of the hole and close the fake tile again.

Back in the main room, I look at the two dead bodies on the floor. Someone would have heard the gunshot and called the cops by now. It's still another twenty-four hours before I'm supposed to meet Whitey and his crew at the Harlem Docks, but I can't stay here. The apartment's been compromised. And when the cops find out it's rented to an ex-con fresh out of Rikers Island, well, the mayor won't want to look soft on crime in an election year. He'll mobilize every cop in the city to hunt me down.

I throw on a coat, sling the poster carrier over my shoulder, and grab Carson's gun from under the bed. I race down four flights of stairs and out the front door. I'm already walking past the restaurants with red roasted ducks hanging in the windows when I hear the distant wail of sirens.

3

Bullets hissed through the air like angry insects, slamming into the soldiers with a series of sickening thuds. Heinrich Schumacher watched the men around him fall. As the French army advanced, the Germans broke formation to find cover. It didn't do any good. The French outnumbered them and had better rifles. The battlefield was littered with bodies, soaked with blood. Positioned behind the thick trunk of a tree, Heinrich checked his ammunition belt and found he was out of bullets. He dropped his rifle and ran, heading back toward Saarbrücken. Someone had to warn them the enemy was coming.

4

There's a spot under the gray behemoth of the Manhattan Bridge where, if you're in just the right place where the slanted concrete support wall meets the iron struts, you can't be seen from the street below. I've used that spot before, back when I had to hide a briefcase filled with fifteen thou in diamonds. But the spot is smaller than I remember, and it hurts my back to have to stay hunched over. It's cold and rainy, and my coat isn't thick enough to keep out the chill.

It would be easier if I could contact Whitey and stay with him until launch time tomorrow night, but I can't risk leading the cops right to him. Or any more like Carson, for that matter.

The sirens of a police car zooming over the bridge make me flinch. They're heading for Brooklyn. It's not me they're looking for, but the sound still draws a cold sweat from my back. It makes me think of Rikers, and that makes the scars on my ribs itch.

When you find yourself hiding under a bridge in the middle of the night, shivering from the cold and wondering if the cops have found the dead bodies in your apartment yet, you have to ask yourself how you got here. I don't have an answer for that. I've been in the game for as long as I can remember. Same with Whitey. We've worked together so long it feels like we grew up together, but people like us don't have childhoods, just a time when we were too small to run and too weak to fight.

Before Whitey there was Costigan, my first boss. He plucked me out of the Angels' Reach group foster home when I was sixteen and gave me a job. He called me X-Ray because I played lookout for him by putting my hands on the wall of a bank or the door of a penthouse apartment to see if the coast was clear inside. Costigan was mid-level, never the biggest player in the game, but notorious throughout the underworld for one thing. If some poor slob crossed him or ratted him out, he'd put a specially made steel cage over the guy's head like a helmet. Inside the cage was a protruding metal plate, covered in tiny, sharp spikes that went in the guy's mouth. "Bite," Costigan would say like the world's most sadistic dentist. When the guy didn't—they never would, not right away—he'd jab his .45 into their necks and repeat, "Bite," until they did.

Costigan also liked to drink, and when he did, he got talkative. One day when he'd had a few too many bottles of Jameson, he decided it was my turn to be lectured. "You know what your problem is, X-Ray? You got no goals, no dreams. No one else can do what you do, but you're happy to be a tool for someone else's gain. You gotta *stand* for something, boy. You gotta have a *cause*. Like me. My cause is to teach these rich motherfuckers a lesson. You think they appreciate what they've got? Hell no. They were born into money, never worked a day in their lives. They don't know what it's like to *need*. So I take it away from them. I teach them what it's like to go without. What's your cause, X-Ray? Why are you in the game?"

I shrugged. "I don't know. To get rich."

Costigan didn't like that answer. He threw the empty Jameson bottle against the wall, grabbed me by the collar, and tossed me out onto the street.

"You disgust me," he spat. "You're nothing."

I never saw him again. I heard that one of the guys he tortured came back and put a butcher knife through the roof of his mouth.

Shivering under the Manhattan Bridge, watching East River rats the size of chihuahuas scamper below and wondering how I wound up here, all I can think of is the question Costigan asked me all those years ago, and my own inability to answer it.

5

Heinrich Schumacher watched the procession from his window. Saarbrücken was an occupied city, under the control of General Charles Frossard and the French army. On the street below he saw soldiers leading a long line of shackled men and women through town. Conspirators, they claimed, trying to overthrow the occupation and insult the glory of Emperor Napoleon III. Marlene, his wife, joined him at the window and took his hand in hers. They watched as the soldiers below dragged a man out of the procession and forced him to his knees on the street. It was Franz Strasser, the baker they bought rolls from every Friday. He was no conspirator, Heinrich thought, just a simple bread-maker who'd always had a warm smile and friendly hello for him. The French soldier hit Franz in the back of the head with the butt of his rifle. Franz fell forward, dazed, then the soldier turned his rifle around and put a bullet through the baker's skull. The bang was so loud it shook the windows. Marlene turned away. "Citizens of Saarbrücken," the soldier shouted in broken, halting German. "This is what lies in store for conspirators and all enemies of the emperor!" Then the procession moved on, leaving the body of Franz Strasser in the middle of the street.

It turned out the French had made a tactical error in taking Saarbrücken. They'd thought it would be the first step toward Berlin, but there was just one, easily defended railway leading to the hinterland, and the rivers only ran along the border, not inland. There was no way through Saarbrücken. And so, frustrated and angry, the French turned to atrocities to pass the time.

That is, until General Frossard heard from a desperate torture victim about a fortune in gold hidden somewhere in the city. Then they had a new mission.

6

By the time I get to the Harlem Docks at midnight the next night, Whitey and the rest of the team are waiting for me on the pier. The windswept, paper-white hair that gives Whitey his nickname glows in the moonlight. I don't recognize the three men standing with him, though. Normally I'm reluctant to pull a job with people I don't know— their skills are unproven, their allegiances unknown—but Whitey calls the shots, and if he trusts them that's good enough for me. Behind them, lolling in the dark, choppy water at the end of the pier, is a sixty-nine-foot Halmatic/Tarquin powerboat, a yacht big enough for twice our number, sleek as a bullet and white as snow, with black-tinted cabin windows. A rowboat hangs by two thick ropes off a hydraulic scaffold at the back.

"Glad you could make it, Sackett," Whitey says, stepping forward to shake my hand. "Let me introduce you to the rest of the team." He nods at a tall, well-manicured slickster in a dark suit. "This is Al. I worked with him a lot while you were gone. He's an expert with locks and booby traps. It's also his boat."

Al nods. "I've heard about you, Sackett. The man with the magic hands. I thought you were still in Rikers."

"Just got out," I say. "Good behaviour." My ribs flare again, and I try to push the image of a flashing shiv from my mind.

"That's why I love this guy," Whitey says, clapping me on the arm. "Five years upriver and it didn't even put any lines on his face."

I force a smile. The lines Rikers gave me aren't on my face.

Whitey points to the next man. "This is Grease. Heavy lifting and ammunitions."

Grease nods, sucking on a toothpick. His name fits him perfectly. He's pure grunt: all muscle, no specialized skill. Next to Grease is another muscleman. He looks antsy, shifting his weight from one foot to the other.

"That's Burns," Whitey says. "Heavy lifting, digging, and disposal."

"And backup ammunitions," Burns says, patting the bulge under his jacket. "Just in case."

I eyeball the new crew. "You've worked with these guys before?"

Al answers, "I have. I can vouch for them."

"I trust Al," Whitey says. "What's bugging you?"

I tell him about Carson, and the smile fades from his face. "But you still have the map?" he asks.

I tap the poster carrier strung across my back. "It's safe."

Whitey nods, but Grease says, "Shit. Killing Carson's only gonna bring more of 'em on us."

Al looks around the dark pier. "If the word's out, we're sitting ducks here. We need to go. Now."

"Agreed," Whitey says. "All hands on deck."

He climbs the side ladder up to the boat's deck. Al follows him up, then Burns. Grease stands behind me on lookout. I put one gloved hand on the ladder, ready to climb up, but then I hear Whitey say, "Al, take the helm. Remember to cut the engines and run dark when we pass Rikers. We don't want to catch the Coast Guard's attention."

I take my hand off the ladder. "What did you say?"

"It'll be viewing distance only, I promise," Whitey answers. "We won't get any closer than we have to."

"You're shitting me, Whitey," I say. "Pulling a job in the shadow of Rikers?"

Behind me, Grease lights a cigarette and laughs. "What's the matter, Sackett? You scared?" He looks up at the deck. "Hey, Whitey, I thought you said this guy's a pro."

"He is. The best in the business. Isn't that right, Sackett?"

I shake my head. "This is crazy. We're talking about the most patrolled water in the East River."

"There's no turning back now. What are you gonna do, stay here and wait for the next wannabe to come at you the way Carson did? Get on board, Sackett. You too, Grease. Time is money."

Whitey is out of his mind, but he's right about there being no point in staying behind. Even if I manage to avoid the police manhunt, the entire criminal underworld is after that map. I'd be dead by lunch.

Grease chuckles. "From everything I've heard about you, Sackett, I thought you'd be able to take the heat. Maybe you got soft while you were in the hole."

I ignore him and climb the ladder. When we're all on board, Al heads for the compass bridge to take the wheel. Whitey guides the rest of the crew into the cabin and shows us the enormous hold at the far end. "It used to be the master bedroom," he explains, tapping the wood-panelled door. "It's forty square feet inside. The walls and door are six inches of reinforced steel. Our own floating Fort Knox, tighter than your grandma's ass when it's locked up. No one can break in."

"Where's the key?" Burns asks.

Whitey yanks his collar to reveal a thin string around his neck. A small silver key dangles from the end.

7

The French officer pointed his rifle at the back of the woman's head. She was kneeling on the street in front of her house, her stringy blonde hair over her face. Two soldiers held her husband and teenage son back. "Where is the gold?" the officer demanded. Heinrich Schumacher ran across the street toward them, shouting for them to stop. "Where is the gold?" the officer asked again. Her husband insisted she had no idea, that none of them knew anything about any gold. "A pity," the officer said. He pulled the trigger and blew a hole through her head. Heinrich skidded to a halt before her fallen body, too late.

The officer addressed the horrified crowd that had gathered. "We will go house to house if we have to. You've seen what happens to those who refuse to give us information." A low moan of terror rose out of the throng. "Now," the officer continued, stepping forward. He grabbed Heinrich by the hair and forced him down on his knees. He put his rifle to the back of Heinrich's head. "Where is the gold?"

8

"Showtime," Whitey says, motioning for us to gather around the dining table bolted to the floor of the cabin. The dull vibration of the motor cuts out suddenly, and the boat rocks for a moment on the waves. My back stiffens. We must be getting close to Rikers. I turn to the window and notice the exterior lights are off too. We're drifting up the East River, through the stretch called Hell Gate. The dark silhouette of Randall's Island looms next the boat. No sign of Rikers yet. I take a deep breath. I never wanted to see that shithole again, and now here I am, all but helplessly floating by it with a bunch of known criminals about to pull a job. If we're caught, the authorities will send me back. And there's no way I'm going back. I'd swallow a bullet first.

The little white intercom on the cabin wall squawks with Al's voice telling us we'll be running silent and dark for the next fifteen minutes.

"What about the lights in the cabin?" I ask. "They can still see us."

Whitey juts a thumb at one of the windows. "Polarized tinting. Light can't get out, infrared can't get in. Now give me the map."

I unstrap the poster carrier, unzip the end, and pull out the map. It feels brittle as I hand it over, as if it'll rip or crumble to dust if I touch it wrong. Whitey unrolls it on the table, pinning the corners down with heavy ceramic coasters. The map is old, the paper yellowing, the edges frayed. Dissected into latitude and longitude grids, it shows landmasses that I recognize right away as two of New York City's boroughs, Queens and the Bronx. At the center of the map is a small island.

I glance at the others around the table, watch their eyes. I don't know what I'm looking for, a shifty glance maybe, a suspicious smirk. The run-in with Carson, being this close to Rikers, it's all got me spooked.

"Shouldn't we wait for Al?" Grease asks.

"He's needed on the bridge," Whitey says. "The Hell Gate currents can really fuck you up. Besides, Al's already been briefed. He was with me when I got the map."

An unexpected twinge of jealousy punches me in the chest. I used to be Whitey's right-hand man, but he replaced me with Al while I was upriver. They probably grew tight over those five years. Now that I'm back, though, where do I fit in? Am I just hired muscle, no different from Burns and Grease?

Whitey puts his finger on the island at the centre of the map. "North Brother Island," he says. "It's been deserted for decades, a ghost town. All that's there now is some overgrown forest, an old decommissioned lighthouse and the remains of the Riverside Hospital for Communicable Diseases. For those of you who left school before puberty, that's where Typhoid Mary lived out her days back in the '30s."

"Great," Grease says. "Are we pulling a job or looking to die from some weird-ass disease?"

Whitey smiles that lopsided way he does whenever he knows a secret. "Ah, but North Brother Island has a place in history for another reason, and that, gentlemen, is what brings us here. Over a century ago, on June 15, 1904, thirteen hundred residents from Manhattan's Little Germany took a joyride to Long Island Sound on a steamboat called the *General Slocum*. It was going to be a church picnic, but a fire broke out on board. The captain panicked and pointed the ship toward the nearest land he could find: North Brother Island. By the time he beached the ship, most of the passengers and crew had died in the fire. More died when they jumped overboard into thirty feet of freezing water. The death toll was over a thousand."

"Shit." Burns shakes his head. "I've never even heard of it."

"Not a lot of people have. It was big news at the time, but then"— he snaps his fingers—"it was completely forgotten after the Triangle Shirtwaist Factory fire a few years later. The *General Slocum* disaster is little more than a historical footnote now, and that is entirely to our advantage. You see, what most people don't know is that hidden in the hold of the *General Slocum* was a fortune in gold bricks. No one knows who it belonged to or why they were bringing it with them."

"Who gives a shit why?" Grease says, chewing his toothpick. "What happened to the gold?"

"The story goes that under the cover of night the survivors moved it from the wreckage and hid it in the hospital. A few bribes for the staff—a little for him, a little for her—and everyone was happy enough to keep their mouths shut about it." Whitey flips the map over. On the other side is the floor plan of a five-story building. He puts his finger on the lowest level. "Right here. According to this map, the gold is buried beneath the cellar. We just don't know exactly where." He looks at me. "That's where you come in, Sackett. You can show us where the gold is."

"And you're sure it's still there?" Grease asks.

"Positive. The Germans might've thought they were coming back for it, but they never did. It's still there, buried in that old hospital, just waiting to be found. It's New York's own El Dorado."

"Except nobody ever got out of El Dorado alive," Burns says. "Isn't that how the story goes?"

A smile slowly creases Whitey's face. "Then it's up to us, gentlemen, to show El Dorado who's boss."

9

Someone in the crowd cried, "Let him go!" Heinrich Schumacher turned, and the cold metal of the rifle barrel scraped the back of his head. Marlene stomped angrily forward, pulling her skirt so the hem wouldn't get trampled under her feet. "That's enough! You should be ashamed of yourselves!" Heinrich felt the French officer's rifle move away from his head and breathed a sigh of relief. But then he heard the soldier ask her where the gold was, and he stiffened. "There is no gold," she insisted. "It's an old wives' tale. You might as well ask me where the gnomes are." A sudden loud explosion startled Heinrich and nearly deafened him. The officer's bullet punched into Marlene, knocking her to the ground. Heinrich cried out and ran toward her. Behind him, the French troops turned and moved on. A pool of blood stained Marlene's dress near her stomach. The crowd gathered around Heinrich as he cradled his wife's head. Her eyelids fluttered. Her chest rose and fell. Heinrich cried with relief. The bullet hadn't killed her.

A bespectacled old man in the crowd leaned over him and took off his bowler hat. "Excuse me," he said. "My name is Crowley. I am a doctor."

10

Up on deck, the wind off the river has a brisk edge. I have to hunch my shoulders in order to light my cigarette. Randall's Island is a black smudge slowly drifting away behind us now. Ahead, I can see the lights from Rikers piercing the dark like bullets. The scars on my ribs start itching so bad I have to turn my back to it, and there's Grease, standing there sucking on a cigarette, the toothpick wedged behind his ear.

"You know," he says, the wind tearing the smoke from his mouth, "I heard when people are in prison too long, when they get out all they can think about is going back. It's the only place that feels safe to them anymore. Rikers is right there. I bet you could swim for it."

"You gonna keep riding my back, Grease?"

"Relax, I'm just yanking your chain." He takes another drag. "Is it true they put you in solitary?"

"Yeah, they did. For six months." I pin that one squarely on my cellmate, a psycho who liked to cut people. He came at me one too many times with a shiv. Cut me right at the ribs, so I put my hands on him. The prison doctors couldn't figure out what killed him, but enough people saw him drop when I touched him that they knew I had something to do with it. They stuck me in solitary as punishment. *Just try working that freaky kung fu shit from here,* the guard said the first time he closed the door. Only two things kept me sane in the six months of darkness that followed. One was putting my hands on the door and watching the guards play poker or flip through channels on their little black-and-white, just so I wouldn't feel so alone. The other was the song. I only heard it sometimes and only at night, a distant melody that somehow penetrated the thick concrete walls. Maybe I dreamt it, I don't know, but whatever it was, it always comforted me, gave me a peaceful night's sleep. Even the rat and spider bites all over my body didn't matter then.

"Six months in solitary is hardcore," Grease says. He looks at my gloves. "So, your hands. Is it true you can do stuff with them? See through walls and shit, whatever you touch?"

"I guess so."

Grease shakes his head. "That must make getting laid really interesting. So how does it work?"

I shrug and toss my cigarette into the water. "If I knew that, I'd make a mint teaching it at the Learning Annex."

He laughs. "So are you like the X-Men or like Spider-Man?"

I squint at him. "What are you talking about?"

"You know, is this something you were born with, like a mutant power, or did it come from an accident, like you got zapped by a super-powered X-ray machine?"

"I have no idea. I've been able to do it since I was a kid," I say. I haven't thought about those days in a long time. My mother was a drug addict who traded sex for her fix. She didn't know who my father was. Could have been any one of her Johns. As I boy, I used to imagine he was someone special, like royalty from some distant land with a funny name. I wished every night that he'd return to take me away, give me a real family that didn't involve drugs and strange men wandering through our apartment in their underwear. Eventually I wised up. He wasn't coming back. He wasn't anyone special. I told myself it doesn't matter where you come from, only where you're going.

Where I went was Angels' Reach, courtesy of Children's Services. At the group foster home, I learned grammar and math and how not to cry when your foster parents beat you with a broom handle. I learned to push it all down, the anger, fear, and resentment, and tie it into a tight knot in my stomach so I could stay numb and stop caring what happened to me. When news of my mother's death came, I took it in stride. I always figured she'd OD one day, anyway. In the end, though, it wasn't the heroin that got her, it was one of her Johns. He cut her up so bad the funeral was closed casket. The knot in my stomach loosened the moment my foster parents and I walked into the mostly empty church and I saw the cheap pine coffin. So much of the rage I felt toward her leaked out right then that I grabbed the casket lid, shook it, trying to pry the coffin open. I screamed and strained and yearned and, in my desperation, something opened up inside me. Suddenly I could see through the lid, could see her inside the box, a gray, sagging, sliced-up thing that looked more like a dummy than a person. That was the first time it happened, and it terrified me. I ran out of the church. Later, my foster parents beat me for causing a scene.

"Mutant then," Grease replies. "I should've figured."

I laugh despite myself. I'm starting to like Grease.

11

Dr. Crowley helped Heinrich Schumacher carry Marlene back to the house. They placed her gently on the couch. Marlene lapsed in and out of consciousness, sometimes mumbling incoherently, other times appearing to sleep soundly. "It's a miracle the bullet didn't do more damage," Crowley said. He worked on her wound right there on the couch, placing towels and sheets under her to catch the blood. After he'd pulled out the bullet and sewn the wound closed, he showed Heinrich how to clean and dress it. Crowley came back to check on her regularly, and after a few days Marlene was fully conscious again, could even talk, though she still needed constant rest and couldn't get up off the couch.

Heinrich was so grateful he offered Crowley everything he had—money, food, his house—but the doctor declined. "However," Crowley said, "there is something you can do for me. Come with me and I will show you."

12

Ahead of us, the island is clearly visible in the moonlight. Standing with the others on deck, I see a thick, tangled mass of trees, a sagging old house half-hidden in the overgrown forest—what's left of the lighthouse, its tower long gone—and cresting the top of the woods, the dark, square shape of a large building: Riverside Hospital.

"Welcome to North Brother Island," Whitey announces. "Your one-stop shop for buried treasure."

Al steers the boat into a narrow, forest-lined cove where we'll be safe from the prying eyes of the Coast Guard, then he drops anchor. We load the rowboat with equipment—shovels, picks, a wheelbarrow—and lower it into the water. With all the gear on board, there's only room left for Whitey and Al. Grease, Burns, and I climb down the ladder, jump into the bitter cold surf and wade alongside it towards the shore. The water feels strange, almost as if there's a dull electrical charge running through it, a vibration that comes up through my legs and into my chest.

"You guys feel that?" I ask.

"What?" Grease says.

"Something in the water. A buzzing."

"I don't feel shit except cold," Burns says.

Grease chuckles. "Next time bring enough drugs for the rest of us, Sackett."

The moment I slosh onto shore, the weird vibration stops. I wring out the hems of my jeans and look around while the others unload the rowboat. The island is overgrown from decades of neglect, the thick foliage forming a natural cover from the moonlight and the dull city glow of the Bronx nearby. We're invisible here.

With the map and a flashlight, Whitey guides us inland toward the hospital. Al carries a big black bag filled with his own equipment. Burns and Grease sling the shovels and picks over their shoulders. I pick up the wheelbarrow and follow at the rear.

The stiff underbrush scrapes at my legs, low tree branches scratch my face. Insects buzz angrily in the bushes. Then the foliage thins, and suddenly we're standing in ankle-high crabgrass in front of the deserted hospital. It's still intact after all this time. Or mostly intact, anyway. The moonlight reveals the glass is gone from the windows, some of them are boarded up, others just big black empty holes. External doors hang by single, stubborn hinges or lay half-rotted on the ground. Vines, creepers, and weeds vein the building's brick facade, poking through the windows and the cracks in the mortar.

"This is your El Dorado?" Grease asks.

"El Asbestos is more like it," Burns replies.

They all laugh, everyone but me. My hackles are up. I felt it in the water, and now I feel it in the air. There's something off about this place.

13

Crowley led Heinrich Schumacher into the Ludwigskirche, the grand stone church at one end of the town square. "There's something you need to see," Crowley explained. "But you must promise not to tell anyone what I'm about to show you." He brought Heinrich into a broom closet in the back of the church, closed the door behind them, then opened another hidden behind some shelves and old mops. He led Heinrich down a flight of stone steps into a vast cavern beneath the church. Heinrich's breath caught in his throat. Arranged along the floor, reflecting the flickering light from the torches affixed to the walls, was a mass of gold bricks.

"The occupiers are leaving Saarbrücken to defend France now that the armies of Prussia and the German Confederation gather on their doorstep," Crowley said. "But once their emperor hears of gold, they'll be back." He turned to the treasure lining the floor. "This is what they were looking for. The Rheingold, or what's left of it. Germany was built on it, and its care was entrusted to the Brotherhood centuries ago." He picked up one of the bricks and pointed to the symbols running along the top. "These runes were carved into the gold at the moment of its forging. They speak of its purpose, and its power. Thurisaz, protection. Uruz, strength. Fehu, wealth. Gebo, gift. Algiz, defender. And this last one, the most important of all: Othila, homeland."

Heinrich balked. Crowley was obviously mad. Surely it couldn't *really* be the Rheingold. That was a myth, a bedtime story of dwarves and giants and gods.

"I assure you it's real," Crowley said. "It is a living thing, the heart of Germany, its soul. It's sacred. It cannot be allowed to fall into the hands of outsiders. You asked me what you could do to thank me, Heinrich. My brethren and I are the gold's keepers, but we're also men of high standing and visibility. We can't leave Saarbrücken unnoticed. But you can. We want you to take the gold away before the French return. Far away, where it can be hidden safely. There's a boat leaving from the Netherlands for America in a few days' time. You and Marlene will be on it, and so will the gold."

14

Rusty old medical equipment and moldy waterlogged mattresses clutter the hospital's main hallway, jamming us up before we've taken ten steps into the building. Burns and Grease clear the way, shoving all the junk against the walls while Whitey checks the map. He points the flashlight at a hallway branching off into the dark. "The cellar should be this way."

A few minutes later we find the metal door to the basement, only it's rusted so tight it might as well be locked. It takes the combined muscle of both Grease and Burns to pry it open, and when they do it flies off its hinges and slams to the floor with a loud clang and a cloud of grime. At first, all I see through the doorway is a wall of dusty cobwebs, but then Whitey brushes them away to reveal stairs leading down into the darkness. Whitey and the others take the stairs single-file, bringing their equipment with them. I leave the wheelbarrow at the top of the steps and hurry after them, not wanting to lose Whitey's light.

The stairs groan under my feet. Each step I take has me convinced the rotting wood is going to break and drop me through the darkness to the floor twenty feet below. I've never been this on edge before. I don't know if it's because this is my first heist since getting out of Rikers or if it's something else. It doesn't matter, I tell myself, a job's a job and money's money. I push the anxiety down into my stomach, the way I always do, and tie it into a tight little knot.

At the bottom of the stairs, Whitey sweeps the enormous room with his flashlight. Garbage, old wooden crates, and rusted chunks of metal piping litter the cement floor. Holes dot the ceiling where plaster and rotten timber have fallen through. The corners are lacy with cobwebs.

Grease rolls the toothpick in his mouth. "This place is a shithole."

"Yeah, but it's the good kind of shithole," Whitey says. "It's a shithole filled with gold." He turns to Al, the booby-trap expert. "Go time, buddy. Make sure this place isn't rigged."

Al opens his black bag. He pulls out a portable halogen lamp, which he hands to Whitey. Whitey sets it on top of a dirt-crusted crate and switches it on. Jagged black shapes leap up the walls in the sudden bright light. My hand is halfway to the .38 in my coat before I realize I've been spooked by nothing, just shadows cast by the lamp.

Al reaches into his bag again and takes out something that looks like an oversized cell phone. He flips it open and points it around. It makes a few squeals and radarlike pings, then he closes it with a nod. "No electronic devices detected. Not a big surprise, though. If they left booby-traps around the gold, they'd be the old-fashioned kind, whatever they had back then. Some wire-and-explosive work, maybe." Al spends another ten minutes using his tools to search the room for signs of more traditional traps. Finally he gives the all clear.

Whitey nods at me. "You're up, Sackett."

I take off my gloves, kneel in the dust and dirt, and put my hands to the floor. I close my eyes. The image I get is blurry and dark. I look deeper, through the cement floor and into the earth below it. I spread my vision out to cover more ground. I move through the rock and soil and root beneath the cellar until I see it, a shape I can only just make out, first cloth, then dark metal rectangles—a big stack of them.

I open my eyes. "It's here."

I blink, suddenly feeling dizzy, and nearly tumble against a nearby crate as I stand up. That's never happened before. Usually it's no big deal to use my hands, but this time's different somehow. It feels as if a part of me didn't just see the gold but *touched* it, and when I did, it made me lightheaded. When I get my balance back, I put my gloves back on and show the guys where they should dig.

Grease grabs a pick. "All right, freakshow, you better be right about this. I don't want to waste time digging through cement only to wind up with my dick in my hand."

"He's right," Whitey says. "He's always right."

Grease and Burns clear the area, then break through the cement floor. While the grunts dig, I look over at Whitey and Al. They have big, excited grins on their faces. They don't feel it, I realize. They don't get that there's something wrong here, something I can't put my finger on even though my instincts are shouting in my ear.

"We've got something," Burns announces a while later, sweaty from exertion. Grease just looks up at me, nods a little. Maybe that's his way of saying he's sorry for doubting me. I walk to the edge of the hole with Al and Whitey right behind me. Whitey holds up the lamp and there in the light we see the tip of an old cloth tarp sticking out of the dirt. Whatever it's covering is big and blocky. I grab a shovel and jump in the hole with them. We dig until we've unearthed enough of the tarp to pull it away.

Grease takes the toothpick from his mouth and mutters, "Holy Jesus."

I've seen a lot of impressive loot in my time—a life-sized crystal tiger, a portrait fashioned from tiny gemstones, a coffin filled with money—but never anything quite like this.

The *General Slocum*'s lost gold. Lamplight reflects off it and shimmers across our faces like water.

I lift one of the bricks out of the hole, the gold bright against the black of my glove. It's heavier than I thought it would be. Shinier too, especially after being buried for a hundred years, tarp or no tarp; it's as if dirt refuses to stick to it. It just rolls off like water. Something that looks like writing covers the top of the brick, but I've never seen letters like these before. They're rough and blocky and remind me more of caveman carvings than an alphabet. For some reason, the more I look at them, the more lightheaded I feel. Part of me wants to put it back in the hole and leave it alone.

Whitey's expression is ecstatic. It takes a moment for him to find his voice. "Take a moment to drink this in, gentlemen. Buried treasure, just like you always dreamed of finding."

We all start grabbing bricks and lugging them up to the wheelbarrow. Everyone's talking excitedly about what they're going to buy with their share, where they'd live, what celebrities they'd fuck. Everyone but me. I don't like this place. I want to be out of here already.

15

Leaving his wife in a neighbor's care, Heinrich Schumacher returned to the Ludwigskirche the next night to let Crowley know he and Marlene had agreed to the plan. "My brethren are waiting for us below," Crowley said. In the cavern, Heinrich saw twelve other men standing in a circle around the gold. They wore hooded robes that covered their faces. Crowley slipped into an identical robe and joined the circle. Heinrich stayed by the stairs, nervous and frightened. If they pulled back their hoods, he wondered, would he recognize any of them? Would they be the shopkeepers and bakers and teachers he saw every day in Saarbrücken? Or would they be devils?

The robed men passed a frightful, curved dagger between them and slit deep red lines into their palms. Their blood fell on the bricks, coating them in crimson, but then the blood seemed to evaporate. No, Heinrich realized with a start, the bricks had absorbed it like thirsty sponges, the blood draining into the carved runes. The robed men chanted and swore an oath to protect the gold always. Swore not to God but to Wotan and Freia and Fafner. Finally Crowley held the dagger out to Heinrich. "A small cut," he said. "That's all that's needed."

Heinrich turned in horror and ran out of the church.

16

It takes a lot longer to get the gold back to the ship than I hoped. It's so heavy we can only fill the wheelbarrow with so much at a time. Same with the rowboat. By the time we load the last of it into the hold, we're sweaty, sore, and tired.

Whitey shuts the wood-panelled door of the hold and locks it with the key around his neck. "Who's got a smoke?" he asks. It's a ritual. Whitey doesn't smoke until the job is complete. I hand him one from my pack and light it for him. He drags deep and blows smoke through his teeth. "To El Dorado, gentlemen!" He raises his cigarette as if he's toasting. "Well done."

"I could use a drink," Burns says, leaning against the wall and wiping the sweat off his brow with his forearm.

"A beer would be great right about now," Grease says. "A nice, cold Bud," he nods at Al, "not one of those fucking Yuppie wheat beers Mr. Suit-And-Tie here drinks."

Al laughs and tries to get Grease in a headlock, but Grease doesn't allow it and slips through Al's grasp. He winds up with Al under his arm, pretending to punch him in the face while making karate noises. Burns hollers, "Let's get ready to rumble!" and I'm laughing so hard my sides hurt. They're all right, this team. I could work with them again.

"Everybody shut the fuck up," Whitey yells suddenly. He holds up his hand. "You hear that?"

I finger the .38 in my jacket. It's as instinctive a reaction as giving Whitey a victory cigarette. "What?"

"I thought I heard something." Whitey's hand is still up. His eyes narrow. "It sounded like a splash. A big one."

"Topside," Al says.

I pull out the gun and head up the stairs toward deck, the others right behind me. By the time we reach the top, they all have their guns out too.

It's gotten darker outside. The moon has sunk behind the island's tree line. The same conditions that shield us from being seen are keeping the light out. I see a bit of starlight and city glow reflecting in the water lapping at the side of the boat, and I can just make out the island's shore, but that's it. I don't like this. Maybe we aren't alone on North Brother Island after all. Maybe Whitey didn't do his homework. With Rikers nearby and the Coast Guard on patrol and the whole goddamn criminal underworld trying to get what we've got, I don't like this at all.

Grease and Al take the flashlight from Whitey and walk toward the back of the boat. When they return, Al says, "The rowboat's gone."

Whitey walks up to him, gets right in his face. "What?"

"The ropes broke," Grease says, chewing his toothpick nervously.

"It must've fallen into the water and drifted away," Al says.

Whitey grabs the flashlight from him and walks to the side of the ship. "It didn't fucking drift away." He starts climbing down the side ladder.

"What the hell are you doing, Whitey?" Al shouts after him. "Let's just set sail!"

"Someone's here," Whitey calls back. He drops into the water and starts wading toward shore, shining the flashlight in front of him. "I don't like being fucked with, and I don't like witnesses. We're marked men if anyone knows what we've got."

"Whitey, come on!" Al shouts.

Whitey's legs splash angrily through the water. "Get your asses down here and help me find these motherfuckers!"

The rest of us climb down the ladder into the water.

"This is fucked," Grease says. "We've got the gold, we should just get the hell out of here."

He looks at me to see if I'm on his side, but I don't answer. Whitey calls the shots, and if he wants to make sure we're in the clear before leaving, then that's what we'll do. Wading toward the island, I keep my eyes open for any movement. The strange hum in the water is back, reverberating through me. It's stronger now. I can feel it in my teeth.

By the time I trudge wet and dripping onto shore, Whitey is aiming the flashlight into the trees. "Sackett, can you see anything in there?" he asks.

"Nothing. Maybe we should get back to the boat, huh?" I feel anxious, as if the buzzing from the water is still inside me. I want to be away from here.

Whitey doesn't speak. He looks around, his jaw set tight.

"The ropes broke and the rowboat drifted away," Al says, wringing water from the legs of his slacks. "That's all it was, Whitey."

Whitey shakes his head. "We're not alone here. I can feel it."

"This place is deserted," Al insists. "You said so yourself. "

Whitey stares into the woods. "Every inch of me feels it."

"Let's just get the hell out of here," Grease says again, chewing his toothpick. He wades back into the water toward the ship.

"Not until I know what's going on," Whitey says.

Grease turns to face us, the water up to his thighs. "Fuck it, Whitey. We'll be safer on the boat anyway."

It's too dark for me to see what rises out of the water behind Grease. It looks like a shadow in the shape of a man, but it doesn't make a sound. It wraps its arms around Grease, and they both fall back into the water with a splash.

Whitey whips the flashlight around too late. It's all over, there's only empty air where Grease stood. The water churns briefly, then stops.

"The fuck was that?" Burns whispers.

I grab the flashlight out of Whitey's hand. I inch toward the water, holding the light parallel to my gun. I scan the water but can't see a thing. The surface is calm and dark, like polished metal. "Grease?"

Whitey breathes hard next to me, shaking his head. "I told you, man. I told you. Someone's here."

The flashlight's beam moves over the water. "Grease?" I call again. Something small and white floats toward me, bobbing on the surface. I stoop to pick it up and hold it in the light.

Grease's toothpick.

In the distance they rise out of the East River, still as statues. Dozens of them. Everywhere I look, heads and shoulders emerge from the water. I point the flashlight, but darkness eats the light before it reaches them.

17

Dr. Crowley came to Heinrich Schumacher's house to apologize for frightening him. Heinrich pulled the old man into the kitchen, away from where Marlene slept on the couch. He hadn't told her about the strange ritual he witnessed in the cavern. "I can't stress enough how important your mission is," Crowley explained. "What I told you wasn't an exaggeration. The gold and Germany are one and the same. The ritual you saw isn't important, you don't even have to believe me, so long as you take the gold to safety. The gold itself must never be spent, not for any reason, so to that end, this is what the Brotherhood has put together for you." Crowley handed him a bag. "It's enough to pay for your voyage, your new life in America, and the best medical treatment for Marlene's recovery. You'll still do it, won't you?" Heinrich looked past Crowley's shoulder at Marlene's sleeping form in the next room. He saw the spot on her dress where the lump of the bandage pushed at the cloth. The best medical treatment for Marlene? He nodded at Crowley. He would do it. For her.

The gold was packed into big, heavy steamer trunks. Crowley personally drove Heinrich and Marlene to the port of Vlissingen in the Netherlands, where an enormous passenger liner waited. He supervised the stewards taking the trunks to the hold while Heinrich brought Marlene to their room. She leaned against him the whole way. Once inside, he placed her gently on the bed. The trip had tired her out. "She needs bed rest," Crowley told him when he came up from the hold, satisfied that the trunks were safe. "Don't let her strain herself. Keep an eye on the wound."

While Marlene slept, Heinrich said goodbye to Crowley outside the room. The old doctor turned to go, then stopped and said, "If anything should happen, remember the words we spoke in the cave. They have more power than you think. And remember what it is you've been charged with. The soul of Germany is in your hands."

As he walked away, Heinrich wondered: What if Crowley was right? What would become of Germany in the years to come without its soul?

18

Branches whip my face as I run inland from the shore. Vines grab for my ankles. I hear the others breathing hard behind me—Whitey, Al, Burns—their feet pounding the ground, snapping twigs, crunching leaves.

"Divers," Al says, out of breath. "Fucking frogmen from the Coast Guard. They must have the island surrounded by now."

Al's right, they must be divers, it's the only thing that makes sense; except, like everything else since we came to North Brother Island, something about them is wrong. They aren't Coast Guard, I'm sure of it, but that's as far as my reasoning gets. Adrenaline and fear have taken pole position, and reason can't even get near the starting line.

The hospital looms up ahead. I pump my legs, running hard, until I reach the open doorway. My lungs are on fire, a painful cramp knots my side. The others stop beside me. Burns bends over, his hands on his knees, wheezing the word "fuck" over and over. I sweep the woods with the flashlight. No movement. We haven't been followed.

Whitey wipes the sweat from his eyes and says, "I don't like leaving the gold like that."

Carson flashes through my mind, him and his thug pushing through the door of my apartment and tying me to the chair. Someone told him about the map. Someone told him where to find me. That same some- one might know about the island, too. "Who knows we're here? Who knows about this place?"

"Just the ones I got the map from," Whitey says.

"Who are they?"

"Some neo-Nazi, Fourth Reich assholes from Germany. They said the gold was rightfully theirs, but they would settle for a cut if we did all the work."

"Ah, fuck," Burns says. He runs his hands through his hair. "So now they want more. They want it all."

Something stirs at the tree line, a black silhouette against the shadows. "Hold up," I whisper. They stop talking. I switch off the flashlight. It takes a moment for my eyes to adjust and catch movement between the trees. Men, a dozen of them, maybe more, approaching from the shore. "They're coming."

The others back into the doorway. Whitey looks into the darkness behind him. "Can we lose them in here?"

"We don't have much choice," Burns says.

"Split up and stay out of sight until they're gone," Whitey says. "If you get caught, don't tell them shit. Not how many of us there are, not what we're here for, or I'll cut out your fucking tongue. Meet back at the boat in an hour."

Burns turns and runs into the building, his footsteps echoing off the walls. Al takes off after him. Whitey turns to me, grabs my arm. "One hour," he repeats, then sprints away.

I stay outside for a moment. I want a better look at who they are, but instinct tells me to bolt. I back through the doorway into the dark corridors of the abandoned hospital.

19

It seemed to Heinrich Schumacher that as time passed aboard the ship, Marlene was getting better. She was able to swallow soup and stand for short periods of time. She could even leave the room for walks if she leaned on him like a crutch. When she took her afternoon rests, Heinrich visited the hold to check on the trunks of gold. Sometimes he thought he felt a hum coming from them, a low vibration that moved through him down to his feet. When he put his hands on the trunks, he heard it through his palms, a haunting song that brought to mind the tiled roofs and green gardens of the land he'd left behind.

Halfway across the Atlantic Ocean, the ship's kitchen staff took ill. Then the janitorial staff. The toilets backed up and eventually stopped working. The water became undrinkable. There was talk of a cholera outbreak. With no fresh water to drink and no way to dress her wounds without risking infection, Marlene's recovery suffered. She slept more and more, no longer able to stand or sit up. She stopped eating. The skin around the bullet wound turned yellow, then purple, spreading outward like a star.

She didn't live to see America. Her body was taken away and quarantined with thirty-five others who'd died from the outbreak. The corpses were wrapped in sheets and dumped into the ocean. Watching from the deck, Heinrich couldn't tell which one was his brave, beautiful Marlene. They were indistinguishable from one another, just white cloth wrapped around oblong shapes. He searched desperately for something familiar, a strand of her hair, a recognizable contour, but then they all sank beneath the waves and were gone.

After that, Heinrich routinely sneaked down to the hold in the middle of the night to listen to the music from the steamer trunks. All alone on a ship full of strangers heading toward a land he'd never seen, the comforting hum of the gold was the only thing that kept him sane. One night he opened a trunk to look at the gold inside and in its shine saw Marlene looking back at him. It filled him up inside like floodwater, filled the emptiness left by her death. He found a shard of broken glass on the floor and cut his palm open on the spot. He let the blood fall on the gold and spoke the words he'd heard in the cavern under the church.

20

Old, decaying wood creaks under my feet as I climb the stairway to the hospital's second floor. The metal banister is corroded. Flakes of rust chip off in the palm of my glove. My footsteps echo loudly through the stairwell. Whoever's after us, whoever those men are outside, I'm sure they can hear me and know exactly where I am. The question is: What will they do if they catch me? Torture me for the gold? Send me back to Rikers? Kill me?

I exit the stairs on the second floor. The flashlight beam bobbles in front of me as I hurry down the hallway, sidestepping recklessly strewn chairs and jumping over old overturned bed frames. I trip on a lone wheelchair wheel, right myself, keep moving, and narrowly avoid falling down a ragged-edged hole in the floor where the plaster and wood have rotted through.

A dim light filters through the dusty air ahead, coming through a glassless window frame. I switch off the flashlight and look out the window at the grounds in front of the hospital. I see them moving below, thirty or forty of them, and now I know why I was so sure they weren't Coast Guard divers. They're not wearing wetsuits. They're not even carrying air tanks.

As they draw closer to the building, I see it's not just men, but women too. They all come to a stop outside the hospital, the men in linen suits, the women in long flared skirts and puffy shirtwaist tops. Water runs down their clothes and drips to the ground at their feet. One stands apart from the others, a middle-aged man with slicked back gray hair. The brass buttons on his blazer glow in the starlight. His head suddenly snaps up to look at me, his expression blank, unreadable. Without a word, the others look up too. Their skin is gray, pale, and wet.

I jump back from the window and flatten myself against the wall, my breath catching in my throat. The flashlight slips out of my hand and lands on the floor with a clunk so loud it might as well be a trumpet announcing my position. It rolls away into the darkness.

Who are they? What do they want? Panic floods through me. I push it down into my stomach. Who they are doesn't matter, I tell myself. Whether they're Coast Guard, neo-Nazi hitmen, or the fucking Manchu army is moot. What matters is that they know exactly where I am, where we all are. What matters is that we're outnumbered.

I lean over and peer out the window again. The grounds in front of the hospital are empty, there is only wet, trampled grass between the forest and the door. They're in the building. I turn back to the corridor, pull the .38 and hold it up by my face. I wish I could see better in the dark.

21

Heinrich Schumacher settled in a predominantly German neighborhood on the Lower East Side of New York City. His new neighbors were intrigued by his grief-numbed eyes and the peculiar steamer trunks that filled his apartment. But what drew them to him most of all was that his whole body hummed with a golden energy—an energy that brought comforting dreams of their homeland.

When he slept, the gold sang to him, easing his loneliness and homesickness. One night, Heinrich woke to strange noises outside his window. He got out of bed and saw a dozen of his neighbors had gathered in front of his building. He opened the door, and, without a word, they entered his apartment like sleepwalkers to stand in a circle around the trunks. The Rheingold had summoned them, he realized. They'd heard it singing and answered the call. He unlatched the trunks for them, and they cut their palms without hesitation, speaking the vow of protection.

The gold called to more and more people over the ensuing years, until, as the nineteenth century turned into the twentieth, half of Little Germany had become the new Brotherhood.

22

I inch back toward the stairwell, holding the .38 ready. The sky outside is a dark indigo from the approaching dawn, but it's still murky in the building. Without the flashlight I have to move slowly so I don't fall through any holes in the floor. This snail's pace is killing me. I have to get to Whitey and the others, tell them the building's been compromised. We have to get back to the boat.

Two shots ring out downstairs, and my heart gives a stiff wrench in my chest. I glance down the stairs, but the stairwell has a low ceiling that prevents me from seeing anything but a small, dim patch of tiled floor at the bottom. I strain to hear something, anything, a voice, Al, Burns, Whitey giving me the all clear, but there's nothing. It occurs to me they may already be dead.

The air changes, grows colder. I can hear what sounds like sloshing water coming from the first floor. A chill sweeps over me.

I descend the stairs slowly, the .38 in front of me. It gets colder the lower I go. The knot in my stomach loosens, releasing the pent-up fear into my bloodstream like a drug. I swallow it, tie the knot again. Getting out of here and back to the ship is all that matters. Make it out alive, get home with the gold, and put this crazy shit behind me. That sounds like a plan.

Before I'm all the way down the stairs, I see them. They practically fill the whole first floor corridor, water dripping from their clothes, their skin. They stand in a loose circle around Burns, who is sweating and shaking so hard the Springfield Pro in his fist rattles like a toy. The shots I heard—they were his. But the Springfield Pro is a nine-millimeter gun, a powerhouse in close quarters, and there isn't a single body on the floor. None of them is wounded, either. They just stand there, surrounding him. Silent, except for the sound of dripping.

I point my gun at the closest one, a bearded man in a tweed jacket, and clear my throat. They all look up at me on the stairs. Not piecemeal the way a normal crowd would, but all at once, heads turning and lifting in perfect unison. They don't make a sound, not even a shocked gasp. Instinct tells me to run, I can feel it tugging at me to get the hell out of there. But I won't leave without Whitey. I owe him that. I owe him more than that.

I pull back the .38's hammer. "Now that I've got your attention, maybe you should all back the fuck up." They just continue to stare.

Burns looks up at me. His eyes are wide, desperate, completely insane. He's broken on some deep, inner level. "Sackett. Look at their clothes." He points at the sopping garments. "They're . . ." He laughs. "They're . . ." He can't finish the sentence, he's laughing so hard.

"Chill," I tell him. I walk down the rest of the stairs. A thin layer of water covers the floor, icy cold even through the soles of my shoes. "The rest of you better find your voices and give me some answers. Who are you? What do you want?"

They stay silent. The room gets colder. One of them steps forward, the older man in the brass-buttoned blazer.

I point the .38 his way. "I'd suggest you stay put, mister. My friends and I, we just want to get back to our boat and get out of your hair. I think that's a plan we can all get behind, don't you?"

The man reaches one hand toward Burns, the movement slow and precise. Burns is still doubled over laughing. He doesn't see it.

"Mister," I say, "you need to step back—"

He puts his hand on Burns's shoulder. Burns stiffens and the laughter cuts off immediately. He looks at me, startled. "Sackett?" he says. His whole face bloats suddenly. He coughs, chokes, and water pours out of his mouth, gallons of it all at once as if his lungs are reservoirs. Burns drops limply to the wet floor. The man with the brass buttons turns to me.

"What did you—?" I start to ask, but then I think, fuck it. Fuck questions. The man reaches for me just as he did for Burns, and I pull the trigger twice. The slugs go into his neck and shoulder. He doesn't even flinch. There's no blood. A clear liquid spills out of the wounds. It takes me a moment to realize it's water.

The knot in my stomach unravels. I turn to run and come face to face with a woman in a cotton dress whose hem is still spilling water like a faucet. She reaches for me with a pale gray hand. I swing the gun around and blow a hole open in her stomach. She doesn't even flinch. Water splashes out of the wound.

I duck aside—she's moving as slow as the man with the brass buttons—and as I pass her, I realize I don't hear anything. Like the others, she stays silent, not even a grunt of annoyance that she couldn't catch me. But it's not just that. I don't hear her breathing. It occurs to me that I haven't heard any of them breathing. Their skin is gray, they're filled with water and they're not breathing. The part of me that's still trying to think rationally says they're not human. They're not even alive.

The crowd moves toward me. They're slow enough to outrun, but there's nowhere to go. There are too many of them in the way. I back up until I hit something hard. The wall, I think with a blaze of panic, but when I reach behind me, I feel a doorknob. Thank God. I turn it and pull the door open. Something heavy falls on my back. I see arms reaching over my shoulders, feel the weight of a head against my neck. I cry out, my heart in my throat, and shove it away. I don't see who it is until the body hits the floor.

Al. He has that same startled look that Burns had, the same bloated face. The front of his suit is stained dark with water. Some of it still dribbles out of his open mouth. He's dead. Burns is dead. There's a good chance Whitey is, too. I'm next. There's no getting around that. The crowd gropes for me with their wet, gray hands.

Something grabs me from behind and pulls me backward through the open doorway. The door slams shut.

23

One day Heinrich Schumacher stopped in the middle of Second Avenue on his daily trek to the newsstand. His breath caught in his throat, his hand clutched at his neck. On the other side of the street was a man his own age whose face was horrifically familiar. His name was Montand and he had been one of General Frossard's officers during the occupation of Saarbrücken. Heinrich was sure of it. Standing on Second Avenue, watching Montand stroll by with a brown bag full of groceries, all the years that had passed since the occupation disappeared. Montand turned his head and caught Heinrich looking at him. He nodded, tipped his hat, and kept walking.

The gold, Heinrich thought, panicking. The French must have tracked it to America, to New York, to his neighborhood. He hurried back to Little Germany, where he called an emergency meeting and told the others what he saw. They had to take the gold somewhere safe, where Montand and the French army wouldn't find it.

Their annual church picnic on Long Island was only a few days away. Their boat had a secure hold. They would take the gold with them, they decided, and find a place on Long Island where it would be safe.

On June 15, 1904, they brought the gold aboard the *General Slocum*.

24

"Quit struggling." The voice in my ear belongs to Whitey. He lets go of me, and I turn around. Whitey is a mess, his clothes disheveled, his white hair sticking out from his scalp in patches as if he's been sleeping on it. "The *General Slocum*," he says. "They're from the *General Slocum*. They—

they've come back for their gold." He's got the same crazy look in his eye Burns did. Whitey has always been like a rock. It scares me that this broke him, turned him to pudding. I don't know what to do. I need Whitey to tell me, but he's too far gone.

I glance around the room. Judging by its small size, it must have been part of the ward, a patient's room. An old rusted bed frame stands upright against the wall. I grab it and pull it toward the door. It is heavy enough to make a good barricade, maybe buy us some time. As I slide it over, a bent corner of the frame gets stuck in a hole in the floor tile. It won't budge. The room grows colder.

"It's their gold," he says as if I didn't hear him the first time. "Don't you see? That's why they're here. They know we took it."

"Whitey, help me." I struggle to pull the bed frame free.

Shadows move in the crack beneath the door, water seeps through as if someone left a tub running on the other side. There's a loud bang on the door. Whitey yelps and hugs himself.

"Whitey, I can't get this free," I say. "Help me."

"They got Al, you know," he says. "I pulled him in here with me, but I couldn't get the door closed in time. One of them touched him. He died right in front of me. Water came out of his mouth."

"Burns too," I tell him.

"All this water," Whitey mutters. "Out of nowhere. Right out of his mouth."

He's a lost cause, totally gone. With one last tug that sends a cramp through my shoulder, I yank the bed frame free and set it against the door. "I don't know how long it'll hold them off," I say. "We can't stay here. We have to keep moving."

Whitey stares at his palms. "Their hands," he says, and I see tears rolling down his cheeks. "You can't let them touch you. Their hands kill you."

I turn to the door. "They're not the only ones."

I peel off my gloves.

Whitey laughs. "You can't kill them, Sackett. They've been dead for a hundred years already. Even bullets don't work. I shot one. Shot him right in the head. He didn't care." He laughs as if it's the funniest thing he's ever heard. "He didn't fucking care."

Something slams against the door, harder than before, and knocks the barricade back. My heart hammers in my chest as the bed frame rocks for a moment as if it's going to fall, before settling back into place. I take a deep breath and approach the door cautiously. I put my bare hands on it and close my eyes. I see wood, the grain, sawdust. I go deeper until I see through to the other side. The gray-haired man with the brass buttons stands right in front of me, his face expressionless, one arm raised to hit the door again. He pauses, cocks his head to the side. His eyes narrow. It's the first time I've seen anything register on their faces. It looks almost like surprise.

He looks right at me and lowers his arm. He lays his hand flat on the door, directly opposite mine. A jolt runs through me, images flash in my mind, crazy visions of marching armies, bodies lying in the middle of the street, curved blades cutting deep, bloody lines into palms. I yank my hand away, open my eyes, and step back.

"What did you see?" Whitey whispers. "What's happening out there? Are they leaving?"

I stammer, trying to find the words. "He knew I was there. Somehow, he knew I could see him. He—he saw me, and then . . ."

"How could he see you through the fucking door?"

I don't answer, because I don't understand it either. I grab Whitey by the elbow and pull him toward a boarded-up window in the far wall. We pull off the planks one by one, each of them crumbling to chunks of sawdust in our hands. With my gloves off, I see the rot inside every piece I pull free, eating away at the wood like a cancer. When we finally clear away all the planks, the sky outside has lightened more. The horizon burns white. The grounds in front of the building are empty. So is the edge of the forest.

I go first, hoisting myself onto the windowsill and through the hole. The cool morning air feels good, reinvigorating, and for a moment I think we might just live through this after all. I turn around to help Whitey out, just in time to hear the bed frame crash aside. The dead of the *General Slocum* pour into the room.

"Move!" I shout. Whitey stretches his arms out toward me. I grab them and pull, trying to ignore the images of muscle, tendon, and bone that flash through my head. Whitey gets halfway out the window before he stops. They've got him by the legs. I pull with everything I've got, but Whitey doesn't budge. He looks at me blankly, eyes glazed. I let go of his arms before the water pours out of his mouth onto the crabgrass and weeds below.

Pale gray hands reach through the window for me. There's nothing left to do but run. I sprint through the lashing tree branches back toward the shore, the boat, the gold. I feel as if I'm running forever but not getting anywhere. Whitey's dead. It's all I can think about. My only friend, the closest thing I've ever had to real family, is dead. I consider stopping, letting them find me because I don't know how to proceed without him, but then I catch a glimpse of shimmering blue water between the trees, the white boat still lolling where Al dropped anchor.

I sprint for the shore, ignoring the pain in my muscles. Suddenly it's sand and rock under my feet instead of dirt and twigs, and I know I'm almost home free. I run out into the surf, splashing waist-high waves around me, and grab the bottom rung of the ship's side ladder.

I pull myself up on deck, wheezing and huffing. I brace myself against the handrail and look to the shore. The man with the brass buttons stands by the water. Behind him are the others. None of them moves.

I dart into the compass bridge and scan the board for the anchor controls, but it's no use. Nothing is labeled. I start hitting random buttons, pulling levers, but the anchor stays down. Frustrated, I go back on deck and see that they've started moving into the water, coming my way. I slam through the door to the cabin. Where can I go? Where would be safe?

My gaze falls on the wood-panelled door at the far end of the room. The hold. Whitey said it was reinforced steel. There's no way they can reach me in there. I try the door, but it's locked. Only then do I remember the key on the string around Whitey's neck. And Whitey's body is in a room all the way back at the abandoned hospital. I slap a palm against the door in frustration and get a brief flash of the gold bricks stacked on the other side. They look small now. Inconsequential. It was hardly worth it.

I open the cabin door and walk back on deck. They wait for me topside, standing perfectly still, water pooling around their shoes, their gray skin glistening in the morning light. Past them, the sparkling blue water of the cove looks wide open, welcoming. I can swim from this place, head for the nearest landmass. I put one foot on the railing, ready to hoist myself overboard, even as Grease's mocking words echo in my mind: *"Rikers is right there. I bet you could swim for it."*

The water around the boat begins to churn, and I freeze. More of them rise to the surface; everywhere I look they're bobbing above the waves. The water is filled with them, more than I can count, with more of them breaking the surface every second. What was it Whitey said about the *General Slocum* disaster?

The death toll was over a thousand.

There's no way out. The man with the brass buttons steps forward, stands in front of me. He holds his hand open, palm up. I knock it away and plant both my hands on his chest. He may already be dead, but I figure maybe I can do some damage before he makes me choke on river water. Instead of seeing the dead man's shriveled heart and empty lungs, though, I see something else.

I see a small, quaint German town with gardens and cobblestone streets and a big stone church. *Saarbrücken,* the name comes to me in a voice not my own. I witness the atrocities of the French occupation. I see a cavern filled with gold, knives slicing across palms as ancient words are spoken. I see the *General Slocum,* the panic and terror as fire breaks out. Lifeboats are stuck immovably to the deck with dried paint; fire hoses are so rotten and frayed they burst apart as soon as they're turned on. People put on life vests and jump into the water, unaware that the cork inside the vests has deteriorated with age and turned to a heavy powder that drags them down into the freezing cold depths. I hear a familiar song, a melody that hums inside me. *The Rheingold!* their voices cry in panic. It's alive. It is Germany. It must be protected. It must always be protected. The images fade, and a name echoes inside my head.

Heinrich Schumacher.

I open my eyes and take my hands off his chest. I look into Heinrich's watery gray eyes and realize I'm still hearing it. The familiar song.

It's coming from the ship's hold. I remember now where I've heard it before. When I was in Rikers, it kept me sane in solitary. Even then the Rheingold sang to me. Even then we were connected. I think about the father I never knew, where he might have come from, what heritage might stand behind me.

For the first time, Heinrich opens his gray-lipped mouth. "You hear it as we do," he says. It's not a question, but I nod anyway. He nods in return. They all do. They seem to sense in me a kindred spirit, one who is like them. I feel it too, a sense of belonging, a desire to keep that beautiful song alive. They crowd around me, stroke my arms, my back, and the glorious cause we share fills me up inside like floodwater, fills me to bursting.

A lifetime ago, Costigan told me I needed a cause. As something sharp cuts across my palm and draws blood, I finally have mine. I speak the words from Heinrich's memories. The names Wotan and Freia and Fafner flow from my mouth in a torrent. I look down at the cut in my palm and see it bathed in falling water.

The gold is safe. No one can penetrate the reinforced hold. We sleep beneath the waves, my brothers and sisters and I, next to Al's sunken yacht, the hole we made in its hull gaping like an open mouth. We sleep and we wait, knowing there will be others who come looking for buried treasure. We sleep and the gold sings to us of a faraway home.

Acknowledgments

The year 2025 marks my twenty-fifth anniversary as a professionally published author. (It also sounds like the far-future setting of a classic science fiction story, and it's mind-boggling to me that we're here now, albeit without the teleportation booths, commercial interplanetary travel, and trusty robot butlers one might have expected.) Releasing a new collection strikes me as a great way to celebrate this anniversary. Most of the stories included here come from the recent years of my career, the 2010s and '20s, a time where my writing evolved closer to weird fiction than the more prototypical horror of my earlier work. (Although you'll still find echoes of that here. I yam what I yam!) The lone exception here is "General Slocum's Gold," an earlier work of mine that was, gratifyingly, nominated for the Bram Stoker Award. It has only been available as a standalone ebook for over a decade now, and I'm delighted to bring it back into print here.

Thank you to everyone who was kind enough to solicit and/or publish the stories in this collection: John Joseph Adams, Rebecca Brewer, Kenneth W. Cain, Andy Cox, Theresa DeLucci, Aaron French, Lois H. Gresh, Kenneth Heard, Monica S. Kuebler, Bracken MacLeod, Darrell Schweitzer, Charles Tyra, and Regina Yau. I appreciate your faith in me and my writing.

I owe a debt of thanks to Teel James Glenn, who asked me some time ago to blurb his Frankenstein's-monster-as-PI-in-1930s-New York City novel *Not Born of Woman*. Reading that excellent novel is what sparked (har har) the idea for "Six Strikes on a Laboratory Lightning Rod."

Thank you, Richard Curtis, for enriching both my writing and my life with your stewardship, friendship, and good humor.

Thank you, Victor LaValle, for your invaluable help with "The Fifth

Horseman," and also for being a friend and all-around inspiration.

Thank you also to my esteemed first readers, who are all incredible, insightful, and extremely patient, and who all made me the writer I am today: Daniel Braum, M. M. De Voe, John C. Foster (the C stands for "critique"), Ben Francisco, Sarah Langan, K. Z. Perry, Stefan Petrucha, Chandler Klang Smith, Lee Thomas, and David Wellington, with the occasional assist from Karen Heuler and Randee Dawn. Thank you all for your friendship, encouragement, and belief in me.

Thank you, Peter Straub. Your kindness and friendship meant so much to me. So did your writing, which was a constant inspiration, always encouraging me to try to be a better writer. I miss you, and I miss all the brilliant novels and stories that were yet to be written when we lost you.

Thank you, Derrick Hussey, S. T. Joshi, and everyone at Hippocampus Press for making this book a reality. I've admired Hippocampus for years, and it's a dream come true to join your ranks.

Thank you, Alexa, for your support, encouragement, and love. Without you, none of this would be possible.

And thank you, my readers, for sticking with me over these past twenty-five years. There's more to come, and I hope you'll stick around for that, too!

Publication History

"Companion" is original to this collection.

"Daughter of Echidna" first appeared in *Giving the Devil His Due,* edited by Rebecca Brewer (Running Wild Press, 2021).

"Every Path Taken" first appeared in *Shadows out of Time,* edited by Darrell Schweitzer (PS Publishing, 2023).

"The Fifth Horseman" first appeared in *Black Static* No. 66 (December 2018).

"The Fire and the Stag" first appeared in *Black Static* No. 63 (June 2018).

"General Slocum's Gold" first appeared as a chapbook (Burning Effigy Press, 2007).

"Lucienne" first appeared in *Cosmic Horror Monthly* No. 11 (November 2023).

"The Rest Is Noise" first appeared in *Dark Fusions: Where Monsters Lurk,* edited by Lois H. Gresh (PS Publishing, 2013).

"Six Strikes on a Laboratory Lightning Rod" is original to this collection.

"Spawning Season" first appeared in *Come Join Us by the Fire,* edited by Theresa DeLucci (Tor Nightfire, 2020).

"Whatever Happened to Solstice Young?" first appeared in *Dark Discoveries* No. 34 (Spring 2016).

www.ingramcontent.com/pod-product-compliance
Lightning Source LLC
Chambersburg PA
CBHW050357030726
47503CB00006B/1893